Malice in the Cotswolds

REBECCA TOPE

Allison & Busby Limited
11 Wardour Mews
London W1F 8AN
allisonandbusby.com

First published in Great Britain by Allison & Busby in 2012.
First published in paperback by Allison & Busby in 2013.
This paperback edition published by Allison & Busby in 2019.

A CIP catalogue record for this book is available from
the British Library.

10 9 8 7 6 5 4 3 2 1

ISBN 978-0-7490-2427-7

Typeset in 10.5/15.5 pt Sabon by
Allison & Busby Ltd.

The paper used for this Allison & Busby publication
has been produced from trees that have been legally sourced
from well-managed and credibly certified forests.

Printed and bound by
CPI Group (UK) Ltd, Croydon, CR0 4YY

For my friend and travel companion
Helen English
Also for Shirley Pick,
reader extraordinary

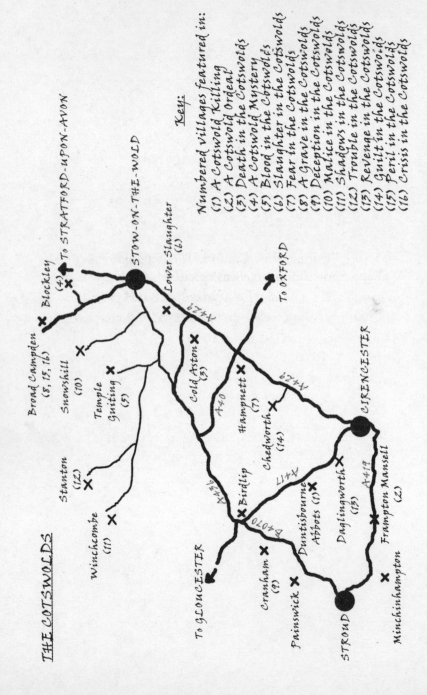

THE COTSWOLDS

TO STRATFORD-UPON-AVON

Blockley (4)

Broad Campden (8, 15, 16)

Snowshill (10)

STOW-ON-THE-WOLD

Stanton (12)

Temple Guiting (5)

Lower Slaughter (6)

Winchcombe (11)

A429

Cold Aston (3)

TO OXFORD

Hampnett (7)

A40

Chedworth (14)

Birdlip

A417

A429

CIRENCESTER

Cranham (9)

Duntisbourne Abbots (1)

Daglingworth (13)

A419

Frampton Mansell (2)

B4070

Painswick

TO GLOUCESTER

STROUD

Minchinhampton

Key:

Numbered villages featured in:
(1) A Cotswold Killing
(2) A Cotswold Ordeal
(3) Death in the Cotswolds
(4) A Cotswold Mystery
(5) Blood in the Cotswolds
(6) Slaughter in the Cotswolds
(7) Fear in the Cotswolds
(8) A Grave in the Cotswolds
(9) Deception in the Cotswolds
(10) Malice in the Cotswolds
(11) Shadows in the Cotswolds
(12) Trouble in the Cotswolds
(13) Revenge in the Cotswolds
(14) Guilt in the Cotswolds
(15) Peril in the Cotswolds
(16) Crisis in the Cotswolds

Author's Note

As with other titles in this series, the action is based in a real village. Snowshill is largely as described, in particular where the pub and the Manor are concerned. But Hyacinth House and others close by have been invented. All characters are the product of my imagination.

Chapter One

Yvonne Parker, owner of Hyacinth House in Snowshill, had an out-of-control air about her, which made Thea want to protect and reassure her, as she apologised repeatedly for being such a nuisance. 'I do hope you'll be able to manage it all,' Yvonne said, with a worried frown. 'It seems such a lot to ask anybody to do. I *hate* leaving it. But—'

'It'll be absolutely fine,' Thea insisted. 'It really doesn't sound too arduous.'

'I suppose it's just routine to you, this sort of work,' said Yvonne wistfully. 'But I've never left it like this before. It's taken me all this time to get up the courage.'

Never before had this particular line been taken by a departing householder. Most of them had been blithely confident of the house-sitter's abilities. Some had left exhaustive instructions, covering eventualities of every kind. A few had culpably failed to warn her of pitfalls. But nobody had yet expressed such reluctance to hand over the responsibility to her.

There was a girlishness to the woman, who had to

be over fifty. Her blonde hair was obviously dyed, with occasional patches where the natural faded colour was still visible. There was puckered flesh at elbow and armpit, as she flapped her arms in explanation of the way her household worked. She wore a tight sleeveless top and cotton cut-off trousers, revealing pale mottled skin on her lower legs. Thea paid very close attention to everything Yvonne said and did, aware that every snippet of information could turn out to be of vital importance.

The Parker homestead comprised two beautiful young Burmese cats, a large garden and four placid-looking cows in a small field at the end of it. 'They're not mine, of course,' said Yvonne. 'They're just here to eat the grass and have a bit of a rest. They're dry.' The cows were fat and docile, it seemed, awaiting their turn to give birth and rejoin the milking herd at a farm half a mile away. Yvonne's easy reference to the cycles of dairy cattle suggested a long involvement with these and other animals. 'If you think there's a problem with the cows, call Pippa on this number, look. She'll come over right away.'

Hyacinth House was modest in size and completely beautiful in appearance. It stood on the south-western edge of Snowshill, a village Thea scarcely knew at all. There was a famous manor house somewhere close by, but she had not yet located it, having only been to see Yvonne on a brief preliminary occasion, three weeks earlier. On that occasion she had found herself staring in disbelief at yet another achingly lovely Cotswold settlement. She had thought it impossible that she could still be stunned by the beauty of the old stone buildings and the way they seemed so carelessly scattered around a church, with a quirky pub for good measure. Snowshill had the same drunken sweeps as Duntisbourne Abbots; the same intriguing walls concealing large mansions as Blockley or Broad Campden – but its short uneven row of gabled houses to the west of the church easily vied with any of the other villages for sheer aesthetic glory. She looked forward to reading up on its history, and learning all about its own special features.

'That sounds easy enough,' she assured Mrs Parker, as they stood admiring the cows from the bottom of the garden. 'And the cats probably won't take much notice of me.' She was deliberately putting emphasis on the least worrying part of her assignment, trying not to think about the greater responsibilities that lay within the house.

Yvonne glanced anxiously at Thea's spaniel, which was nosing around the garden. 'They're not used to dogs,' she said.

'I won't let her bother them. She's very good in that respect.'

'Of course, it's the *things* you'll be worrying about,' said Yvonne, as if reading Thea's mind.

Things was an understatement. The house was densely packed with ornaments, pictures, books, wall hangings, candles, bowls and much more. The ornaments were ceramic, wood, stone and glass. A great many of them were made of glass. They were displayed on long shelves mostly, in the main living room. But many sat on low tables, window sills, mantelpieces, and on top of other furniture, not just in the living room, but all over the house. Everywhere Thea looked there were accumulations of Yvonne's *things*.

The garden was similarly overstocked, with not an inch of bare ground to be seen – even the minute lawn grew lush and green. The colours were bright, if not positively gaudy. Reds, purples and vivid oranges ran riot. Thea could identify crocosmia, calendula, standard roses, lavatera, rampant geraniums – all in peak season in this, the last week of July.

'Don't worry about dusting anything,' Yvonne pleaded. 'It's much too hazardous. I like to pretend I'm suffering from the Snowshill syndrome, if you know what that is. Have you been to the Manor?'

Thea shook her head. 'No, but I do know a bit about it, and how it's filled to bursting with some sort of eccentric collection. I'll pay a visit while I'm here.'

'It makes my stuff look quite modest,' said Yvonne, with a rare smile. 'Ten or twelve rooms, at least, all absolutely full of things from around the world. We think it's wonderful.'

'The village itself has a bit of a crammed feeling,' Thea observed. 'Houses pushed into small spaces, on all these strange levels. It's even more chaotic than Blockley.'

'Mmm.' Yvonne's attention had wandered, and she glanced at her watch. 'I'm going to have to leave you in another twenty minutes or so, and I haven't quite finished packing yet. Are you *sure* it's going to be all right?'

Thea wondered uneasily whether news of her previous two years spent moving from one Cotswold village to another had filtered through to this woman. Had she heard stories of the house-sitter's involvement in violent death and sudden crises, which were making her nervous? 'Yes, I'm sure,' she said firmly. 'Everything's going to be fine.'

Still the woman made no decisive move to finish her preparations. 'Where exactly are you going?' Thea asked, more for the sake of conversation than anything else. She had been given a mobile number for emergencies, but little further information. She thought she recalled a mention of France on her previous visit, but wasn't sure.

Yvonne grimaced, her pale blue eyes closing for a moment. 'Oh! Well . . . um . . . London, actually. Crouch End, if you know where that is.'

'Not exactly. Sounds interesting.'

'It's near Highgate. I'm going to see my husband,' she added unexpectedly.

It took Thea a few seconds to work out what was odd about this remark. 'I see,' she lied.

'Well, he's my ex-husband now, of course. We were divorced not long ago, and haven't seen each other since he left, five years ago. He's between houses, or something. He wants to talk to me about boring legal stuff, I suppose. Our daughter's getting married in September, and I have to be sure he'll do right by her. I ought to have gone before now, but I can't go anywhere in term time.' She looked to Thea as if she was dreading the coming encounter, but was putting a brave face on it.

'I don't imagine that'll be much fun,' Thea sympathised, wondering how such a task could possibly take two weeks of anybody's time. Would Yvonne be staying in the same house as her ex? Wouldn't he have found a new woman after such a long time? 'I thought you were going to France, actually.'

'Oh, yes, I am. That's next week. I'm not spending long with Victor. My sister has a house near Avignon,

13

and I'll probably need a shoulder to cry on. I did tell you I teach French, didn't I? I haven't been there for nearly twenty years, which is a dreadful thing to admit. I often feel an awful fraud, teaching it to children when I've barely been to the actual country. I haven't been *anywhere* since . . .' She looked sadly around her lovely garden. 'I've been keeping busy here.'

'So I see.'

'It . . . I mean . . . I was quite ill for a long time. The shock and everything. I didn't want to see people. It was all so *humiliating*. And now, with the cats, and the things . . . I couldn't just *leave* it, you see. You do understand, don't you?'

Thea made what she could of the garbled revelations. Yvonne had probably assumed that her marriage was permanent. Safe and solid and reliable, just as Thea's own had been before her husband had been snatched from her one calm and cloudy day. The children raised, the finances secure, the habits established. And then the swine had pushed Yvonne Parker over a cliff and very probably replaced her with somebody else. As they did. At least, some of them did.

'Yes, I understand,' she said. 'Trust me. Everything will be all right here. It's only for two weeks. I'll make sure the weeds don't take over while you're away.'

'I expect he'll claim to be short of money, as usual. He'll say Belinda can afford to pay for her own wedding. If I had my way, we'd leave him out of it completely, but the children insist he should pull his weight.'

She was sounding more assertive, Thea noted, once she

started to talk about her offspring. 'Where does she live?' she asked. 'Your daughter, I mean.'

'Wales. Her fiancé's a farmer. It's all very romantic.' Her eyes went dreamy, and Thea tried to share the emotion, rather than imagining rainswept uplands and recalcitrant sheep. 'It's going to be a traditional village wedding, with everything home-made and authentic.'

'Lovely,' said Thea. 'My daughter's more likely to use a local registry office and a Manchester pub.'

'Oh? Is she engaged?'

'Actually no. She does have a boyfriend, but I don't think marriage is on the cards at all. She's very young.'

Yvonne's worried frown was back, the crease between the blue eyes deepening. Despite the momentary flicker of something more substantial, Thea's strongest impression was of a faded creature overwhelmed by life's surprises, hair lifeless and clothes hanging shapelessly around her. Defeat and helplessness seeped out of her, making Thea want to take her in hand and brighten her life in some way.

'You've done wonders in the garden,' she said bracingly. 'It must have been some consolation.'

The response was gratifying. 'It saved my sanity,' Yvonne said, with a wide-eyed smile. 'Blake next door took pity on me and let me use some of his ground as well – do you see?' She waved at an extra triangle of land, which began halfway down the adjacent garden and widened as it approached the road, leaving a modest wedge for Blake himself to tend. Seemingly he was not missing the donated area. His part was mainly a space for car parking, boasting little more than a small rowan tree rather too close to the house. The red berries were in full glory. Yvonne continued to explain. 'We even had the fence moved. Mark says there'll be the most dreadful legal complications if either of us ever wants to sell, but I don't think there will. Blake's very good. You'll probably meet him later today. He's called Blake Grossman and he lives here with his girlfriend.'

'Right. And who's Mark?'

'My son. He's always worrying about what's legal. I've no idea where he got that from.'

It was Thea's turn to glance at her watch. The spaniel was eyeing her impatiently, waiting for something to happen.

'Oh, gosh, I must get on,' cried Yvonne, noting the glance. 'You'll think I'm never going at this rate. It'll take me ages to get there.' She shivered. 'I hate driving in London. I never know where I'm going. I ought to get a satnav thing, I suppose, but I could never manage to work it.'

Thea herself would have been hard pressed to drive from Snowshill to Crouch End, so made no attempt to advise. She'd have been tempted to suggest the train, under the circumstances, but guessed there might be issues involving fear of crowds or panic over timetables.

'So I ask Blake if I get into difficulties?' she queried. 'And I see there's another house just over there.' She nodded at a medium-sized building on the other side of the road and slightly further down the hill that led into the village centre. It had mature trees growing around it, and a wrought iron gate firmly closed across its drive.

'That's Janice and Ruby,' said Yvonne distractedly. 'I wouldn't think you'll see them. They're not very sociable. What sort of difficulties?' she asked with a frown.

'Well . . . you know.' Thea wished she'd had the sense to keep quiet. She did know better than to specify possible disasters, however. 'Unforeseen events,' she laughed. 'Forget I said anything. It'll all be absolutely fine.'

Finally, the green Peugeot set out, leaving Thea and Hepzibah to explore Hyacinth House in peace.

The house was old, with thick walls and low ceilings. The kitchen was small, with steps leading down to a shadowy dining room at the back of the house. Most of the ground floor was devoted to a rectangular living room which Yvonne had packed with furniture on which to display her ornaments. There was not a speck of dust to be seen. The glass and china figurines, jugs and plates jostled with all the other objects in deliberate patterns that slowly came into focus. Colours had been assembled together, so that blues were in one corner, greens in another, opposite the reds and pinks. It was an art gallery and a museum, a personal folly and a passionate collection. Thea wondered if Yvonne had started it all as a replacement for the errant husband – or had it contributed towards driving him away? What would happen if a careless move broke the arm off a shepherdess or the handle from a jug? Would Yvonne scream or cry or go into a sulk? And how, for heaven's sake, was all this clutter consistent with the possession of two young cats?

The cats had a routine which Yvonne had described in detail. They had their own saggy armchair in the dining room, covered with a colourful blanket. They also had an elaborate climbing arrangement with platforms, a tunnel, scratching post and dangling toys. They could go in and out of the house at will, via a tiny scullery off the kitchen. But they were most definitely not permitted outside at night. The cat flap must be firmly locked, once Thea was sure they were both inside, when darkness fell. They were then confined to the kitchen until morning. A litter tray was provided, but was seldom used.

'Their names are Julius and Jennings,' Yvonne had said. 'But they don't really answer to them.'

'They're beautiful animals,' Thea had said admiringly. One was a dark chocolate colour ('That one is Jennings,' said Yvonne) and the other a pale yellowy-grey. 'Are they from the same litter?'

'Yes. They were rejects, actually. The breeder wanted females, and got landed with all boys. She kept the best one and sold these off. She insisted they were neutered. They were done last week, poor things.'

Thea had made no comment, hoping there would be no delayed reactions to the surgery, under her care. 'I assume they're never allowed in the living room?' she asked.

'One at a time is okay. They're very careful, moving so delicately it's like magic, but if they're playing, things can get a bit rough. Are you happy with that? It does mean keeping the door shut all the time.' Both women had eyed Thea's dog and its long plumy tail.

'That's fine,' said Thea heartily. 'And Hepzie's not tall enough to cause any trouble.'

If their roles had been reversed, she did not think she'd have agreed to the inclusion of a spaniel in the house-sitting deal. Dogs knocked things over – everybody knew that. But it was July, and with any luck they could spend almost all their time outside.

On the map, Snowshill had looked tiny, with a pub, phone box and the prominent National Trust manor. Contour lines suggested chaotic sweeping slopes and rises, and there was little evidence of woodland. Her previous house-sitting commission had been at Cranham, to the south, a rather untypical village containing numerous post-war bungalows, surrounded by dense woods. The contrast between the two was dramatic. There did not appear to be any houses in Snowshill under a century old. It was a very contained little settlement, with none of the straggle that had enlarged such places as Blockley and even Broad Campden. No major roads came within two or three miles, which Thea supposed made it more of an adventurous goal for many of the tourists who found their way to Snowshill Manor. Hyacinth House was to the south-west of the village centre, on a small road leading up to sudden wide expanses of cornfields. There was a patch of grass outside the gate, between the garden wall and the single-track road, with space for two or three cars. There was no garage, although Blake-next-door had found space for one on his side. A track ran at right angles to the road, passing Blake's house, and giving him access to his garage. Yvonne's front garden was adjacent to a small field which rose to a patch of trees. Beyond that was the village.

It was eleven on a Saturday morning, and hazy sunshine lent a typical muted light to the landscape, as Thea slowly scanned the hills around her.

Yvonne's beloved front garden included a tiny patch

of lawn, furnished with a somewhat utilitarian wooden seat. Thea made herself a mug of coffee and went out to sit on the seat, intending to savour her surroundings. The low front wall was adorned with a vigorous climbing rose, which had ventured over onto the broad grass verge beyond, where she had been ordered to leave her car. A little group of people walked past, pausing to admire the garden and the handsome old house. Although the parking for Snowshill Manor was on the other side of the village, she realised she could expect to be included in the impromptu sightseeing tours that people took while waiting for it to be time for lunch at the pub. The whole settlement was so small that a five-minute walk in any direction would take people well beyond the actual village. As she watched the strollers disappear, she heard a tuneless whistling approach from the track beyond Blake's garden. Peering curiously across the flower beds, she caught sight of a short blond haircut on a boy who seemed to be aged about ten, coming in her direction.

Before she could call out a greeting, or ask herself whether he was with family or friends, there was a sharp zipping sound, of air being torn apart by rapid movement. A *thwack* followed, and then another.

'Hey!' she shouted, jumping to her feet. 'What do you think you're doing?'

The boy met her eye, full on, his face taut with ill will and triumph. He uttered a syllable that sounded like *Yah!* and broke into a run.

Thea went to the gate and surveyed the verge below Yvonne's garden wall. Six or seven bright-red roses lay murdered on the grass. She went out and gathered them up, holding them to her nose for a final valedictory sniff. They smelt of joy and love and long sweet summers.

With tears in her eyes, she carried them back to the seat on the lawn, shedding petals in her wake.

Chapter Two

She sat holding the flowers and thinking about wanton destruction, when a voice hailed her from somewhere over her right shoulder. 'Oh, hello?'

'Who's that?' said Thea, twisting round on the wooden slats. 'Are you calling me?'

'It's me. Blake. Next door. Hang on. I'll come over.' And before she could respond, he was standing in front of her, grinning like a labrador.

'Hello,' said Thea, without enthusiasm. 'Yvonne told me about you.'

'Oh dear! What did she say?'

'Only that you were a good neighbour.' *Too good*, she thought sourly, *if you come over like this every five minutes*.

'That's nice.' He was in his late thirties, she thought, and not bad-looking. His mouth was fleshy, his black hair rather long, and he smiled too much. He struck her as an improbable owner of a substantial Cotswold residence. 'She's such a sweet lady, isn't she?'

'Well . . . I don't really know her. She seemed very pleasant.'

'She's had a hard time. I do what I can for her – electrics and so forth. The wiring in this house isn't very modern, I'm afraid.'

'Are you an electrician?'

He laughed merrily. 'Oh, no. But I'm reasonably handy. Eloise always says so, anyway. That's my girlfriend,' he added, in response to Thea's raised eyebrows.

'Does she live here as well?'

'Sort of. She's doing a degree, so she's away in term time. And now she's gone off to Palestine of all places. Honestly, it's embarrassing. My parents would go ballistic if they knew. Not that they're Zionists or anything, but even so—'

'You're Jewish,' said Thea with a nod. 'Right.'

'Guilty as charged. Metropolitan intellectuals, for the most part. My uncle is something very impressive at the LSE and he lives in Hampstead.'

She had no idea how to reply, although it seemed her unduly direct reference to his race had caused no offence. Since her daughter had taken up with a black police detective, she had become far less wary about the whole business. She had discovered that there was no need to positively discriminate in favour of certain groups. Some people from ethnic minorities could be every bit as repellent as those of her own colour.

'My name's Thea Osborne,' she told Blake. 'And this is Hepzibah. She always comes with me when I'm house-sitting.'

'Sweet,' he gushed. 'Eloise can't wait to have a dog, but I've told her not until we're married. It gives me a hold over her, you see.' He grinned again, to indicate the lack of seriousness in this remark.

The massacred roses lay in a pathetic heap on the seat, wilting rapidly. 'A boy chopped the heads off some of the ramblers,' she said, hoping to dispel her own sadness by passing it to somebody else.

'What? *Ramblers?* My God! How many? Where are the bodies?'

Hysteria gripped her, without warning, and she giggled helplessly for some moments. 'No, no. Rambling *roses*. Look.'

'How beastly. But I suppose boys will be boys. Summer holidays just started and he'll be bored already.'

'He looked as if he'd escaped from an outing from the local remand centre,' said Thea tightly. 'He'll be off into the woods, setting snares for unwary wildlife next.'

'Sounds like young Stevie Horsfall to me. Did he have yellow hair and freckles?'

'I didn't notice freckles, but the hair was right. Who is he?'

Blake shrugged, with a hint of rebuke at the question. 'He's just a boy. Lives down the track – see?' He indicated a point behind his own house.

'Not really. Where does it lead?'

'Down to a farm, but his mum's got a little house halfway along. It's only a minute or two from here. But don't worry – I don't imagine he'll bother you again. He generally concentrates on tormenting Janice and Ruby over the way.'

Not very sociable, Yvonne had said about the two women. 'Oh?'

'He's got nobody to play with. But I would keep an eye on your dog, all the same. There's something about boys and dogs, isn't there?'

Thea had visions of tin cans tied to her spaniel's tail, and worse. 'Heavens! That sounds terrible.'

'No, no. He's just a boy,' the man repeated, absently. He was staring at the sky somewhere behind the house. 'There's a lark – can you hear it?'

Blake was sounding evasive to Thea, but she chose not to demand further detail. She listened to the joyous bird for a minute, in silence. 'It'll be August next week,' she observed inconsequentially. 'It's been a nice summer so far.'

'Have you been busy with the house-sitting work? Flitting from place to place, never resting long in one spot?'

She gave him a narrow look. 'Something like that,' she nodded. 'But I generally get three or four weeks at home between commissions. I don't do it full-time.'

'Even so,' he said doubtfully. 'It's an unusual existence. Living out of a suitcase, as they say. Not to mention your dog.' Hepzie was sitting a small distance away, ignoring the visitor in favour of something interesting in her own rear end. Her coat had grown shaggy over the past few months and there were a few lumps in the skirts at the back. 'Who could do with a trim, if I might venture to comment,' added Blake.

Thea resisted the temptation to make a snappy defence. 'True,' she admitted. 'I know it's perverse of me, but I prefer her a bit unkempt. She becomes a completely different dog after a haircut.'

She thought fleetingly of Phil Hollis, her former boyfriend, who had also nagged about getting the spaniel tidied up. Now there was no boyfriend, and it seemed that total strangers felt justified in filling the gap.

'I gather you and Yvonne are good friends?' she changed the subject.

'You gather correctly.' His smile could only be perceived as patronising and she felt a stab of resentment. There was a sense of being played with, or teased, and this was not something she had ever enjoyed.

She waited in vain for further elaboration. This man, then, was no gossip, which was cause for mild regret. It would have been interesting to learn more about the estranged husband and his circumstances. 'I suppose I should come to you if there are any problems, then? She didn't leave any names or numbers other than a farmer called Pippa. I've just got her mobile for emergencies.'

'I'd certainly have been happy to help if needed,' he agreed, with a little inclination of the head. 'But I'm afraid I won't be here after tomorrow. I'm going to be following Eloise out to hotter climes, actually.'

'Oh, well,' she said. 'Let's hope everything will go smoothly.'

'It's only two weeks, isn't it? I don't imagine anything much will go wrong in that time.'

Thea shuddered inwardly. *Don't say that*, she wanted to shout at him. Instead, she sighed and smiled and said nothing.

* * *

Sporadic clusters of exploring walkers went past all afternoon, an experience Thea had never had before in the Cotswolds. She had stayed almost entirely in small villages on the way to nowhere, where every visitor was an event. Not only did Snowshill boast the eccentric Manor, but there were extensive gardens that attracted their own swathe of trippers. The car park was a long walk from the Manor, a deliberate ploy beloved by the National Trust to force everyone to use their legs and traverse the grounds before reaching the main attraction. 'We'll go and have a look next week,' Thea promised the dog. 'If you're allowed in, which is doubtful.'

The interior of Hyacinth House grew no more inviting as the day progressed. Outside was warm enough to make the garden a far better prospect, despite the people having a good look at the flowers over the wall. Where most Cotswold properties had the larger area of garden at the back, this one was almost entirely at the front. Only a shady patio, a clump of trees and a high hedge offered themselves in the rear, making it an unappealing place to sit. On the map, a footpath was marked plunging down a steep hill to some woodland on the other side of the road, but she was in no mood for exercise, especially where such a declivity was involved.

The best aspect was definitely from the front. The views were harmonious in all directions. Even turning one's back on the landscape gave a pleasing picture of the facade of the house with its mellow colours and balanced shapes. The windows were set at exactly the right points, the roof suitably weathered, the size ideal for an ordinary family. Everything about it looked perfect. Only Yvonne's excesses had spoilt the rooms inside, making them hazardous in the clutter of fragile objects and unrestful to the eye.

She was just deciding that it must be almost time to feed the cats, when the telephone rang from the hallway, a few feet inside the open front door.

Yvonne had left no instructions regarding messages, but common sense ordained that she must answer it.

A man's voice burst loudly in her ear, before she had managed to utter more than a syllable. 'Vonny? Where the hell are you? I've been watching out for hours now. You said you'd be here by two. It's nearly five, and there you are, not even left yet. Couldn't you have called me, instead of keeping me hanging around here all afternoon? I have got things to do, you know.'

'This is Thea Osborne, the house-sitter,' she eventually succeeded in telling him. 'Yvonne left here at eleven.'

'What?'

'She left Snowshill at eleven. Even with Saturday traffic, she ought to be in London by now.'

'Of course she ought. There's no problem with the traffic. The silly cow's probably got herself lost.'

For six hours? Thea seriously doubted that. 'Surely not,' she said mildly. 'She would have called you.'

'Precisely. That's what I *said*.'

'But sometimes it can take ages, if there's an accident holding up the traffic. I assume she's using the M4. You know what motorways can be like.'

'She's not answering her mobile. I tried it. Three times.'

Only now was he starting to sound worried. 'Where the devil has the idiot woman got to, then?'

'As far as I could tell, she had every intention of driving directly to you. I mean, she's gone to the trouble of employing me to watch over the house. I really don't know what to suggest.'

'Well, I don't see how she can be lost. It's easy enough to find.'

'But she hasn't been there before – is that right?'

'Actually, no.' His voice faltered. 'No, she hasn't.'

'Oh, well . . .' Her own voice was losing conviction. Six hours really was a long time to spend trying to get to north London. Nobody went silent for that long in these days of perpetual communication. Except when they couldn't get a mobile signal or the battery died. That could happen, of course. 'There's probably been some sort of hold-up,' she repeated feebly, thinking that unless Yvonne herself had been injured, she had no justification for allowing so much time to pass without making contact. Although she could very easily have lost her nerve, changed her mind . . . been abducted? Of course not. There was no need to invent wild explanations of that sort.

'Thank you for your help, anyway,' he said, suddenly formal.

'Will you ask her to call me when she turns up? Just to put my mind at rest?'

'Of course,' he said, leaving her doubting that he would do anything of the sort.

She spent the next hour restlessly moving from kitchen to living room, upstairs to her bedroom and out into the garden, holding her phone as if it were welded to her hand. Yvonne or her husband would use the landline in the house to call her, but somehow the mobile made her feel connected to the wider world – a feeling she had acquired only in recent months. Before that she had regarded it as more of an irritation than something useful. Since her daughter had given her a new model last Christmas, she had been discovering more and more functions in its repertoire, designed to give her access to virtually everything that was being done, thought or said across the entire globe. Almost against her own nature, she was finding it intoxicating. There were apps for things she had never dreamt could be provided so quickly, and for so little cost.

'Hello again,' came a man's voice, the second time she found herself roaming restlessly around the garden.

'Oh . . . Blake. Hi.'

'Everything okay?'

'Not really. It seems that Yvonne never reached London. Her husband's worried about her.'

'My God!' The reaction did nothing to soothe Thea. 'She must have got into trouble, then. She's been gone *all day*.' He made it sound like a month.

'Yes. I thought perhaps she'd called in on somebody on the way, as a sudden whim. Or just . . . changed her mind.' She shrugged at this temptingly normal idea. Something about the failed marriage, Yvonne's nervousness that morning, the husband's tone, made it seem rather plausible that the woman had deviated from her original plan, that she had got cold feet and decided instead to go and stay with a distant cousin in Beaconsfield or Haslemere.

'She's been psyching herself up for this for ages,' he said, almost to himself. 'The final showdown with bloody Victor.'

'But aren't they divorced? Wasn't that the time for a showdown?'

He wrinkled his nose. 'She just signed everything that was put in front of her, whether it was fair or not. It didn't do much to sort out the emotional side of things. She hasn't been able to face up to a meeting ever since . . . well, for years. We talked it over endlessly. She wouldn't chicken out of it now. I know she wouldn't.' He sounded less certain than his words.

'If she hasn't seen him for a long time, it must be hard for her.' Thea fumbled to express her vague understanding of the situation. 'I mean, that sort of thing – it looms bigger and bigger in your mind, doesn't it?'

'She wouldn't do it now, if it wasn't for Belinda.'

Thea nodded. 'Yes, she told me. She wants him to come to the wedding.'

'She wants him to *pay* for it. I'm not sure anybody wants him to show up as well.' He laughed, and added, 'I've got something of a similar problem myself, as it happens. Eloise's dad is almost as out of favour as Victor is. All we can think of is to get married in the Caribbean or somewhere, with no family at all.'

'Bit drastic,' remarked Thea.

'It's a drastic business,' he said severely. 'So much can go wrong – as Vonny would tell you if she was here.'

'I assume Victor took up with another woman?'

Blake's eyelids dropped, giving him a sly appearance. He turned his head aside and examined the colourful flowers intently. 'That's what we all assumed. But Vonny would never say exactly what happened to split them up.'

'Probably too painful to talk about. She said she felt humiliated.'

'Poor old girl. She really does need to move on.'

Thea felt uneasy, now that gossip seemed to be finally under way. That Victor had behaved badly seemed axiomatic – and her impression of him from his phone call had not been favourable. But more pressing now was the question of what might have happened to Yvonne in the course of the day.

Blake, however, seemed to have settled any initial worries he might have been feeling, and was intent on conveying what he knew of the couple. 'I don't get why he's in Crouch End,' he said, with a little pout of puzzlement. 'He was renting a swish apartment in Hampstead Garden Suburb as far as I knew. Don't you love the sound of Hampstead Garden Suburb?' he added incongruously. 'It conjures such a lot in those three words.'

'The point is, I'm not quite sure of my position, if my employer's missing,' Thea said, with some emphasis. 'I ought to find out whether she's okay.' She refrained from mentioning that she had previously experienced the death of a homeowner whilst caring for the house, and it had led to considerable confusion and complication. She was not keen for a repetition.

'I can understand how you feel,' he said, as if this was a brilliantly helpful remark. 'But I don't suppose she'll stay lost for long. I know old Vonny pretty well. She's a survivor.'

The implication was that Blake regarded himself as in some sort of relationship with Yvonne, the exact nature of which was unclear. 'It's a pity *you* couldn't have watched the house,' she said tiredly, 'instead of going off on holiday.'

'I know,' he said carelessly. 'Terribly bad timing. Plus I don't like cats very much.'

I see, thought Thea suspiciously. *So it's possibly rather auspicious timing, after all.* Something about this man struck her as slightly too good to be true, as if he was playing a part, when his real attention was somewhere quite different. Which it probably was, with his girlfriend in Palestine and his own bags needing to be packed. But she had been given reason to think he actually cared what happened to Hyacinth House, its owner and its temporary sitter. Not just because the gardens had become connected, but from something less definable and more to do with feelings. Besides, he was, at that moment, all she had.

'I'll be left on my own, then,' she said, feeling a daft kinship with the despised Victor. 'How long will you be gone?'

'Only five days. Back next Thursday, all being well. It's business actually, not a holiday. Can't be ducked, or I'd have helped poor old Vonny out, of course.'

'Well . . .' she began helplessly. 'Not much I can do, I suppose. The cats still have to be fed.'

'True. And the homestead guarded. You'll be fine,' he assured her, with the sort of expression that suggested quite the opposite.

She nodded and turned away. In her hand, the phone jingled and she read a message on the screen:

Mum – I need to talk to you. Can you call me asap? Jess.

Chapter Three

Her daughter was a probationary police officer in Manchester; a bright confident girl who had coped bravely with the loss of her father when she was nineteen, scarcely breaking step on her career path. Thea had been less successful in adapting to unimagined widowhood, the house-sitting a desperate attempt at distraction a year after Carl's fatal accident. It had worked well, on the whole.

Jessica answered the phone within seconds. 'What's the matter?' Thea demanded.

The answer came without prevarication. 'It's Paul. He's dumped me.' The voice was thick with tears and Thea's heart turned a painful somersault.

'Oh, darling! When?'

'Yesterday. He was so *horrible* about it. He tried to do it in a text and when I phoned him he said *terrible* things to me. Some of them about you.'

'But *why*?' It was a silly question, but words were proving difficult. This was a totally shocking turn of events. Last time she'd seen Jessica and Paul, she'd begun to worry that they might be planning permanent togetherness. Had the young detective been aware of her reservations, which she thought she had kept well hidden?

'He says we're both racist, and he never felt comfortable around you.'

Likewise, thought Thea. But it had nothing to do with his race and everything to do with his arrogant insensitive personality. She had also begun to suspect the existence of a hidden streak of cruelty in her last encounter with him, which Jessica now appeared to be confirming.

'But surely . . .' Again words were hard to find. 'You poor girl. You sound dreadfully upset.'

'I've been crying all day. I had to call in sick. I can't go to work like this.'

'It's the shock.'

'It's much more than that. I had no *idea*. He must have lied to me the whole time, pretending he felt the same as me about us. I feel like a victim, absolutely powerless to do anything about it.'

Thea could readily understand that – the helplessness in the face of implacable forces working against you. The bruised and battered emotions that nothing could assuage. 'Do you want to come here?' she asked, with a sense of history repeating itself. Over the many house-sitting commissions she'd undertaken, her two sisters had used her as a refuge, one after the other. Jessica too had joined her once or twice. In general, such episodes turned out badly and Thea had concluded she preferred to have the places to herself. Although there were exceptions, she inwardly admitted.

'No, no. I can't. It wouldn't help. Not at the moment, anyway. I never know what I'm going to find when I visit you in one of your houses.'

'I know.' Thea forced a laugh. 'And this one's already getting complicated.'

'Don't tell me.'

'Well . . .'

'No, I mean it. *Don't tell me*. I've got enough to worry about.' The tear-choked voice was sounding stronger, for which Thea was thankful.

'Okay. Have you got someone there you can cry on? What about Sasha?'

'Yeah, she's been great. It happened to her last year, so she understands. She says she never liked Paul anyway. I wish she'd told me sooner.'

'You wouldn't have listened. That's what girlfriends do – they wait on the sidelines, ready to pick up the pieces. That's all they *can* do.'

Thea had never met Sasha, and had not realised how close the two girls were until Jessica made some casual mention of the effect her relationship with Paul was having on the friendship. It seemed the boyfriend had insisted on exclusive rights over her, virtually banning all outings with Sasha or other female friends.

'Right.' Jessica sounded doubtful, as if wary of accepting any pearls of maternal wisdom. 'Maybe.'

'Some things don't change,' her mother told her. 'Certainly not this sort of thing. I do know how it feels, honestly.'

'So what about your undertaker friend?' Jessica asked, in an apparent change of subject.

'What about him?'

'Have you seen him lately?'

'His wife's in hospital, fighting for her life, as far as I know. He's unlikely to have time to think about me.' *No*, she thought. *That isn't what I meant to say.*

'Poor chap. I forgot there was a wife.'

'Of course there is. Don't you remember when he went off to phone her, in Broad Campden? How that led to all sorts of trouble?'

'Vaguely, now you mention it. That seems ages ago now.'

'Four months,' said Thea, thinking that it did indeed seem very much longer. A lot had happened in the meantime. She also wished that her daughter had not raised the subject of Drew Slocombe. No good at all could come of it.

'Anyway – thanks for listening. I might call you again if I need to vent, if that's okay?'

'Of course it is. It's called "venting" now, is it?'

'Keep up, Ma. You're nowhere near as old as you like to pretend. Haven't you signed on to Twitter yet? That'll keep you in the mainstream. Or Facebook.'

'I just might do that. Don't write me off yet.'

Jessica gave a faint sniff of laughter. 'Thanks, anyway. I feel a bit better now.'

'That's what I'm here for,' said her mother, in all sincerity. 'You'll be okay, you know. Don't let him damage you. He's not worth it.'

'Tell me that again in a few weeks' time. At the moment, I still think I love him. If he turned up now with a bunch of flowers, I'd take him back in a heartbeat.'

'I imagine you would,' said Thea, aware that her timing

had been off. 'But it would never be the same after this. Phone me again tomorrow, will you? I want to be kept informed. Whatever happens, don't brood on your own. Go out and see people.' The idea of her daughter sitting in her flat, weeping over the unworthy boyfriend, made her want to abandon Snowshill and rush to Jessica's side. 'When are you supposed to be at work next?'

'Tomorrow. I don't know whether I can face it. I might see *him*.'

'Well, turn up if you can. Don't let him think he's won.'

'I didn't know we were in a fight,' the girl wailed. 'I thought he loved me.'

Thea made a wordless murmur of sympathy, and the conversation ended.

She spent the evening stewing over the beast that was Detective Constable Paul Middleman. That he could hurt her stalwart Jess was outrageous, and entirely unnecessary. Why couldn't he have finished with her in a dignified manner, letting her down gently, finding the courage to talk it over with her in an adult fashion? And to throw in wild accusations about racism was thoroughly despicable. As far as Thea had been able to see, his ethnicity had been readily assimilated into the relationship, a mildly interesting detail that came second to their work and their feelings for each other. At least, so she had assured herself, as it slowly dawned on her that he really wasn't a very nice person. The discomfort this realisation brought with it was almost entirely due to fears for Jessica's happiness – of course it was. But it also contained a thread of worry that it wasn't comfortable to dislike a black person. She had talked about it briefly with Drew, who had reassuringly understood.

She ought not to be thinking about Drew. During her recent stint in Cranham, looking after a handsome manor house and an old man in its lodge, Drew had come to visit her. But she had not seen him since then. His wife, Karen, had collapsed at the beginning of June and was still in hospital almost two months later. Thea had phoned for news once or twice, only to be given a terse 'no change' and an unspoken instruction to stay out of his life. *And quite right too*, she told herself firmly. Never mind that they had worked so well as a team, that his children had taken to her with enthusiasm, that she hugely admired his alternative funeral business. All his attention and time must go to Karen, obviously it must. Having been shot in the head a few years earlier, Karen had never quite returned to her former self; now, it seemed, some unidentified damage had been simmering deep in her brain, only to erupt, dramatically and shatteringly for the family.

But what if Karen died? nagged a wicked little voice. *What would happen then?* But she wouldn't die. The doctors would work out a treatment, would devise a brilliant piece of microsurgery that would restore her to perfect robustness. That was what they did – especially when the patient was a thirty-six-year-old mother of two. Nobody was going to let her die without an epic medical struggle.

Jessica – that was where her thoughts ought to lie. Her poor unhappy daughter, suffering her first major romantic reversal, humiliated and betrayed. Thea could well understand the difficulties Jess would have in going back to work and facing the dubious sympathy of her colleagues. Police officers were notoriously flippant about matters of the heart. Jokes would be made, callous remarks exchanged. The loss of dignity would be impossible to conceal, when both parties were working in the same team. Paul would be in and out of her workspace, forcing Jessica to speak to him in the line of duty. The best hope was that an unusually sensitive senior officer would ensure that this didn't happen for at least a few days. There would probably be lectures about the folly of embarking on a relationship with a close working colleague. There were probably rules against it, which would be virtually impossible to enforce, but which did make good sense. The girl would learn some useful lessons in the course of her suffering, but Thea knew all too well that this would bring no consolation at all in the short term.

And Yvonne Parker, who had gone missing. This was another urgent subject that she ought to be thinking about. It mattered a great deal, after all. If the woman didn't turn up, then she, Thea, was unlikely to be paid for her work. She would have to apply to the husband, or possibly the son or the soon-to-be-married daughter living somewhere in Wales.

She mentally tested a variety of hypotheses as to where her employer might have gone. The story about her broken marriage already had two versions which did not entirely match up. Something odd and mysterious had led to the departure of Victor, according to Blake from next door. Yvonne herself had said something about being humiliated and made ill by the break-up. She had not appeared to be

41

especially secretive about it, despite Blake's implications. If she had experienced a powerful loss of nerve, somewhere on the M4, that didn't strike Thea as altogether unexpected. She was very likely cowering anonymously in a B&B while she tried to regain her courage. Given her timid dithering manner, this seemed altogether plausible. Other more dramatic ideas were dismissed. Loss of memory; abduction; a deliberate plan involving extensive lies and deceits – all felt utterly wrong in the light of the woman's personality. Even the possibility that she had been the victim of violence felt unconvincing. Why would anybody bother to kidnap such a feeble creature?

But if she hadn't materialised by the end of the next day, something would have to be done. Victor might call the police, of course, if he was as genuinely worried as he sounded. Thea herself would feel increasingly impelled to take action, if only to inform Yvonne's husband that she needed some sort of assurance that she would be paid.

She ate a scrappy meal and took the dog outside to catch the last rays of the summer sun. The village in the hollow down to the left seemed to be comatose and there was a peaceful silence. Lights were coming on in the few windows she could see from the garden, and she noticed a watery beam coming from amongst the crocosmia in one of Yvonne's flower beds. Closer examination showed it to be a solar-powered light, placed inexplicably amidst the flowers. Over the next ten minutes she found three more, barely visible in the densely packed beds. Once darkness fell, they might make better sense, she supposed. Having charged themselves up during the sunny day, they could well give a healthy light – perhaps even enough to prove annoying to anybody eager to avoid light pollution, as Thea was.

Idly, she poked about, searching for more of the lights. No two were the same, and she assumed they must form another kind of collection, like the stuff in the house. As she gently moved the tall flowers aside, without any warning she was attacked by an unseen assailant, which inflicted a sharp pain in her lower arm. It was impossibly intense and she ran blindly onto the tiny lawn, swiping at the affected spot, in case the attacker was still there. 'What on earth was it?' she demanded shrilly of the indifferent garden. Her dog was close by, watching her with a wholly unhelpful alertness. 'Oooh,' she moaned as the pain got steadily worse. She cradled her arm, swaying from side to side, gripped by a deepening agony, trying to think lucidly.

With muddled intentions, she made for the house. It seemed she could walk quite steadily, her faculties still functioning. Had it been a snake, she wondered? Surely she would have seen it. It could only have been an insect of some kind – but what could have such a terrible sting as this? Normally an assault by a wasp or bee hurt acutely for a minute or two and then abated. This was still as bad as at first, if not worse.

She went into the kitchen and switched on the bright central light. The place on her arm was already swelling and red. She held it under the cold tap, which made little difference, and tried to remember what one was meant to do. Hold the arm up high? Or did that send the poison directly to your heart and kill you? Suck it out? Rub it with butter? In the bathroom there was probably an assortment of remedies such as antihistamine or that chalky pink stuff she could never remember the name of. It was meant for sunburn, which implied a cooling effect. The arm was still swelling, she noted, and really very hot. The pain seemed to have reached the bone, a circle of aching wrongness that made her want to cry.

'Can I help?'

The voice came from the doorway, and she flinched, part alarmed, part ready to throw herself onto any possible rescuer.

'I've been stung,' she gasped. 'It's agony.'

'Hornet,' nodded Blake calmly. 'There's a nest of them in your roof. I thought that must be it, so I brought this.' He held out a tube of ointment, and proceeded to unscrew the cap.

Chapter Four

The ointment made little immediate difference, but the mere fact of another person taking charge had a soothing effect, at least to start with. Then questions began to form. 'Were you watching me? In the garden?' she asked, with a frown. The idea was distinctly unwelcome.

'No, of course not. I heard you moaning and came out to see what had happened. My door and windows were open, and you did make quite a noise.'

'Did I?' She could only remember uttering one soft complaint. 'I thought it might have been a snake. I don't think I've ever seen a hornet.'

'They're increasing, apparently, but they're not usually aggressive. They look exactly like wasps, only three times the size – at least.'

'This one was definitely aggressive. I didn't do anything to provoke it. Am I allergic, do you think?'

'You are very swollen. Lucky it wasn't your throat, or you might have been choked to death.' The relish in his voice was unmistakable.

'I've never known such pain. I didn't know where to put myself.'

'Is it better now?'

'A bit. Either that, or I'm getting used to it. I'll be scared to go outside again after this.'

'Honestly, you don't have to be. It's not likely to happen again.'

'Have *you* ever been stung by one?'

He shook his head with a rueful smile. 'Actually, I think they're rather beautiful. I know that sounds crazy, but it's true.'

'I'll take your word for it. Why doesn't Yvonne have the nest destroyed? Why didn't she *tell* me about it?'

'She'd never do that. Live and let live is her motto when it comes to nature.'

'You're both mad, then,' said Thea with feeling. 'I've a good mind to call the council first thing in the morning.'

His eyes widened and the smile vanished. 'Don't you dare!' he flashed. 'You have no right to do anything of the kind.'

'The way I see it, I've got a *duty* to do it. What if they stung a small child? It could be fatal.'

'Nonsense. They hardly ever sting anybody at all. Just leave well alone, you silly woman.'

Her rescuer had turned into an adversary, which felt deeply unfair in her weakened condition. She lifted her chin, and fought back a renewed urge to cry. 'Well, don't let me keep you,' she said coldly. 'You must have packing to do.'

'What? Oh . . . yes. I mean, no, it's all done. But I'll go, if you think you'll be all right.'

'I'm fine. Thanks for the ointment.'

'I'll leave it with you, in case you want some more. It should start working any moment now.'

'Yes . . . it is, I think. And the swelling seems to have stopped. Thanks again.'

She waited in vain for an apology for his rudeness. 'No word from Yvonne?' The subject change was offensive to Thea's sensitive feelings and she merely shrugged and shook her head.

'I guess we'd have heard if she'd had an accident. But I must admit I'm worried. She can't be coping as well as I thought she would.'

'Coping with what?'

'People. Surprises. Unkindness. The usual things.' He gave her a direct look. 'You probably wouldn't understand. I don't detect much vulnerability in your robust little soul.'

She took it as blatant criticism, the effect of which was to once again make her want to cry. She had rapidly come to hate Hyacinth House and Snowshill and everything that had happened through the long day since she had left her home in Witney at 9 a.m. 'Mind your own business,' she hissed, turning away from him. 'Now please go away.'

He went, with a faint smile and not a vestige of apology.

She took Hepzie up to bed with her at ten-fifteen, closing the windows tightly against any possible incursion from hornets. The thought of a nest of them somewhere just above her head was terrifying. Her arm throbbed, still fiery to the touch. The room felt airless and she fetched a large glass of water for thirsty awakenings during the night. The

47

bedroom was marginally less cluttered than the rest of the house, but still contained too much furniture and a crazy excess of ornaments. A deep-red wax sculpture sat proudly on the mantelpiece over the tiled fireplace. It was shaped like a fantasy castle, with twisty turrets and shadowy grottoes, which she found appealing in spite of herself. The fragility of it, combined with the obvious imaginative work that had gone into it, raised paradoxes in her mind, echoing Blake's accusation that she herself was unnaturally strong. It carried implications of a lack of femininity, and worse – a lack of empathy and consideration for others. This she emphatically rejected, as she rehearsed the many occasions when she had been kind to people. Hadn't she offered her daughter all the sympathy and attention anybody could wish for, that very day?

But these fragments of self-justification were eclipsed by memories of much less benign conduct, particularly towards her former boyfriend, Phil Hollis. She was never going to forgive herself for the way she had shown such selfish impatience over his damaged back, when they were in Temple Guiting. Every time she thought about it, she accused herself more deeply of cruel and callous behaviour. She had even told Drew Slocombe about it, as if to warn him about her darker side. He had laughed it off and claimed to be equally cold-hearted at times. She had not believed him for a moment.

She drifted off to sleep, eventually, after an hour or more of jumbled thinking, most of it uncomfortable. Her dreams when they came involved her sister Jocelyn, whose life was never easy and who at times needed more help than the family willingly gave. She dreamt that Joss was being attacked by a gang of small boys with sticks while her own husband and children looked on uncaringly.

When she woke on Sunday morning, the dream was still vivid, its message seemingly important. Something to do with victims and wanton cruelty and the necessity of giving assistance without asking questions or making excuses.

'Hmm,' she said to her dog. 'I wonder what that's really all about.'

A car horn pipped in the road outside and she got up to see what it was. Blake was walking quickly down his crooked garden path, wheeling a heavy-looking bag behind him. The driver did not get out, but from the dispassionate nod Blake gave him, Thea concluded that it was a taxi of some sort. 'Have fun,' she muttered, unsure as to whether or not she was glad of his departure.

The phone rang at nine-fifteen. It was Yvonne Parker, full of gushing apology. 'Victor told me he phoned you yesterday, because I was late. I'm really so terribly sorry for worrying you. Everything's perfectly all right. I just . . .' she faltered. 'I lost my nerve, I suppose. When I saw the place he lives in, I just turned round and went to find a hotel for the night. I needed to have a proper think before I could face him. Of course, he's furious with me.' She gave a little giggle and Thea guessed that the man himself was listening.

'The place he lives in?' she queried, thinking that Crouch End was rather a good address as far as she was aware.

'It's an awful little flat in a shared house. He told me he'd rented somewhere while he looked for a new house, but I never dreamed it would be something so small.'

Plainly, Victor was *not* listening, Thea decided. She made a sympathetic sound and waited for further disclosures. 'Anyway, he's gone out to get some milk. We're supposed to be getting down to business over coffee.' The laugh she gave was decidedly forced.

'Well, I'm glad you're all right. I wish I could tell Blake, but he's gone already. We were worried about you.'

Yvonne laughed. 'Oh, Blake's always like that. He's like an old mother hen, isn't he?'

'He seems to be,' she agreed, not really wanting to talk about Blake. Instead, she wanted to ask a dozen questions: What did Victor say about her delay? How was it possible that she hadn't known how he was living? Was she going to bunk up with him in the bedsit? And could she, Thea, please call the council about the hornets?

'I was stung last night by a hornet,' she said, slightly too loudly. 'Blake says there's a nest in the roof.'

'Oh God. You weren't, were you? Was it in the house?'

'No, the garden. But really, it's a serious health hazard. They ought to be exterminated.'

'Oh, no. The poor things don't deserve that. I'm so sorry you were stung, but they honestly aren't a bit aggressive. That's the first sting there's been. You were just unlucky. It won't happen again.'

'You can't know that. I'll be scared to use the garden.' It was the first time this had properly occurred to her and the idea was shattering. 'I'll feel as if I'm under siege.'

'No, no. It'll be fine. Is the sting still bad this morning?'

Thea examined the place on her arm. She could

clearly see the point where the sting went in, with the surrounding flesh still tender and stretched. 'It's swollen and itchy,' she reported.

'Oh dear. Where is it exactly?'

'On my arm. A couple of inches above the wrist.'

'That's a sensitive place,' Yvonne sympathised. 'I really am sorry. But please don't let it bother you. It's only a small nest, and they won't be troublesome for another month yet, at least. It was just bad luck,' she repeated. Her voice sounded stronger than Thea had so far heard it, the insistence hard to withstand.

'Well . . .' she began reluctantly. 'It isn't really fair . . .'

'I'll pay you extra for the injury,' said Yvonne quickly. 'And if it happens again, then I suppose you will have to call somebody to get rid of them. I just hope it won't come to that. Is that all right?'

'It'll have to be, I suppose,' said Thea grudgingly. 'And thank you for letting me know you were all right. I might have reported you as missing, otherwise.'

Yvonne gave a little shriek, either of amusement or alarm. 'Gosh – don't do that,' she said.

When she'd gone, Thea realised she had cast herself as the stern voice of common sense and responsible action. Never seeing herself as exactly feckless, she was nonetheless capable of breaking a few rules when it suited her, and defying some of the more bureaucratic authority that seemed designed to obstruct for the sake of it. How had she come to be such an upright citizen all of a sudden?

Somehow the resolution of the mystery of Yvonne's whereabouts during Saturday afternoon left her feeling more troubled than before. Yvonne's apparent ignorance of her husband's circumstances felt very strange, particularly as Blake-next-door seemed so confident that he knew most of the story. The purported reason for Yvonne's visit was basically to do with money for Belinda's wedding – and now there seemed good reason to think Victor was perhaps rather short of cash. Thea's natural curiosity burgeoned as she tried to construct a convincing narrative to explain the Parker family's situation. After all, she told herself, if a person invited you into their home and gave you full jurisdiction over it, even paying you to fill that role, you had every right to enquire into the background. There were things a house-sitter needed to know, if she was to do a good job.

The threat of the hornets receded somewhat as her arm began to feel more normal. It was Sunday morning, the day was dry and she had no immediate tasks to perform. Time, then, to go and make the acquaintance of the cows in the field behind the house. Before embarking on her new career in the Cotswolds she had never imagined the existence of these small patches of land belonging to so many individual houses. With the decline of traditional agriculture it seemed that homeowners had managed to snap up odd acreages as small farms were swallowed up by massive agribusinesses. Awkward shapes, large trees, steep slopes and ancient restrictions all led to the ready sacrifice of these unprofitable nooks. They made little difference to a farm of five hundred acres or more, and a massive improvement to the value and quality of a family house. Yvonne seemed to have no use for her amenity, however. Somewhere there must still be a small farm with more cattle than was comfortable, so that these few had overflowed into an auxiliary field.

These creatures plainly came from a dairy farm. Yvonne had said they were due to calve shortly, and were enjoying a short holiday from the relentless milking routine. They were all black and white, with prominent hip bones and little sign of any spare flesh. Their pregnancies swelled their sides, giving an impression of flagons on legs, viewed from the front. Two looked to be past their prime, with flaccid udders all too visible. They turned their big monochrome faces to her in idle curiosity when she went to the small gate to view them.

The grass seemed plentiful on the small uneven field, and she remained for several minutes watching them snatch mouthfuls of it, swallowing it whole. They were like efficient harvesting machines, moving forward and scything the grass in a pattern that seemed random, but might not have been. The rhythm was soothing and timeless. Ungulates such as these had been mowing grass for millennia, all across the world, and she liked to trace the bygone links down the centuries, from the first concerted efforts by man to slaughter and eat the beasts, through to a realisation that their milk was good to drink and their hides made excellent coverings. She found herself approving of animals with a purpose. *Unlike those damned hornets,* she thought crossly.

Then one of the cows made an ungainly leap forward, emitting a low bellow as she moved. Before Thea could understand what had happened, another animal did the same thing. Were they being stung, as Thea had been? She could see no swarming insects. Instead, as the second cow gave a startled jump, she saw a stone roll to the ground. A few moments later, a third missile came into view, this time missing the cows and landing in the hedge close to Thea, with a rustle and a clunk.

'Hey!' she called, to the invisible attacker. 'Stop that!' Across the field there was a wide metal gate, opening onto the track beyond Blake's house. She glimpsed a small fair head, and immediately made the link with the nasty little boy who had chopped down the roses the day before.

The blond head bobbed out of sight. Furiously, Thea ran through the garden of Hyacinth House and out into the road. Fifteen yards to the right, she turned into the opening onto the track, her faithful spaniel trotting after her.

There was no sign of the boy. A small house stood further down the track, on the other side from the field containing the cows. Her rage unabated, Thea marched along and rapped loudly on the front door, before noticing that it was so festooned with clematis and ivy that it could not have been opened for years.

'What do you want?' came a harsh female voice.

'Does a boy live here, with fair hair? About nine or ten?'

'What if he does?' The woman had come into view from the side of the house, apparently ready to do battle. She was short, tanned and confident. Her hair was a tangle of numerous shades from the yellow of fresh cheese to the dull brown of winter mud. Her accent was rough and she appeared to be in her late forties. If she hadn't been obviously living in a house, Thea would have taken her for a gypsy from an earlier era.

'He's been throwing stones at the cows in Yvonne Parker's field. And yesterday he cut the heads off her roses. He's a menace. Are you his mother?'

'If you're talking about my Stevie, then yes, I'm his mother. What's it to do with you?'

'I'm in charge of Yvonne's house. I can't let the cows in her field get hurt. Besides, it's a vile thing to do. What's the matter with the little beast?'

Too late she realised this was a dangerous question. She braced herself for the news that the kid was autistic or had Down's syndrome, or was in the grip of some dreadful personality disorder.

But it seemed she had struck a chord. 'You just leave him to me.' The expression was grim, the eyes darting past Thea apparently in search of the delinquent. 'I'll see it doesn't happen again. Bloody little pest. Never does a thing he's told. The cows aren't really hurt, are they?'

'Startled more than hurt, I think. But why would he do such a thing?'

'You might well ask.' The sigh that followed was more exasperated than defeated. 'I'll see he doesn't do it again, don't worry. One of these days I'm going to kill him, if he goes on like this.'

There didn't seem to be much more for Thea to say. The woman's expression was complicated – anger, impatience and a dash of anxiety were all in evidence and all made sense. It was unlikely that this was the first complaint against the boy, and the attentions of the police could not be far away if his recent behaviour was typical.

'Right, then,' she blustered. 'Thank you. Perhaps his

father . . . ?' She knew it was another risky remark, but it was meant as an opening for the woman to disclose some reason for the delinquency of her son. It backfired.

'Never mind his father,' came the snarling response. 'I'm quite able to deal with my own child, thank you very much.' She glanced over her shoulder as if worried about being overheard. 'Don't you go talking about his father,' she warned in a low voice, 'when you know nothing at all about us, and not likely to, neither.'

'Sorry. Just tell him I don't think much of the way he's been acting, all right?'

The woman gave a quick nod, and rolled her eyes insolently. There seemed to be some grounds for expecting that she would chastise the child. Thinking of the deliberate attempt to hurt the cows, Thea shivered. If young Stevie really wanted to inflict pain and injury, what defence did she and her dog have? He lived only yards from Hyacinth House, and might well have conceived a grudge against her already, thanks to her reporting him to his mother.

'Stevie! Where are you? Come here, you little bugger.' The woman's voice rang out unselfconsciously through the quiet Sunday lane. There was no immediate sign that the boy was making any move to obey.

Thea lingered, to see what would happen next. 'Stevie!' roared the woman again.

'What?' came a child's high call from somewhere behind the little house.

'Come here. There's a lady says you've been hurting them cows. What have I told you?'

56

No reply, but a moment later, the woman went on, 'There you are. Now stay where I can see you. You're not to be trusted out of my sight . . .'

Thea moved away and the voice faded into a mumble.

Maybe he wasn't such a little monster after all, she mused – just a bored lonely kid, as Blake had suggested, in the first days of the endless summer holiday.

She had coffee in the kitchen of Hyacinth House and planned the next stage of her explorations. 'Come on,' she said to the dog, when the drink was finished. 'Let's find your lead and go for another little walk. As far as I can see it'll take all of ten minutes to explore the village, but we may as well give it a go.'

Passing the home of Janice and Ruby, she slowed for a good look at it. Made of the identical stone to Hyacinth House, it was a very different shape – taller, with gables. A copper beech tree dominated the front garden, along with something even more exotic that Thea thought might be an aspen. The handsome gate that had been closed the day before now stood slightly open. 'Morning,' came a female voice behind her. 'Are you the house-sitter?'

Thea turned to be faced with the bosom of a tall woman. A *very* tall woman. She looked up into a soft face framed with short mid-brown hair. A face that suggested self-sufficiency, good sense, patience – characteristics that would normally befit an older woman. This one was some years short of forty, if Thea was any judge. 'Yes, I'm Thea Osborne,' she said. 'Your house is lovely. Assuming this *is* where you live?' she added.

'I'm Janice Williams,' the woman nodded. 'I've just been

after that damned Stevie again. He's been in the garden. I can always tell.'

'He seems to be quite a little menace,' said Thea with feeling. It was surprisingly good to find an ally against the delinquent. 'He chopped the flowers off Yvonne's roses yesterday. Today he's been throwing stones at cows.' She paused. It was only fifteen minutes since she had left the Horsfall cottage. 'Have you seen him just now?'

'An hour ago. Why?'

'Oh, sorry. I always ask too many questions. It's a bad habit.'

'I imagine you feel a need to understand the place, if you're going to be here for a few weeks,' said Janice, understandingly.

Here, Thea realised, was another person who could easily have fed Yvonne Parker's cats. It was becoming increasingly clear that she had other less obvious roles to perform. Like guarding the roses from Stevie Horsfall.

'Mum!' A girl's voice came from somewhere behind the copper beech. 'What are you doing?'

'Coming, Rube,' Janice called back.

The daughter of the house came slowly down the short drive, her head cocked enquiringly at the sight of Thea. She seemed to be about sixteen. She was probably five feet ten, making her at least an inch shorter than her mother. Together they made a formidable pair. 'This is Thea,' Janice introduced. 'My daughter, Ruby. Stevie's been up to his tricks again,' she added.

Ruby was fair-haired, with the natural grace of a girl her age, but she had hard lines in her face, her jaw chiselled from stone. She kicked angrily at a small stone, and ground her teeth. 'It can't go on,' she growled. 'We've got six weeks of it, if we don't do something. There won't be a flower left in the garden, otherwise. The gate doesn't stop him.'

'We could pay to send him to a summer camp,' said Janice lightly.

'Or get a Rottweiler,' said the girl.

Thea had the impression that it was a well-rehearsed conversation. The lurking sense of helplessness and frustration was all too apparent. 'It must be a real pain,' she sympathised.

'You understand why Yvonne felt she had to get a house-sitter,' said Janice. 'We'll have to do the same if we decide to go away. I don't suppose you're free, are you?' She laughed to indicate a lack of seriousness. 'Don't worry,' she added. 'We'll leave it until September, when at least he'll be at school for most of the day.'

'We can't, Mum,' said Ruby with exaggerated composure. 'I'll be at college.'

'Oh, well . . .' Janice tailed off.

'I expect I'll see you again,' said Thea, aware that she was detaining them. 'I'm off to do some exploring.'

Although tiny on the map, the village was so multi-levelled that it felt as if a plunge down one of the steep little side streets might open out into a whole new area of settlement, much as it did in Blockley. The sporadic summer traffic heading for the Manor was easily negotiated as she led the spaniel cautiously along the narrow road into the village. She could see the yellow church with a squat tower, a triangle of buildings set around it. The first landmark she noticed was a pale stone wall with strange circular shapes set into it. It bordered the route to the pub: a quiet untravelled street, several feet lower than the slightly larger and busier road to her right.

Jumbled was the word that came to mind as she scanned the scene before her. Then she quickly adjusted her impression to something more admiring. No two roofs were the same, the whole picture offering very few straight lines. The hill that rose close by felt protective on this sunny morning – in other seasons it might well seem more of a threatening, looming presence. The colours of the stone were variations on the usual Cotswold creamy-yellow, the scents all of natural vegetation and warm earth. There was honeysuckle somewhere, her nose informed her.

Nobody greeted her. There was activity in the tiny car park next to the Snowshill Arms, and people were talking somewhere close by, but she and her dog attracted no attention. Because, she realised, this was a village inured to strangers. Thousands of people came every year to see the Manor, and many of them would take a little walk down this very street, call in at the pub and perhaps the church, take a few photos and drive away again. On a summer Sunday, the only surprise was that she was not part of a much larger throng of pedestrian visitors. Most of them seemed to be firmly inside their cars.

All the houses looked satisfyingly old to her reasonably tutored eye. There was no modern sprawl on the outskirts of Snowshill, as there was in Cranham and other places. Here there remained a sense of isolation, thanks to the long featureless approach from virtually every side along rising ground, which lent itself to the growing of corn rather than the erection of dwellings. The tourists could be redefined as pilgrims to the small oasis without too much whimsy. The pub itself was plainly of ancient origins, any urge to modernise thwarted by the lack of space and impossible levels.

She admitted to herself that she was in no rush to return to Hyacinth House, with the hornets and the malicious Stevie. The cats had yet to manifest any interest in her, content to eat the food she provided and leave it at that. Perhaps she ought to climb the nearest hill, which one guidebook had claimed to be the most significant feature in the area. Oat Hill was, apparently, the highest point for some miles. It certainly looked steep, and she doubted her stamina was sufficient to comfortably reach the summit.

It was also nearly lunchtime and she was hungry. Never eager to venture into a pub on her own, she decided not to seek sustenance there. It probably refused admittance to dogs, anyway. Instead, she would take a quick exploratory walk around the church, emerging onto the higher street from which she might be able to see the famous Manor.

This, she confirmed to herself, was indeed the heart of the village, with very few further houses to be discovered. Surrounding the church was a modest area of grass, with one small patch outside the church wall, to the north, that might at a stretch designate itself as the village green. It boasted a wooden seat for good measure.

The church was much more in harmony with its immediate landscape than many she had seen, the low tower making no attempt to compete with the hills surrounding it. The houses clustered companionably on every side, quietly ignoring the tourists and pretending it was still the eighteenth century. There was no hint of a service going on in the church, despite the day of the week. After all, she told herself, this was hardly a village of sufficient size to warrant a full-time vicar – and that meant fortnightly or even monthly Sunday services. As she passed between church and pub, she noted a board listing several small churches in the same group, all represented by the same overworked clergyman.

A young man was standing close by, taking photographs of the buildings, carefully considering his angles, squinting at the sky before getting down on one knee and pointing his lens at the church tower. Thea was tempted to creep up behind him to share in the view he was capturing, but she resisted. He was unlikely to take kindly to a spaniel tangling her lead in his ankles just as he found the perfect frame.

There was nothing left to do and she began to feel conspicuous, dawdling aimlessly through the little streets. She could perhaps find somewhere quiet and send a text to Jessica. *Somewhere quiet*, she repeated to herself with a smile. That would not be difficult. Like many another Cotswold village, quietness was the default condition. Isolated, and secluded as well in this instance, even with the famous Manor no distance away and visitors part of the backdrop. Snowshill was not as utterly deserted as Frampton Mansell or Duntisbourne Abbots had been, but it was still very far from busy.

She sat on the seat provided, her back to the church wall, and extracted the BlackBerry from her pocket. After several months, it still gave her a little thrill as she tapped a finger on one icon after another, keyed in the message and sent it winging its way to her daughter. The signal was strong, and she wondered whether she should contact anybody else to ease her growing sense of loneliness.

But who? Drew was the first name that sprang to mind, but she really couldn't call him on an unjustified whim. Her mother would be pleased to chat, but the sort of exchange she could offer was not what Thea was looking for. She always felt restless and somehow uneasy after speaking to her mother, as if more had been required of her than she had been able to give. She had two sisters and a brother, but they would all draw alarmed conclusions from a sudden phone call in the middle of a Sunday.

Instead, she idly thumbed some of the options on the screen, and found herself reading a list of websites featuring Snowshill. The ability to do this without a phone line or a computer, out in the open air, was still a great novelty and she could hardly believe it when it worked.

She followed a blog, selected at random, in which a keen walker had passed through this very spot a year ago, and seen a ghost in the Gents of the Snowshill Arms. Convinced of its authenticity, he had researched the history of the area and discovered a monastery on the site, with taverns and inns provided for travellers. Always fascinated by history, Thea lost herself in imaginings of bygone days on the very spot where she was sitting.

It passed a very pleasant twenty minutes, Hepzie contentedly flopped at her side. At the end of it, she had perused a repetitive series of accounts of the Manor and the man who had bought it in 1919, who dabbled in black magic in the attics and entertained famous writers, several of whom found his growing collection of bizarre objects more than a little strange. Lots of people were perfectly certain that there were ghosts abroad in Snowshill, though almost entirely confined to the eccentric Manor. Nobody else had seen a wraith in the Gents at the pub.

And still the boyish features of Drew Slocombe hovered before her mind's eye, more insistent than any ghost could be. She wanted to know how his wife was doing, whether his business was suffering badly while he was occupied at Karen's bedside, and what was happening to his children.

Then, within five minutes, as if she had conjured him by the power of thought, a text popped up on the screen.

Are you in the Cotswolds again? If so, would you be able to go and see Mrs Simmonds' grave? I haven't been for months as you can imagine. The field could do with a check, too. Best, Drew.

It was such a polite and formal message, she laughed aloud, startling her dog. Perhaps Drew too had a shiny new phone which could compose and send messages almost telepathically, with little of the painful laborious thumbing that there had been a year or two before. He certainly seemed to have mastered it at last.

She sent a quick reply.

No problem. Hope things are ok? Thea.

A shadow falling across her legs made her look up. A tall woman stood over her, her back to the sun, making her face hard to see clearly. 'You've been sitting there for ages, playing with that phone.' The tone held a hint of accusation.

'I was reading about Snowshill. Did you know that Charles Paget Wade was a vampire?'

'Rubbish. Of course he wasn't.'

'It's a good story, though. Especially these days when vampires are all the rage.'

'"All the rage"?' The repetition of the phrase was made with amused scorn. 'What an old-fashioned thing to say.'

'I'm not making a very good impression, am I?' said Thea, rather seriously. 'Let me stand up, and I won't feel at such a disadvantage.'

'Don't bother. I'll sit down. I could do with a rest.'

The newcomer sank onto the wooden seat and turned sideways, offering a hand. 'I'm Clara Beauchamp,' she said formally. 'I live here.'

'Pleased to meet you. I'm Thea Osborne, house-sitting for Yvonne Parker. I assume you know her?'

'Oh yes. We never thought she'd finally bite the bullet, though. You know, she hasn't seen Victor since he left. And that's been years now.'

'Five, apparently.'

'Blimey! Is it really? Feels like last week.'

Thea wanted to retort *'Blimey'? Isn't that a bit old-fashioned?* but she kept her peace. 'Do you know a badly behaved child called Stevie? Must be nine or ten, and appears to run wild.'

Clara Beauchamp's face tightened. 'Little swine. He's the bane of all our lives. You should watch out for that dog of yours.' Hepzie met the woman's eye with placid unconcern.

'His mother struck me as more than capable of keeping him under control, if she made the effort. If he's like that now, what'll he be doing when he's sixteen?'

'She does her best, I suppose. I never thought I'd say it, but it's tempting to think the kid was born bad. The whole exercise was doomed from the start.'

'Oh?' Thea met the woman's eyes, registering her as roughly her own age, big-boned and fair-haired. A faint whiff of horse seemed to emanate from her, which probably explained Hepzie's interested sniffing of her legs.

'It's a long story. And a lot of it's just gossip and supposition, anyway. Two centuries ago, she'd have been labelled as a witch.'

'Witches *and* vampires! I seem to have blundered into a time warp here.' And indeed, that was how she was beginning to feel. Genuinely feral children were definitely unknown in the twenty-first century.

'This village hasn't changed so very much in that time, in some respects. The Manor has always brought visitors who spread stories about it and give Snowshill a reputation for weirdness.' She waved an expressive hand at a high wall beyond the pub. Beyond it Thea could just see a roof, apparently belonging to a large old building.

'Is *that* the Manor?' she said with a frown. 'I thought it was a mile or more away, from the signs.'

Clara Beauchamp laughed. 'It's a trick. You have to drive nearly half a mile to the car park, and then walk back on yourself. You can't even get in on foot from the centre of the village.'

'I'm amazed,' Thea confessed. 'That seems like something in a dream, or maybe an optical illusion.' She shook her head, wondering why she found it so startling. 'And those little houses. They've all got National Trust colours to the paintwork.' She was focused on a row of small dwellings that looked like almshouses. The dark greeny-blue was repeated on a doorway at the end of the Manor wall. The sense of unreality intensified.

Clara laughed again. 'It's always good fun, watching people realise how it all fits together. Often they come back three or four times before the penny drops.'

'It's a whole other world,' said Thea, not quite sure that she liked it.

'We *are* rather cut off,' Clara agreed. 'Especially when it snows. And it *does* snow here, quite a lot. The parish council even has a snow warden, would you believe?'

'Stevie,' prompted Thea. 'Tell me more.'

'Okay – his mother, Gudrun, is a single parent, had him when she was forty-four. Her only one. Invested everything in him. Spoilt him rotten, so he thinks he rules the world.'

'Good-run?' Thea repeated. 'Is that what you said?'

'G-U-D-R-U-N. Like in *Women in Love*, the D.H. Lawrence novel. It's Swedish or German or something, I think. Awful name, if you ask me.'

'She doesn't look remotely Scandinavian.'

'No. I assume her mother liked the book, same as mine. Except it was *Sons and Lovers* in my case.'

Thea grimaced helplessly. 'You've lost me. I don't think I've ever read any Lawrence.'

Clara Beauchamp's cheerful laugh erupted for a third time. 'You're too young. Our mothers were mad about him – yours too, I expect. He was "all the rage" in the sixties, apparently. In any case, it gives me and Gudrun something in common.' She used her fingers to draw the inverted commas in the air.

Precious little, thought Thea, remembering the gypsy-like woman. 'She must be a lot older than she looks. I guessed about forty-eight.'

'She'll be fifty-four next week, as it happens. She was born two days before my eldest sister – who is furious about it, because on a bad day she can look at least sixty. Not fair at all when you consider how much she spends on anti-ageing stuff. Gudrun just has the right bones and skin, apparently.'

'Does Stevie have a father?'

Clara's face constricted, her mouth clamped shut. Thea waited, head slightly cocked, eyes wide. The reply, when it came, was disappointing. 'Nobody knows who he was. There are various malicious stories but I don't believe any of them. Gudrun has never told a soul, to my knowledge. Certainly, if she has, that person knows how to keep a secret.'

'I get the impression that you like her?' Thea hazarded. 'You think Gudrun's all right?'

'That's entirely the wrong question. She's elemental, a free spirit, a force to be reckoned with. It's not a matter of *liking* her. Most of us just gaze on with open mouths as she forges through life without a second thought. Gudrun gets what she wants, without ever thinking about it. Even when it turns out to be a huge mistake, she doesn't agonise, like other people would.'

'So you're saying Stevie was a huge mistake?'

'Oh yes. About as huge as they come.'

'Poor little chap,' said Thea sadly.

Chapter Five

Sunday lunch was a late affair, comprising a bowl of soup and a cheese sandwich. Catering for herself during the house-sitting commissions was sometimes difficult and frequently boring. Now and then she would be given free access to a well-stocked freezer, as part of the deal. More usually, she was expected to fend for herself, driving ten miles or more to a supermarket in one of the larger towns. Often she grabbed basic necessities in small expensive village shops, or those attached to petrol stations. Occasional meals in local pubs were disproportionately welcomed, as a result.

It had been a relief to meet and talk to Clara Beauchamp, who had vaguely offered her company one evening in the following week, if Thea felt the need. 'I live with my boyfriend, half a mile from here,' she said. 'And my mother's in that house there.' She had pointed to a classic Cotswold cottage halfway down the street. 'I work in Cirencester, so I'm never here during the day. Rupert's in town all week, so it would be nice if you could come over. I've got Yvonne's landline number – I'll call you. Or should I take yours?' She eyed the BlackBerry still in Thea's hand.

With a small effort, Thea recited her mobile number. *How Phil would approve*, she thought ruefully. Only a year before, she had been wilfully technophobic, much to her lover's irritation. Now, not only was she enthusiastically using the thing, the yet more resistant Drew Slocombe was blithely sending texts, and perhaps even developing a website for his business.

Now she wished she had somebody she might phone for a long lazy Sunday chat, mentally reviewing possible candidates. Still mildly haunted by her dream of the night before, she paused at the thought of her sister Jocelyn, revising her earlier careless dismissal of the idea of calling her. Two years earlier Joss had spent a few days with her in Frampton Mansell, and since then they had seen little of each other. There were five children in the family, which meant there were very few opportunities for long lazy chats, besides which, it was not their habit to call each other. But it was worth a try, perhaps, especially in the light of the dream.

Jocelyn's husband answered the phone, sounding impatient. 'Oh, Thea . . . hello. What's the trouble?'

'No trouble at all. I just wondered if I could have a little chat with Joss.'

'She's upstairs. Hang on.'

Already Thea was regretting the impulse. Casual conversations about nothing were a waste of time. Her family had never gone in for such stuff, which meant that Jocelyn would leap to the same conclusion as her husband had, and assume there was a problem.

'Thea? What's the matter?'

'Nothing. I'm bored, that's all. Are you busy?'

'No more than usual. Where are you?'

'Snowshill, if you know where that is.'

'Not the foggiest. Is it snowing?'

'Not today. Apparently it does, quite a lot, in the due season.'

'Is it nice?'

'It's fantastically lovely. Same gorgeous old houses as there are all over the region. Plus a famous manor for good measure.'

'Sounds okay.'

'How about you? What're you doing for the summer? Mum said you might go to the Shetlands – can that be right? With the whole family?'

'Yes, it's all fixed. We leave on Wednesday and get the ferry. Everybody's wildly excited.'

'What an adventure. Lucky I caught you, then.'

'Thea – are you really okay? You sound odd. Sort of *drained*. What's the house like? Have you got loads to do?'

'It's stuffed full of knick-knacks. Hepzie and I daren't move in case we break something. But no, there's hardly any work. That's why I'm bored.'

'Have you met any people?'

'One or two. Nobody interesting. Oh – Jessica's boyfriend has dumped her. She's dreadfully upset, poor girl.'

'The swine! You never did like him, did you?'

'Not much. But I didn't think he'd be as rotten as this. He did it by text, apparently.'

'They've all forgotten how to speak face-to-face. Mine are getting to be the same.'

'I've got very fond of my BlackBerry, I must admit.'

'Pooh! A BlackBerry is very yesterday, dear. It's moved on since then.'

'Don't tell me that. I don't think I could face starting again with something else. Anyway – it does so many things, how can a new version be any better?'

'Don't ask me. Anyway, I can hear ructions in the garden. I'll have to go. I'm sure you'll have a lovely time there. The weather's good, and you can go and explore that manor.'

'Yes, I can. Go on then and quell the riot. And have a lovely holiday.'

'Thanks, we will. Bye, then.'

Thea disconnected the call with a rare feeling of warm sisterhood. She should value Jocelyn more highly, spend more time with her, keep up the bond between them. Their older brother, Damien, was difficult and distant, since becoming a committed Christian and trying to make them see how fulfilled and inspired he was. When they politely wished him well, but failed to adopt the same all-consuming faith, he had withdrawn from them. Their sister Emily was distant for other reasons, which nobody in the family could bring themselves to discuss.

Her arm was almost better, the terrible pain of the hornet sting almost as forgotten as the much more distant throes of childbirth – which had been far from excruciating anyway. Nonetheless, she harboured a persistent nervousness about the front garden, as well as an irritation with the overstuffed interior of the house. Sitting in the kitchen, she sipped coffee and wondered where she might spend the afternoon.

Yvonne's cats were slowly coming to accept her presence, slinking sinuously across the floor to crouch under the table, side by side. Hepzibah ignored them, having found a chair to her liking in the living room. It was positioned beneath the window, where sunshine fell for most of the afternoon. Thea had removed a hand-embroidered cushion from the seat and permitted the dog to curl up on the upholstery, promising herself that she would give it a thorough brushing on her final day.

As on the previous day, traffic flow past the house was sporadic as people headed for Snowshill Manor. Where did they all come from, she wondered? How far afield would people travel to see a motley accumulation of Japanese armoury, old clocks, Victorian toys, boxes, machines and a thousand other things? You looked, but couldn't touch. As far as she could understand it, there was no narrative, little chronology and a strong sense of pointless eccentricity. Yes, she would have to go and see it for herself, but the real interest lay in what had been hidden away in the secret attic room, which the National Trust had very sensibly banished to more esoteric realms where such objects were better understood. Nobody could accuse the National Trust of having any truck with witchcraft, with their wholesome teas and carefully labelled gardens.

Somehow she had entangled the sinister-sounding Charles Paget Wade with the delinquent lad, Stevie. There was a hint of malevolence surrounding them both – Wade with his sudden startling leaps from hidden passages, Stevie with his sticks and stones designed to damage. Wade had spent his younger years in the West Indies, amongst practitioners of voodoo and wild tales of zombies and black magic. Stevie had presumably spent his entire life being spoilt and indulged by his mother in a remote English village. Even the neighbours who regarded him as a menace appeared to accept him as a necessary element in their lives. Yvonne had given no advance warning of his predations. Perhaps he had just been having a bad day, and should be given a chance to redeem himself – especially after Clara's disclosures, minimal though they had been.

There was a limited range of choices as to how to pass the afternoon. She could drive to a local beauty spot and walk the dog again. She could wander back down the track past Gudrun's house and follow the official footpath leading to Dulverton Wood. Or, she remembered, she could go to Broad Campden and check out Drew's incipient burial ground. He had put the whole enterprise on hold when his wife fell ill, but the local council had already given outline permission for him to establish a modestly sized woodland cemetery, and he had effortlessly gained ownership of a house in the middle of the village. Funny he hadn't asked her to go and look at that as well, she thought. As far as she knew it was standing empty, with no firm plans for its future.

Outside, the sky was clouding over, some thickening grey areas hinting at rain. That would be very bad news, confining her to the house and all its oppressive contents.

'Come on, then,' she called the dog. 'We'll just go for a little drive, shall we? I need to get milk and fruit, anyway.'

Her car was parked just beyond the front hedge, there being no allotted space for vehicles within the official curtilage of the house. Hyacinth House did not possess so much as a garden shed. The lawnmower and a few tools lived under a flimsy overhanging device at the back of the house, supported by two wooden posts, without walls or doors.

As she reached the small gate which opened onto the road, she unlocked the car from a yard or so distant with the button on her keyring. The driver's side was closest to the wall, so she went to the passenger door to admit the dog, who had been sniffing at something just beyond the vehicle. Then she walked around the front, heading for the driver's door. But she never reached it. Lying crumpled on the grass, face down, legs sprawling, was a small body with very fair hair.

Chapter Six

Her mind froze, her only sensation a violent urge to find the child's mother and bring her to him. He belonged to her with a primitive irrational sense of rightness that could not be resisted. Having paused only to turn him over and ascertain from the inert white face and tightly constricted neck that he was dead, she went flying down the track to Gudrun's cottage. Not, she noted later, across the road to Janice and Ruby. Nor into the village where she could stand by the church and scream for help. Only one thought filled her head – the mother must be summoned.

Breathlessly, she ran round to the back, following a brick path becoming slippery in the first minutes of a heavy rain shower. 'Gudrun!' she shouted, throwing as much breath and energy into the word as she could muster. 'Are you there?'

There was a sound from within the house of a chair being scraped over a stone floor, and then a low 'Yeah? Who's that?'

'It's me,' called Thea unhelpfully, and threw open the door, unable to wait for Gudrun to gather herself.

'What d'you want? I was just having a bit of a rest. I was cutting up logs all morning.' She looked out at the sky. 'Raining, is it? Thought it would. Where's Stevie got to? Has he been up to his mischief again?'

'He's at my house – I mean, Yvonne's house. You've got to come. He's—' For the first time, she wondered what in the world she was thinking of, fetching the woman to witness the cruel killing of her only child. She almost backed away, hands aloft, saying she was sorry, it was nothing, just a silly mistake. Instead she looked away, focusing on the tidy pile of logs in a lean-to shed a few yards away.

'What? He's what? Hurt himself, you mean? Wait a minute – let me get my boots on.' Gudrun thrust her feet into a pair of black wellingtons standing just inside the door. 'Did you call an ambulance? How bad is he? Can't he walk?'

Thea led the way back up to the road, saying nothing. She could barely hear the questions being fired at her, her mind full of the image of the boy's small lifeless face, and the tight cord around his neck.

He lay where she'd left him, the rain starting to form a faint frosting on his clothes. As Gudrun rushed past her, her head twisting from side to side as she searched for her child, not seeing him at first, Thea found herself swaying in the closest she had ever come to a faint. How had she ever managed to fetch the woman? Her legs couldn't possibly have found such strength. How could such a gigantic catastrophe be happening, here before her eyes?

Everything had gone silent. Gudrun gathered up the limp body and clutched it to her breast, her eyes staring unfocused, straight ahead. Now and then she shook the boy, as if to force life into him. Her fingers toyed with the ligature round his neck, but made no serious attempt to remove it. It was as if she made no connection between it and the cause of the child's death. Thea choked slightly, as she slowly realised what had been done to young Stevie, how terrifying it must have been for him to feel it digging into his tender skin.

The BlackBerry was in her pocket, as always. She tremblingly took it out and tried to remember what to do to summon the police. Gudrun should have been shrieking at her, galvanising her into action, instead of just sitting there in the rain rocking her boy. Two or three cars passed a few yards away, one every half-minute or so. How could they fail to know what was happening, how badly they were needed? Too much time was passing; something was supposed to happen. When it did, it was far from useful.

Tears began to course down Thea's face of their own accord. Something had welled up like a great wave from deep inside her and erupted out of her eyes. Her chest pumped the fluid out, as if it were her lifeblood. It was much too terrible to deal with. Nothing so bad as this had ever happened before, not in the whole history of the world. Gudrun's face bore witness to that. Gudrun had turned to stone, as dead and useless as the child in her arms.

It was the spaniel, yapping impatiently from inside Thea's car, that set things in motion at last.

Thea had been involved in sudden and violent deaths before, not least that of her own husband, Carl, over three years earlier. This was nothing like any of them. The police officers, when they arrived, evidently had the same reaction. A deliberately garotted child was way beyond the experience of almost anybody in the country. Children might accidentally hang themselves from carelessly placed ropes or lines, which was ghastly and terrible enough – but this had been done with malice. The weapon appeared to be a sort of plastic-coated string, which must have been held tightly in place for several minutes, before the attacker tied it in a knot at the side of the child's head. It was bright green – the sort of innocent item everybody had neatly coiled in their box of oddments. It was not an obvious means of killing someone, being rather springy and disinclined to stay where one put it. These details emerged in short fragments from the low conversation that went on around Thea's car throughout the remainder of the afternoon.

Thea and a policewoman led Gudrun into Hyacinth House, but she stayed only moments before running outside again to see what was happening to her boy. She was like a bulldozer, with wide powerful shoulders and short strong legs. Nobody felt up to tackling her physically, and in no other way did she pay the slightest attention to the people around her. There was no place for consolation or sweet tea or sedatives. Her distress was far beyond anything on offer, impossible to assuage or divert.

And yet Thea was already catching odd glances between the milling officers, which suggested ideas that were at first quite horrifying. They eyed Gudrun's muscular frame, and muttered about Stevie being a known troublemaker, a real handful for a single mum. They cocked sceptical brows at her display of maternal grief, which had, over the course of an hour or so, mutated from silent horror to loud moans. Anger was not far away, Thea guessed – and then things would become far more difficult.

But the child himself remained the central focus. A doctor knelt gently over him, listening to his heart and palpating the violated neck. A photographer grimly captured the scene, swallowing hard as he bent close to the area of trauma. The little knot of curious villagers assembled at the gate was held back by a uniformed officer. Unable to see anything, thanks to Thea's sheltering car, they drifted away quite soon.

And then Gladwin arrived.

Detective Superintendent Sonia Gladwin was well known to Thea, and very much liked. She had transferred from Cumbria, where the climate and people had shaped her into a person of adaptability and great good sense. She was approaching forty, a thin energetic mother of twin sons and generally content with her life. She had never seen a garotted child before, either.

'My God, Thea! What's going on here?'

She ought not to have addressed the house-sitter before the police officers at the scene, but nobody appeared to take exception. Gladwin's gender was a central part of her approach to the job, something she made no attempt to deny or conceal. She behaved as a woman generally behaved: going soft over baby animals, looking for the emotional angle in a case, making outrageous intuitive leaps and cajoling colleagues instead of yelling at them. As far as Thea could tell, it worked extremely well.

'I found him. He lives just over there, down that track. I'd already met his mother, and seen him around, since I got here yesterday.'

'And somebody killed him?' Like the photographer, she swallowed hard before moving to view the body. Thea knew better than to follow, even if she had wanted to. It was a crime scene, potentially rich with invisible clues, and everyone was required to keep a good distance away, the police hoping the earlier invasions of both Thea and Gudrun would not have already obliterated anything of significance. It was raining harder now, and the chance of finding helpfully relevant threads and hairs and flakes of skin had to be close to zero. Nonetheless, rules were rules and the area was now forbidden territory. It had to be meticulously examined for signs of a violent struggle.

'Unless he did it to himself,' said a uniformed male officer. 'The doc thinks that's unlikely.'

Gladwin's expression silenced him very effectively.

'You're right in the middle of this one, then,' she said to Thea. 'Again.'

'Don't,' begged Thea. 'I tempted fate by thinking things were really going to be rather dull here. Except when the homeowner went missing, of course,' she added carelessly.

'What?'

'It's not important. She was soon found again. And from what I've seen and heard of Stevie, he was . . . well . . .'

She tailed off, unable to voice anything condemnatory of the pathetic little figure, who had certainly never done anything to deserve such a dreadful end. He should have lived, and grown up to become a responsible citizen, using his talents to good effect. She put a hand to her own throat, as she had seen a number of the assembled officers do unconsciously. 'Poor little boy,' she murmured. 'How could anybody be so cruel?'

'I have to talk to the doctor and the others. I'll see you in the house in a little while. We'll have to deal with the mother first. She's looking rather explosive.'

'I'm not going anywhere,' said Thea, thinking it would be good to sit down and let go of some of the emotions she was fighting to control. She felt choked and clogged with misery. 'Can I let the dog out now?'

Gladwin frowned, until Thea indicated the frantic animal still shut inside the car, which had been shunted three or four yards away, to leave space for the numerous police officials. 'I thought she'd better stay there for the time being, but she'll go mad if I don't rescue her soon.'

For answer, Gladwin herself went and opened the passenger door of the car. The spaniel flew out, ears flapping, and jumped up at Thea's legs in an ecstasy of relief. Thea pushed her down, and took hold of her collar. 'Come on, you. I'll have to shut you in the house now. You'll only be a nuisance out here.'

She took herself to a corner of the living room, amongst the clutter of shelved units and crowded cabinets, and closed her eyes. The feeling of overwhelming cruelty surged all around, with a sense of something demonic and loathsome lurking close by. She had already been foolish enough to entertain fantasies about witches and vampires, letting the supernatural add spice to the blandness of the day. Now the real world had turned far more threatening and malevolent than any demon or bloodsucker ever could. She almost found herself hoping that Gudrun had indeed murdered her own son. That would at least contain the dreadful wrongness, and make some slight sense of what had happened. Mothers lost their wits in the strain and pressure of dealing with an impossible child; it was terrible and tragic, but not evil. People could crack, their weakness emerging as a fit of appalling violence, and they finished up by harming themselves more terribly than anybody else. Except for the slaughtered child, of course, who had lost absolutely everything.

But if Gudrun *had* done it, then was it possible that Thea herself had added the final straw to her breaking back? Could it be that her report of his stone-throwing was just one more unbearable event in a tightening chain of awful acts that forced her to accept that her son was out of control? Thea recalled her conversations with the Williams mother and daughter, and with Clara Beauchamp, only hours ago. All three confirmed Thea's own impressions of a child running wild and free, with a nasty malicious streak that alarmed them. Had it alarmed them enough to tip them over into killing him? Was that even imaginable? She thought of the tall composed Janice, with her iron-jawed daughter. Could they have flipped, driven to homicide by the attacks on their garden?

It was tempting to believe anything rather than that it had been Gudrun who killed the boy. How could that suspicion possibly square with the annihilation she had witnessed in the woman, as she slowly understood what had happened? Nobody could act as well as that. Of *course* she hadn't done it; the idea was insane.

But somebody had, and who could possibly have such passionate antipathy to the boy – whatever awful things he might have done – other than his mother who lived with him every day and knew, perhaps, what he was capable of?

Gladwin walked into the house without fanfare at seven and stayed for half an hour. Thea made coffee and found some cheese and biscuits, which they ate together like old friends.

'Are you okay?' Gladwin asked.

'Very much not. That poor little boy. I can't stop thinking about him. His white face, and thin little legs.'

'Didn't you hear anything? It was right outside this house. Why didn't you see what was happening?'

Thea blinked at her. 'I never thought of that. I was in the kitchen, I think, and it looks over the back. Hepzie was on the chair in here. At least – I'm assuming it happened in the middle of the day sometime.'

'He was still warm. We're guessing something like three in the afternoon, or a bit earlier.'

Thea winced at the stark implications. She had been speaking to Jocelyn, or washing a plate, or simply being idle and inattentive while a dreadful act was being committed only yards away. She swallowed, and tried to speak lucidly.

'I don't know – but I was probably in the kitchen. I phoned my sister. I walked around the village this morning, and got back here around half past one.'

'You haven't used the car today?'

'No.'

'So you might not have seen him if he'd been there when you got back from the village?'

'No. I just came in through the gate. Hepzie might have noticed, though, if he'd been behind the car.'

'I'm afraid Hepzie doesn't make a very good witness.'

'No.' She didn't laugh or even smile. It was like being under a rough brown blanket that smothered all normal tendencies to lightness or humour.

'You know . . .' Gladwin said slowly, looking at the floor, 'there have been moments when I could have strangled my own boys. I can just about imagine having a piece of string in my hands for something else, and whipping it round the little wretch's neck in a crazy moment, just to shut him up for a minute or show him a lesson. Can't you?'

'I've got a girl,' said Thea. 'It's probably different.' She thought about Jocelyn's children, and especially her favourite nephew, Noel. He was sweetly affectionate, a smiling cooperative little chap who endured the teasing from his four older siblings as if it was his due. Even through serious ructions between his parents, he remained his same pliable, contented little self. 'So, no, I can't think how that might happen. Besides – what about the string? If she was chasing after him for some reason, I suppose she could have just had it in her hand. And why would he run up here?' As she spoke, the scene offered itself to

86

her imagination, all too vividly. Stevie having infuriated his mother, dodging her slaps perhaps, defying her, saying something intolerably insolent. Then running up the track, into the road, past Blake's house and then finally being caught outside Hyacinth House. What more natural, then, than to cower behind Thea's car, in the hope of evading the irate woman? By the time she found him, her temper would be far beyond control, the string a handy means of restraining him.

'She can't possibly have meant to kill him,' she said, feeling again a phantom ligature below her own ear, pushing at the delicate vulnerable area of neck where the carotid artery pulsed. 'She just pulled it too tight. If it was her, I mean. But it *wasn't*, Sonia. I just know it wasn't.'

'Right,' nodded Gladwin, with professional neutrality. 'So, when you found him, you ran down to her cottage, or whatever it is, to tell her? Did you know he was dead then?'

'Yes, to both questions. If there'd been any doubt, I'm sure I would have summoned help.'

'You don't sound sure.'

'How can I know exactly what I'd do? I wasn't thinking in any normal way. I just reacted on instinct, and that sent me running for his mother.'

'How did you know where she lived?'

'I saw them yesterday. I mean, I followed the boy to his house and spoke to his mother.'

Gladwin went very still and closed her eyes. 'And . . . ?' she prompted.

'He'd been misbehaving,' Thea evaded.

'You complained about him?' the detective guessed.

'Clever you. He was throwing stones at the cows.'

'Thea, *please* don't tell me that she said she'd kill him. That didn't happen, did it?'

Thea's clenched silence answered the question.

'Oh, God,' moaned the detective. 'I can hear the prosecution already.'

'She didn't mean it. We've all said it a hundred times. The whole *village* must want to kill him. He was a brat. Everybody says so. Except Blake. He seems to think it's just normal boyish high spirits.'

'I assume you'll tell me who "everybody" is, as well as this Blake person. First let's finish the story. What was she doing when you got to her house?'

'I don't know. She sounded as if she might have been having a nap, funnily enough. Sort of bleary.'

'That doesn't work, does it?' Gladwin's voice remained low and strained. Anybody overhearing the conversation would have utterly failed to identify her as a senior police detective. 'Not if she'd gone berserk and killed him by mistake. It fits better with a cold deliberate murder.'

'Nobody coldly and deliberately kills their own child.'

'Men do, sometimes. They think it's the best thing for all concerned.'

'Really? Perhaps Gudrun thought that. Perhaps she thought he was going to turn into a psychopathic monster, and was better off dead.' She considered miserably. 'Yes, that would make quite a lot of sense.' Then she shook herself. 'But it wasn't her,' she repeated. 'You have to believe me.'

'We're running much too far ahead,' Gladwin checked herself. 'Supposition, that's all this is. Not even that, before we get the PM results. We're being entirely too female about it.'

It was the closest Thea came to a smile, but it never reached her lips. Amongst the smothering blanket of pain and horror there was a warm thread of relief that it was Gladwin in charge, and not a well-intentioned but outraged man. Men automatically became disproportionately judgemental when confronted with a delinquent woman. A woman who killed her own child was monstrous, beyond all normal bounds. This attitude made sense from a variety of cultural and biological viewpoints, but it often obscured the truth of what had happened. It was going to be easier to defend Gudrun to Gladwin – and defending Gudrun was what all her instincts were demanding of her.

'I'm so glad it's you,' she said.

'Glad to be Gladwin,' quipped the detective. She even managed a smile. 'Look – we're keeping the media quiet until tomorrow. They've got wind of it, of course, and there might be some camera crews on your doorstep, but nobody's to know who was killed, okay? For the time being, we need to sort ourselves out and decide how much to say. Abigail's working on it now.'

'Abigail?'

'Media liaison. Delicate work, I can tell you. She does a good job. Everybody loves her, including the reptiles from the tabloids. She has them right where she wants them. It's a miracle.'

'So I can't tell anybody?'

'Not until tomorrow. Midday, let's say. It'll be out by then, anyway, but we'll have a go at controlling it.'

'You think there'll be a lynch mob out for Gudrun?'

Gladwin rolled her eyes. 'It's all too horribly possible,' she confirmed.

Thea went cold, thinking of her own role in the tragic business. 'I won't say anything,' she promised.

Chapter Seven

The rain brought an early twilight, the sky almost dark by nine o'clock. Stevie's body had finally been removed, Thea's car having been carefully reversed into the road to make way for the undertaker's vehicle. Gudrun was taken away somewhere – where *did* someone go when the whole purpose of their existence had suddenly collapsed? Perhaps she had a large extended family to take her in. On the whole, Thea thought this unlikely.

There were still people coming and going outside, up to nine-thirty. The fact that a serious crime had been committed was impossible to conceal, and Thea was alarmed to find a journalist and cameraman on her doorstep when she went to answer the bell. 'I have no intention of speaking to you,' she said, and slammed the door in their faces. This was a disastrous turn of events, something she ought to have anticipated. Was she to be besieged for days in this impossible house, imprisoned with the knick-knacks for the next two weeks? Could she make an escape from the back, running through the field and up into the woods?

When the phone rang, she decided to ignore it. It would only be the press, trying another approach. But it rang repeatedly, and she faced a choice of unplugging it or answering it. The former was very much her preference – after all, the important people all knew her mobile number – but it felt too much like a violation of her responsibilities to Yvonne Parker. 'Daft,' she muttered to herself. But she could not forget that she was in another woman's house, paid to step into her shoes for a fortnight and ensure that all was as well as possible on her return. The fact that Hyacinth House would be on the TV news, in the papers, on innumerable websites, in all its recognisable glory, was beyond Thea's control. She could, however, maintain some vestige of dutiful behaviour, and answer Yvonne's telephone.

'Mum? What's going on?'

Was it Jessica? Thea wondered in puzzlement. It didn't *sound* like her. 'Um . . . ?' she said.

'Who's that? Have I got the right number?'

'This is Hyacinth House,' said Thea, trying to assemble her faculties.

'But you're not my mother. Who *are* you?'

'The house-sitter. Are you Yvonne's daughter?' She searched her memory. 'Belinda, is it?'

'Why has she got a house-sitter? She never goes anywhere.'

'She's gone to see your father. In London.' Too late, she wondered whether it was diplomatic to convey this news. Had Yvonne not told the girl for a reason? Were the wedding arrangements some sort of secret surprise?

'Oh. But the house has just been on the news – something's happened. They just said "an incident", but it's obviously something terrible.'

'Yes, but I'm not allowed to talk about it. You needn't worry. Your mother's perfectly all right.'

'How do you know she is? You don't know what a brute my father can be.'

'Well . . .' There was really nothing to say to that, of course. The complications of the Parker family felt entirely irrelevant on that particular evening.

'When is she due back?'

'In a fortnight. She's going to France to see her sister as well.'

'To see Auntie Sim? You're joking! She'd never do that. She's scared stiff of flying, and the tunnel's almost as bad.'

Again Thea failed to respond. She was far too drained to care about Yvonne Parker's phobias. Normally she might have made friendly efforts to elicit more detail. Had Belinda really said 'Auntie Sim', for instance? It was too much effort to question it. 'I'm sorry,' she said. 'I only know what she told me.'

'Obviously. Look – I'm coming over tomorrow, to see for myself what's been going on. My mother would never just swan off like that. She never wants to see my father again. My God – just wait till I tell Mark about this. He isn't going to believe it for a second.'

'But – aren't you in Wales? Isn't that a long drive?'

'I'm just over the border. It'll take me an hour, A44 all the way. I need to see for myself,' she repeated in a distracted tone. 'Oh, but no, I can't. We've got to sort the lambs tomorrow. You're quite sure Mum's okay, are you?'

'I am sure. At least, nothing that's happening here is to do with her. It's something else entirely. They'll release details tomorrow, so you'll have to wait till then.' She knew she ought to make an effort to pacify Belinda. After all, she wouldn't like it if she saw her mother's house on the news, with police tape all over the place and a very sinister vagueness about exactly what had happened. But she felt too drained to do a satisfactory job. 'I'm sorry,' she attempted. 'It must have been an awful shock. Phone me again tomorrow, if you like. I'll be able to talk more freely then.'

'I'll phone my father,' came the cool reply. 'Thank you.'

She went to bed in a miasma of gloom, having given the dog barely a minute to relieve herself outside the back door. The SOCOs or whatever they were had gone home for the night, as had the press people. It was blessedly silent, but where the previous night she had listened for vicious hornets in the roof, this time she had far more lethal human beings to worry about – somebody out there was capable of murdering a child, and therefore surely quite apt to do something every bit as terrible again.

She was just drifting into a shallow sleep when the face of her daughter swam before her mind's eye. She hadn't even checked to see whether a new message had arrived. Had Jess gone to work as advised? Had she seen Paul? Was she feeling better or worse? The worries kept her awake for another hour, only to be followed by thoughts of Drew Slocombe, who wanted her to go and check his property in Broad Campden. In a nightmarish merry-go-round, Yvonne Parker replaced Drew, and somehow Jocelyn returned to bother her. Why, she asked herself, had she dreamed about her younger sister the night before? She had sounded fine on the phone, setting off on a family adventure that made Thea feel quite envious.

And how was the wretched Gudrun facing the first night without her little boy?

And were the hornets dormant now that the sun had disappeared?

The doorbell woke her from a profound slumber that had lasted less than two hours. Her tossing and turning through most of the night had so annoyed her dog that it had jumped off the bed and made a nest in a corner of the room on a woven wool rug. Her yaps were more instantly disturbing than the rather fainter bell, ringing down in the hall.

'Who's that?' Thea groaned. 'What time is it?'

Her watch informed her that it was half past seven. With a sense of helplessness, she stumbled down the stairs in her pyjamas, wishing she had the strength of character to simply ignore whoever it was.

It was a young man, with prominent blue eyes and wavy brown hair, which appeared to have missed its morning brushing. 'Sorry, sorry,' he gushed with theatrical exaggeration, seeing her pyjamas. 'I'm Mark Parker. I couldn't wait any longer. I set out at first light. What in the world's happened here? Linny says the house was on the news, but they wouldn't give any details. She would have come herself, but she's got to do something complicated with lambs.'

'Mark Parker,' she repeated, dozily distracted by the rhyming name. She recalled a Miriam Ingram she had met a while ago, not to mention her husband Graham. She should start a collection.

'Vonny's son,' he elaborated. 'She's gone off somewhere without telling us, according to my sister. I thought I should come and make sure you haven't murdered her.'

The tactlessness of this remark took Thea's breath away. She threw a long look at the police tape across the grass beyond the front gate. He had the grace to flush. 'It looks to me as if there *has* been a murder,' he defended himself.

'Come in,' she said. 'I'll get dressed.' She remembered a comment from Yvonne to the effect that her son worried about legalities, at least where the shared garden was concerned. Did that extend to a need to assure himself that the house-sitter was fully law-abiding?

'No, no. It's all right. I just wanted to see if you were real. If you were still here. I suppose you've got to watch out for those blasted cats, as if anybody couldn't just drop in and see to them. I don't mean this rudely, but I imagine you don't come cheap and she's in no position to throw money around like that. But my mother hasn't been very rational for a while now.'

Thea shook her head impatiently. Not just legalities, but finances, it seemed, came under this man's area of concern. Yvonne Parker felt altogether irrelevant to her on this new morning that already threatened to be every bit as horrible as the previous afternoon had been. Stevie was still dead, and once the police authorised the media to release some facts, there would be far too much attention on Snowshill and Hyacinth House.

But Mark Parker was waiting for a response, his eyebrows raised. 'I think she was worried about her things,' she said weakly.

'Oh!' He swiped splayed fingers through his hair. 'The *things*. Of course. Look – why don't you go out for a little walk and I'll quickly set fire to the whole damned place?'

His jokes were not improving tastewise, she noted. She didn't even smile. 'Wouldn't that be illegal?' she said tartly.

'Sorry,' he said again. 'I can't help it.'

'You've got Tourette's syndrome?'

'What? No, of course not. I'm just – oh, I don't know. Trying to make you like me, I suppose.'

Her unamused gaze conveyed very clearly that he was approaching this goal in quite the wrong way.

'So they let you stay here – the police, I mean? Isn't that a bit weird? I mean . . .' He turned to look again at the police tape and Thea's awkwardly positioned car. His own vehicle was further up the road, a splash of red just visible over the hedge. 'Who was it that got killed? Was it somebody I knew?'

'I'm not allowed to tell you.'

'Why the hell not? That's insane.'

'I'm just doing what they asked. It helps with their initial investigations, I suppose. But it'll leak out any time now.' She changed the subject. 'You lived here, did you, as a child?'

He nodded. 'Here until I was twenty-five, actually. They more or less had to throw me out.'

'How long ago was that?' He didn't look much past twenty-five.

'Five years. Then Dad buggered off, and I suggested coming back to keep Mum company, but she wouldn't let me.'

'Right,' said Thea vaguely.

'What if the killer comes back? Aren't you scared?'

She shrugged. Something of his manner must be contagious, she thought. 'Not unless you're him,' she said.

'Me?' He threw up his hands. 'Not likely. I'm the ultimate wimp, anybody can tell you. Our Linny's always worn the trousers in the Parker family.'

'She phoned me.'

'Yes, I know. That's why I'm here.'

'Yes. Sorry. I'm not properly awake yet.'

They were standing awkwardly on the threshold, the spaniel restlessly circling them, hoping for the breakfast routine to start, whereby she received a biscuit and a few minutes out of doors. Mark continued speaking, his tone insistent, eager to gain her full attention. 'You told Linny that Mum had gone to see our disgraced father, and presumably discovered his sordid lifestyle.'

Thea nodded. 'She seemed a bit surprised.'

'It's not the way it looks, actually. He's between houses, so to speak, but he's pretty well heeled these days. He's done some kind of deal with an Indian outfit, very much to his advantage. I have no idea of the details, but it sounds fairly amazing. It's handy for him, moving in with the new girlfriend, while he decides what comes next.'

It felt entirely irrelevant to Thea's immediate concerns, and she barely registered what he had said. 'So?' she said. 'None of that explains why you've come here at crack of dawn, and then won't even step inside the house. Your mother's arrangements are her own business, aren't they? Does she have to tell you everything she's doing?'

His expression turned sulky. 'I told you why I'm here.'

'You wanted to make sure I hadn't killed your mother?'

'Is that what I said? How awful of me. Take no notice.'

'I'm not. But if you won't come in, then I'm closing the door and getting myself some breakfast.'

He pushed a hand through his hair again and heaved a sigh. 'Okay, I'll come in for a minute, then. I don't suppose you're making coffee, are you? That might settle me down. I get a bit crazy these light mornings. It's all wrong, don't you think? The sun should never come up before eight. It's disorienting.'

'I like them,' she said. 'It makes me sad that the days are already getting shorter.'

'There you go, then,' he said, meaninglessly. 'I'm a night owl. A vampire. A creature of the shadows. Shows how bothered I was, coming here so early. The thing is, I have to be at work by nine, seventy miles away. I expect I'll be late.'

'You will if you stop for coffee.'

'I have to have the coffee,' he said seriously. 'Taking the wider view, it is definitely necessary. I can't drive without it.'

She gave him a mug of strong instant, adding plenty of milk to cool it down. 'I like your dog,' he said. Until then, she hadn't thought he had even noticed there *was* a dog. 'I always wanted a dog.'

'Where do you live?'

'Kington. It's a remote little Herefordshire town, almost in Wales. Linny's a couple of miles over the border. We like to think it means we can exist separately, but of course that's ridiculous.'

'You're not twins, are you?'

He snorted. 'Not even biological siblings, let alone twins. We were adopted, first me, then her. There's less than a year between us. We always said we're even closer than most twins. It's all rather odd, when you stop to think about it.'

'You don't seem the slightest bit bothered by what's happened,' she reproached him impatiently. All she could think about was the pathetic child's limp body. Mark Parker could have told her he was a surviving conjoined twin or a foundling left under a moorland gorse bush and she would scarcely have listened to him.

'Because you won't tell me anything about it,' he flashed back. 'Do you want me to torture the details out of you? I'm sorry, but I happen to be more interested in my parents and whatever unholy mess they're making of all our lives. I blame Belinda, actually. What does she want to go and get married for, anyway?'

Thea shrugged and pointed to the clock on the wall. 'You're going to be seriously late,' she warned him.

'Yeah,' he said without moving. 'First time in five years. I've been at their beck and call all weekend, I might tell you. I guess they'll cut me some slack, after that.' He put on a bad American accent, which failed to elicit a smile from Thea, although she did feel a slight thawing towards him. Somehow her defences were collapsing in the face of his banter. She had encountered men like him before, wolves in the guise of placid llamas, amusingly self-deprecating, hiding their real motives. Or perhaps this one was the real article, trained from birth to gain popularity by making people smile, and acquiring the habit as a second skin, with no sinister undertones. Just an element of inadequacy and low self-esteem.

'What work do you do?' she asked him.

'It would take a while to explain, but it involves the welfare of children in hospital. All terribly insecure, the way things are. One of those nice idealistic jobs dreamt up by New Labour when there was plenty of money sloshing about. Now they're starting to think maybe people's own families could do it for free. Trouble is, they won't, half the time.'

He smiled and shrugged helplessly, and she envisaged him dressed as a Pierrot, entertaining sick children and persuading them to eat their hospital food.

She groped in vain for the central significance of his visit. Nothing seemed to justify such a time-consuming effort, risking her non-cooperation by arriving at such an unearthly hour. 'Do you want to search the house for your mother's body?' she asked, forcing a steely note into her voice. 'Your sister's going to want to know you did a thorough job.'

'Oh, she doesn't know I've come. She'd think I was mad. Well, she *already* thinks that. Let's just say she wouldn't be happy about it. But I *can* act independently every now and then, and I have been worried about Mum for a bit now.'

'So?'

'I can see you're not a murderer,' he said simply. 'Besides, nobody would really murder my mum. She's too . . . I don't know. Bland, maybe. People don't notice her. It was all a stupid panic, when we saw the house on the telly.'

She wanted to respond with assurances that this was quite understandable, but found herself unable to do so. After he had gone, she felt irritated and bewildered by this strange visitation from a man who had felt untrustworthy. When he'd persuaded himself that nobody had hurt his mother, he had drifted into a relaxed flippancy that seemed callous to Thea.

Mark's visit was no more than a dreamlike interlude, made more unreal by the fact that she was still in her dressing gown. There had been some sort of near-physical barrier to making any reference to the child, Stevie, well beyond a dutiful obedience to Gladwin's injunction. The boy had been pushing at the edge of her mind throughout the conversation with Mark Parker, and yet the tone and content of their exchanges prevented her from properly thinking about him.

Yvonne Parker had been given even scantier attention over the past twenty-four hours or so. She had made that reassuring phone call the previous morning and thereby removed herself from Thea's list of worries. The horror and tragedy of the child's murder had completely blotted her out. And there was no good reason to readmit her now. She could have had no connection with Stevie's death, even if she knew him as a persistent nuisance – which was far from certain. Yvonne was a schoolteacher; she probably knew how to deal with annoying children. It was even possible that young Stevie was at her school, she thought, before remembering that the woman taught French and was therefore obviously at a secondary school, which Stevie had not yet reached.

The cats were in the kitchen when she went back downstairs having finally got dressed, impatient for their morning biscuits. Although not entirely reconciled to the interloper, they had apparently decided to make the best of the disappearance of their rightful owner. Eyeing the closed door, beyond which was the untrustworthy spaniel, they delicately crunched the food in unison. 'You really are very pretty things,' Thea told them. 'And absolutely no trouble, thank goodness.' It was true what Mark had said, she admitted to herself. Anybody could have dropped in twice a day and ensured that the cats got their meals. Yvonne's motive for employing a house-sitter had to lie beyond the care of these easy creatures.

She felt caught in a strangely paradoxical state: having too much to think about and too little to actually *do*. There were literally no tasks awaiting her until late afternoon, when again she had to feed the cats. It was all too likely that she was going to end up dusting the sprawling collection of objects and perhaps even mentally cataloguing them according to date, or place of origin, or aesthetic appeal. And she would do the same with the buildings of Snowshill: listing the many gorgeous houses in order of merit or interest.

And all the time she would be thinking about young Stevie and his mother, and Gladwin's suspicions, and the terrible things people were capable of doing to each other.

Chapter Eight

At eight-thirty, twenty minutes after Mark departed, the police team reappeared wearing white suits and face masks and crawling assiduously over the grass where Stevie had been lying. This might go on for days, Thea realised, with mixed feelings. They cast a pall of tragedy over the whole village, but at least they gave Thea something to watch – and they might even accept refreshments from her if she offered. She had to keep Hepzie firmly indoors, or only let out at the back on a lead. She wondered frustratedly what had become of Gudrun, and how she was coping with the police questions. Had she maintained a stunned and traumatised silence, or had she understood her doubtful position and ranted and raved at her accusers? Had anyone spoken up for her, volunteering to sit with her in her misery? What did police guidelines ordain in a situation like this? As far as Thea could see, there was no hard evidence that Gudrun had murdered her own child, which surely meant she could not be kept in custody. And what did the locals make of it? What would the ghost of Charles Paget Wade think of any suggestion that the most taboo crime of them all might have been committed on his doorstep?

Snowshill was a dauntingly small place. The residents would inevitably all know each other and pass on their opinions of what precisely happened. It had been plain from her meeting with Janice and Ruby, and then with Clara Beauchamp, that Stevie was a universal menace. Gladwin would have to interrogate everyone in the village, accumulating a list of the boy's misdemeanours. There might even be a guilty satisfaction rippling just below the surface, beneath the genuine horror, at the knowledge that at least he wasn't going to terrorise their animals or massacre their flowers ever again. And perhaps he did worse than that; perhaps he bullied their small children and damaged their cars as well. But this was a respectable English village, where emotions seldom went beyond an occasional raised voice across a garden fence or an impatiently hooted car horn. It was unimaginable that a child could be slaughtered simply because he was a nuisance.

Thea's natural curiosity gradually began to assert itself as the morning progressed, sparked by the comments Clara had made and fuelled by further remarks from Blake-next-door. It was annoying that he should take himself off just when she would have liked somebody to talk to. She could hardly expect Gladwin to devote much time to filling her in on what had been discovered, even if Thea was the principal witness to the aftermath of the murder. She had found dead bodies before and had become important to the police investigations as a result. This time she felt a dread she hadn't previously known; an emotion worse than the fear that had gripped her in Hampnett. She felt a dark malicious spirit lurking close by, embodied fancifully in the hornet that had attacked her when she least expected it and then disappeared from sight. She had thought this spirit resided in the boy Stevie, but with his death it became obvious that it lay elsewhere, and Stevie was just another victim.

Now here she was, cooped up in a house she should have liked for its beautiful proportions and heavy protective walls, but actually found oppressive and even hostile. The atmosphere of malice extended through those thick walls and filled the house itself. A spikiness, perhaps, a suspicion that many of Yvonne's collectables could be brought into use as weapons if the occasion demanded it. There were heavy stone objects, for a start, and a great deal of glass that could quickly be rendered lethal. Candleholders with sharp metal prongs could stab you, and one or two of the old electric lamps probably had such dodgy wiring they could electrocute you. It felt like the home of someone planning deviously sly means of harming someone, once seen through this kind of lens.

Madness, Thea scolded herself sternly. The woman who owned this house was a timid creature who had quailed at the simple task of finding a house in north London, where maps and signs abounded. She was dependent on her neighbour for almost everything. And yet . . . she held down a job teaching teenagers a foreign language, which couldn't be entirely easy. It would be unwise to take her wholly at face value, and it would be very interesting to unravel the complicated history of her marriage to the bewildering Victor. Victor who lived in a small scruffy flat, but had made a lot of money; who had left the marital home for reasons that remained obscure, and had apparently finally been confronted by a wife who had overcome her own reluctance because of the needs of her daughter. On the phone he had sounded impatient, even contemptuous, towards Yvonne. His children appeared to have few illusions about him. The more she thought about him, the more Thea wished she could meet him and draw her own conclusions about his character.

And then, the blessed Gladwin came back at ten, and saved Thea from further plunges into fantastic imaginings.

'He wasn't killed out there,' she said, with minimal preamble. 'The body was moved.'

It was a bigger relief than Thea could have anticipated. There had been nothing she could have done to prevent it, then, if only she'd been listening hard or watching more closely. 'How long before? I mean—'

'About an hour, apparently. Hard to say for sure, but the blood in his veins had pooled significantly on his left side, and you said you found him lying on his face. I'm assuming you didn't move him.'

'I'm afraid I did. I turned him over. He was lying on his face when I first found him. And then his mother picked him right up and cradled him.'

'Which is why your testimony is going to be absolutely crucial.'

'Oh dear.'

'It's not as bad as it sounds. There's sure to be a bit of forensic evidence to support you – grass residue on his front, for example. They'd mowed that verge only a couple of days ago and left the trimmings just lying. Very helpful, that.'

'Gosh.'

'So now we ask ourselves why he was dumped just there, behind your car. Even someone walking past wouldn't have seen him. The chances that it would be you, and only you, were very high.'

'You're saying somebody deliberately wanted to horrify me, as some sort of attack on me? But I don't *know* anybody here.'

'You met Gudrun and complained to her about her boy.'

'Yes.' Thea's eyes widened in disbelief. 'But you're not suggesting she killed him, threw him at my feet, as it were, to say "There! See what you've made me do!" That would be completely insane.'

'Yes – and yet there's a ghastly logic to it, don't you think?'

'There might be if he was a pet rabbit – although even then it's a horrible thought. Nobody would do that to their own child. They just wouldn't. I don't believe it.' She forced herself to relive the moments when she went to fetch Gudrun, in an instinctive desire to reunite mother and child. 'No, she didn't do it. She was much too appalled. Worse than that – *annihilated*. How is she now?' she remembered to ask.

'I haven't seen her. She's got a Family Liaison girl with her. According to her, Gudrun's more or less catatonic.'

'Poor woman.'

'Indeed.'

'Coffee?' Thea invited. Gladwin accepted, and as she boiled the kettle, Thea said idly, 'This is the second time this morning I've made coffee for somebody, and it's not even ten-thirty yet.'

'Oh?'

'Mark Parker turned up ridiculously early. He'd seen all the commotion on the news and came to check it out for himself. This is his mother's house,' she added belatedly.

'Where does he live?'

'Somewhere on the Welsh border. I can't remember exactly.'

'How very strange. Were you still in bed?'

'Yes, I was fast asleep. It was only half past seven.'

'So tell me about the family. Are they connected to Gudrun and her kid somehow?'

'Not that I know of, apart from living close by. There's Yvonne, the mother, who's gone to London to see her husband for the first time in ages. They've got two adopted children, aged around thirty, brother and sister, Belinda and Mark. Yvonne intends to insist that her husband contributes towards the cost of Belinda's wedding. They broke up five years ago, or thereabouts. He lives in Crouch End, in a flat that Yvonne regards as scruffy, but has plenty of money and is expecting to make more any day now. Then he'll probably buy a new house.' She frowned. 'Or did I just make that bit up? And she couldn't face it on Saturday, so she stayed at a B&B or something, and went there first thing Sunday morning.'

Gladwin's mouth was open, and she was absently rubbing her neck. 'It's a miracle,' she gasped.

'What?'

'That you've gleaned all that in two days, when you tell me you haven't seen anybody since you got here. Do you have some sort of hotline to the Recording Angel?'

'I didn't say I haven't seen anybody. I talked to Blake-next-door, and Janice and Ruby, plus Clara Beauchamp – and now Mark. And Vonny told me a few things, before she left.'

'Vonny?'

'That's what they all call her.'

Gladwin took the coffee and wandered out into the hall, and then into the living room. Thea followed her, braced for the reaction. 'Blimey! What a lot of stuff!' She started to examine some of the displays. 'Is there a theme to it that I'm missing?' she asked, after a few minutes.

'Not that I can see. She says it's the Snowshill Syndrome, and she got it from the Paget chap and the Manor. You know about Snowshill Manor?'

'Remind me.'

Thea summed up the eccentricities of the collection in a few words, finishing with the confession that she had not yet seen it for herself, merely read about it on various websites. 'I suppose I'll have to go and have a look one day soon,' she said.

'And it's near Snowshill?'

'It's right *in* Snowshill, a quarter of a mile from here. But you have to walk or drive so far to get into it that it feels as if it's somewhere else. Like the opposite of a mirage,' she added obscurely. 'I mean it feels far but is actually close. It's all National Trust now.'

Gladwin gave a puzzled nod. 'I never heard of it before.'

'That's forgivable,' smiled Thea. 'I hadn't either until a few weeks ago. This place isn't really in the middle of things. There are barely even any signs to it until you get a mile or two away. I'm almost scared to go out anywhere in case I can't find my way back again.'

Simultaneously they both reined back from the chit-chat and recalled themselves to the urgent matter confronting them. The detective noted down the names of the residents Thea had spoken to, with their comments about Stevie. 'I'm being outrageously unprofessional again,' she reproached herself. 'The truth is, I'm having trouble facing up to this. It's far too close to home.'

'I keep thinking of the media comments,' shivered Thea. 'I guess it won't be long before they start making insinuations.'

'They're not allowed to. It would make a fair trial impossible.'

'I hadn't noticed that stopping them, especially recently.'

'True. It makes everything a lot more difficult.' Gladwin spoke absently, her thin face turned to the window overlooking the field behind the house.

'Does it, though? At least it means you'll have to find absolutely certain evidence before bringing a prosecution. That's a good thing, isn't it? Think of those cases where innocent women have been charged with smothering their babies, because the police relied too much on half-baked experts. If Gudrun didn't do it, and ends up in court, that would be ten times worse for her – like torture. Barbaric and cruel.'

'"If",' said Gladwin gloomily. 'It's a big "if".'

'Come on!' Thea found a seam of energetic resistance to this attitude. 'You can't possibly have any real proof yet. And if I'm called as a witness—'

'Oh, you will be,' said the detective.

'Well, then, I'll be a witness for the defence. I saw absolutely nothing in her behaviour to suggest guilt. Not a thing.'

'Good. That's good. Thank you.'

'What?'

'I was basically testing you, I'm afraid. Just checking for weak spots, if you like. In this sort of case, you really do have to think the unthinkable, but I'm with you. I don't believe she did it, either.'

'But you have to keep an open mind.'

'I do. And what I believe really has very little to do with it.'

Chapter Nine

Nothing felt any better after Gladwin had gone. The forces of cruelty and ignorance and prejudice and salaciousness were going to be very hard to resist in the coming days, she suspected. Something was still simmering out there, waiting to turn the screw a bit tighter. Since Saturday morning, almost nothing pleasant had happened. Even the reputedly generous Blake had been insolent and patronising. Clara Beauchamp had also carried an air of superiority in her local knowledge and refusal to offer any enlightenment about any of it. Stevie had been a little beast and his mother defiant.

Then Jessica had splurged her troubles and Drew had made a demand that she had, so far that day, forgotten almost completely.

She could perhaps go over to Broad Campden and do Drew's bidding. It would be nice to have a reason to speak to him again, when she gave her report of the state of his field there, containing one solitary grave. She had no obligation to play detective and start questioning villagers about Stevie Horsfall. She could leave all that to Gladwin and her team. It was definitely none of her business, as virtually everybody she knew would tell her.

Except possibly Drew Slocombe, who understood the uncomfortable mixture of curiosity and outrage that all too often led to undue interference with police business whenever an innocent victim demanded retribution.

Opening her trusty Explorer map, she was startled to discover that Broad Campden was effectively within walking distance of Snowshill. Four or five miles, connected by a road in a virtually straight line, once clear of Snowshill. She wouldn't walk it, of course. The round trip would be beyond her comfort zone especially along small roads with nowhere safe for pedestrians. But it confirmed her sense of the whole Cotswolds region as deceptively small. The villages – hundreds of them – were densely packed into an area measuring roughly thirty miles square. And yet the distinctiveness of every single settlement was undeniable. No two were the same, even where their names suggested otherwise. Upper and Lower Slaughter were quite different from each other, as were Bourton-on-the-Hill and Bourton-on-the-Water. The land twisted and heaved in giddy directions, with huge extended vistas one moment, and tiny hidden dells the next. Snowshill was a prime example of that. The lowest point, just south of the church, was shaded by trees, the road leading mysteriously out of the village, only to bring you within seconds to a sweeping upland expanse of cornfields and views to Broadway and beyond.

She made herself a sandwich, filled a plastic bottle with

tap water, and gave the dog the good news that they were going out.

Only then did it occur to her that she might not be allowed to use her car; that it might comprise part of the forensic examination that was plainly set to last for a long time yet. She thought about it for a moment, and then went to speak to one of the robotic officers meticulously collecting invisible flecks from the ground outside Yvonne Parker's fence.

'Is it all right if I take my car?' she asked.

He stood up and stared at her with dark eyes. The mask over his nose and mouth gave him a medical aura, and she half expected to see a scalpel in his gloved hand. 'I have no idea,' he said in a muffled voice. 'Jimmy – can the lady use her car?' he called to a colleague.

'What – the Fiesta? 'Spose so. The kid wasn't in it, was he? Nobody's said.'

'He *definitely* wasn't in it,' Thea asserted with some force. 'He was *behind* it, that's all.'

'Might have prints on it, though,' mused Jimmy. 'Let's have a quick look.' He walked the few yards to where Thea had pulled her car onto the roadside grass outside Blake's fence. He produced a gadget that she couldn't properly see and ran it expertly over the car's paintwork. How, she wondered, could any criminal ever hope to get away with anything these days? There were technologies for everything now, where invisible specks of blood, sweat, hair, and skin could be detected and identified and used as evidence against you. In theory, at least, every move a person made could be traced, which should, of course, have made crime obsolete. The reality was quite astonishingly different. All the technologies cost large sums of money, the operatives were fallible and let their own flakes of skin contaminate the samples. The criminals could still outwit the forces of the law if they managed to conceal the crime in the first place, or to frame somebody else by judicious sprinkling of their DNA at the scene.

And Gudrun's DNA would be there in abundance, because she had huddled on the grass with the body of her child. She had very probably touched the car, as well. Surely the search was already hopelessly compromised.

'Go on, then,' said Jimmy, after a minute or two. 'This isn't going to be any help to us.'

'Thanks,' she said, carefully unlocking the car and putting the spaniel onto the back seat. 'Stay there, Heps,' she ordered. 'Not long before you can have a nice run.'

She had to think about the first stage of the route, emerging onto a road she wasn't sure about. Snowshill was bordered by a grid of small single-track roads, and it was all too easy to start charging off in quite the wrong direction. But turning left would only take her back to the upper level of the village, so she went to the right. Then left, at the sign for the place that grew and sold lavender, then right at a small insignificant crossroad. 'No, wait!' she told herself aloud. 'This isn't right. This goes to the place where the A44 meets the A424.' She rummaged in her bag for the map, which she had sensibly left folded to the right sheet. 'Yes, darn it. But there's nowhere to turn round.' Besides, it was a pretty route, with ripening corn on either side, and she could remedy the mistake quite easily when she reached the main road.

And so she turned left again onto the A44, and right onto the B4081, and everything was well after all. She smiled at the thought of a satellite tracking her journey, wondering at the zigzags she had performed when there was a perfectly straight route from A to B. *Let them wonder*, she thought defiantly. *It's none of their business.* Sometimes she acknowledged that she might be growing very slightly paranoid about the age of surveillance she was living in.

Broad Campden was almost startlingly familiar as she approached from the north-west, passing a house in which she had spent a dramatic evening, as well as one she had called home for two weeks or so. The flamboyant yew hedge with its topiary, the odd little church, the pub that refused entry to dogs – nothing had changed. She took the road towards Blockley, and there was Drew's field, still innocuously anonymous, apart from the laminated council notice pinned to a tree by the gate, in which Drew's intention to establish a green burial ground was announced in such language as to make the idea unremarkable. Whatever the planning department might think of the suggestion, they would prefer not to attract much interest. When the public got wind of any new project, they were liable to cause trouble. Much better to just discuss it amongst themselves and let it through on a nod, if possible.

The road helpfully widened at just the right spot for parking, not far from the gate. When they had buried Mrs Simmonds, four or five vehicles had managed to squeeze themselves in, without obstructing passing traffic. In fact, it appeared that a de facto parking area was already forming itself, the grass flattened and sick-looking, the hedge somehow yielding ground.

She let the dog out and together they went into the field. Conscientiously, she closed the slightly rickety gate behind her.

The most obvious change since March was the length of the grass. Clearly unmown, it stood knee-high, dotted with buttercups and a few purple thistles, but mostly a delicious variety of feathery seed heads. Butterflies flickered in the sunshine, and Hepzie went yapping off after what was probably a rabbit.

She stood in rapture at the scene. It was a small area, with trees on two sides, sloping very gently upwards to its southern edge. The sun had emerged after a cloudy start, bathing the whole field in a light that turned golden as it fell on the ripened grass. She knew little more than the rudiments of agriculture – that grass was cut for hay, in early summer, or kept as grazing for animals. Either way, you seldom encountered whole acreages of gone-to-seed grass heads like this. She plucked a few and arranged them in her hand, three distinct sorts, with a faint idea of laying them on Greta's grave.

The grave itself had no grass growing on it, suggesting that somebody had been to keep it clear. There were relatives, as well as local friends, who evidently missed Greta enough to render her remains this small service. *What a wonderful place to lie!* Thea thought, almost enviously. How much nicer than a churchyard with its obsessive tidiness and constant irrelevant visitors walking past without knowing or caring who you were. How clever and wise and brave of

Drew Slocombe to find a way of making this possible for people, and how foolish of the majority that they did not avail themselves of his talents.

She tried to remember just what it was he wanted her to do. She could find the message again on her phone, but the peace and ancient beauty of her surroundings made her reluctant to introduce modern electronics into it. The phone was in her pocket, but she chose to leave it there. All he wanted was that she come and have a look, as far as she could recall. Graves could be vandalised, with terrible consequences. There could be cattle in the field, having broken through a fence, trampling the tidy mound of earth, which had still not quite settled after four months and a bit.

And he could perhaps really have wanted just to make contact with her, using the grave as an excuse. Or, more worthily, he might have wished to remind her of Greta, who had been a very nice person and deserved to be remembered for a while longer.

Having spent many minutes simply soaking in the atmosphere, she heard a car approach, more slowly than was normal for the relatively straight road. It then unmistakably stopped, close to hers, thirty or forty yards away, beyond the thick screening hedge. Was somebody else coming to visit Greta? Her immediate involuntary leap of guilt surprised her. She had every reason to be here, after all, even without her connection to Drew. It was more a feeling that any human presence was an intrusion, that the grave was in fact best left alone, as Greta herself would have wanted. She had severed most of her intimate ties with the living, before she died. If they persisted in tending her grave, then she might well have maintained that they were doing it for their own peace of mind, and not from any concern for her.

Two people were talking, at the gate, and would see Thea at any moment, even if she didn't stand up. The long grass went a long way towards concealing her, but still her head and shoulders were in plain view. And her dog was around somewhere, all too liable to run and greet the newcomers by scrabbling at their legs.

But the couple were so caught up in conversation that they paused before opening the gate. In the still summer air, Thea could hear almost every word.

'It isn't going to come to that – of course it isn't. I don't know how you can even think it.'

'Sorry, love, but I think we've got to. It's been eight weeks now, with no change.'

'But she's still there, inside. You can tell by the way her eyes flicker when you talk to her. What are you suggesting we do?'

'It won't be up to us, will it? There isn't a *we* here, Maggs, however much you might feel part of the family.'

Thea's heart contracted in a painful spasm. This was Maggs? Maggs, business partner of Drew, wife of an ex-policeman, very nearly part of the Slocombe family, whatever the man might be saying now. Thea's initial guilty instinct magnified a thousandfold. She contemplated crawling, Indian-style, towards the sheltering trees, hoping the tall grass would hide her. But it was much too late for that. She heard the gate drag open, the welcoming yap of her dog, the surprised sounds as they realised somebody was already at the grave.

Mustering what dignity she could, Thea stood up and faced them. The man was well over six feet tall, his wife much much shorter. They were a comical pair, visually, and it seemed they knew it. 'Hello!' called Maggs, slightly too loudly. 'That's your car out there, then. We did wonder.'

'Yes,' said Thea. 'Hello.' She might yet, of course, conceal her identity. She had never met either of these people before, and could easily pretend to be a niece or friend of Greta Simmonds. But the spaniel might give her away. She imagined the conversation back in Somerset, when Drew asked for a report. *We met a woman, small, with a cocker spaniel. She didn't say who she was*. He would know immediately, and wonder at the secretiveness, and feel a shadow of the guilt that led to it. By silent mutual consent, Drew and Thea were determined to do nothing that could cause feelings of guilt. It wasn't what they'd *done* that sent her emotions into freefall, she realised helplessly. There were aspects of oneself that remained stubbornly beyond control. 'I'm Thea Osborne,' she said, feeling as if she'd just jumped off an uncomfortably high cliff.

Maggs's eyes widened and then narrowed in her dark face, her mouth doing much the same as astonishment was followed by something like rage. 'What? The house-sitter who's been trying to get your claws into Drew? Why are *you* here?'

'He asked me to come and have a look at the grave. And I knew Greta.'

'Oh yes, and you had a secret rendezvous with him in Cranham, not so long ago. Stephanie told me all about it. When his wife was so ill, you had him running after you – and taking his kids along as well.'

Retention of dignity became the prime necessity. Thea said nothing, but caught the eye of her accuser's tall husband, and thought she saw the promise of rescue in it. 'Maggs,' he said gently. 'Go easy, now.'

'No!' she spat. 'It needs saying. She's taking advantage. You know Drew's always been a soft touch for a woman in distress. There was that Genevieve, years ago. I saw the way he looked then, and now it's happening again.' She was addressing her husband more than Thea, despite fixing her angry black eyes on Thea's face throughout. 'And it's not right,' she finished.

Still Thea said nothing, her throat tight with shock at the attack. Shamefully she took refuge in her dog, who had come enquiringly up to her. She bent down and fondled the long ears, which were sprinkled with grass seeds. 'You're wrong,' she managed to choke out. 'There's nothing at all between me and Drew.'

'So why are you here?' Maggs flashed back, repeating her earlier question. Thea had observed the young woman's involuntary softening as she noticed the dog, and instinctively increased her attentions to the ears. If anybody could defuse a hostile situation, it was Hepzibah.

But there was no convincingly ingenuous reply to be made to Maggs's question. 'I told you – he asked me to check it was all right. And I knew Greta,' she reiterated weakly.

'Oh. Right. Best friends, I suppose.'

They were going round in a circle, hostility sparking off Maggs in an incontinence that Thea had only seen in children. It was debilitatingly alarming.

'Listen,' she managed. 'Just listen. You're completely wrong. I don't understand your problem.'

'You would if you saw how Karen is,' Maggs said bitterly.

'I heard you just now, talking about her,' Thea said bravely. 'It sounds dreadful.'

The husband took his chance. 'Maggs is upset,' he said quickly. 'She's been with Drew and his family since Steph was a baby. It's the only job she's ever had.'

'Don't! Don't *defend* me. I don't need that. Let me speak for myself.'

He sighed gently and put a hand on her shoulder. He was some years older than her, Thea noticed, with a fatherly air about him. She struggled to remember the admiring things Drew had said about Maggs – that she was wise and funny and fearless, that he could never have kept the business afloat without her and the children relied on her like a second mother.

'I'm sorry you've got such a poor idea about me,' she said. 'I really don't think I deserve it.'

Maggs shook her husband's hand away. 'You don't understand how Drew sees you. His home life is such torture at the moment, he's bound to be tempted by an escape to somebody like you – somebody who doesn't know Karen, who's pretty and bright and amusing. *Plus*,' her eyes glittered furiously, 'you've offered him the one thing he finds totally irresistible.'

Thea interrupted, assuming she knew what was coming. 'You're wrong there – I'm not in any distress, and haven't been at any stage since I met him. It was *him*, actually, who needed somebody to speak up for him.'

'I wasn't going to say that. What you might not realise is that Drew Slocombe has always fancied himself as an amateur detective. He loves mysteries and complicated motives, and ferreting out people's secrets. And you, bloody Thea Osborne, seem to be perpetually at the heart of the very thing he most enjoys.'

The glimpse of humour, the girlish exasperation, and the unmistakable desire to squat down and make a fuss of the spaniel all gave Thea some encouragement. 'I see,' she said calmly. 'I mean – I do see how it must look. But why can't he have a bit of distraction, if that's what he wants? I'm in no doubt that he's a brilliant husband and father, before anything else. You really don't have to protect him from me, I promise you.'

Maggs continued to scowl, but her husband, who belatedly introduced himself as Den Cooper, cleverly took the lead in petting the dog and eventually she relaxed enough to follow suit. Hepzie played up to their attentions, to the point of rolling over and displaying her vulnerable pink belly. Sensing that this was the closest they would get to a rapprochement, Den wordlessly encouraged Thea to go.

She found herself ploughing stiffly through the long grass which had turned from a natural glory into an annoying impediment in the space of half an hour. She was angry by the time she reached the car – with herself, with Drew and with Hepzie who panted with goofy joy on the back seat, with no inkling of her mistress's state of mind.

She found the straight route back, without even thinking about it. Inwardly she reran Maggs's accusations a thousand times, increasing her own emotional reactions in the process. Although she was pleased at the way she'd defended herself, rather than spinelessly agreeing to all the charges against her, that didn't ameliorate the feelings of victimisation. She had been attacked as severely as if Maggs had taken a cudgel to her. There had been no civilised half measures, no polite concealments within velvet tones. The girl had laid into her without restraint. The man beside her had been unable to prevent her from having her say, and had done very little to dilute the aggression. Maggs *hated* her, before she had even met her, and saw no reason why her feelings should remain hidden. If the encounter had ended on a slightly easier note, that did little to soften the genuine feelings that had been exposed.

Maggs's plain purpose had been to ensure that Thea and Drew had nothing more to do with each other. Maggs saw Thea as a threat, not only to Drew and Karen, it seemed, but to the children and probably herself as well. Even in her shaken self-pity, Thea could dimly see that there was a logic to this. Obviously she was 'the other woman' in Maggs's eyes, poised to snatch Drew up the moment his wife abandoned her struggle. There was a small kernel of truth to this, of course. That was the problem.

Maggs might lay claim to a number of justifications for her behaviour. She was desperately upset about Karen's condition, frightened that it would be decided to switch off the supporting machinery and let her die. From what she had gathered, Karen was a nice person, a good mother, a faultless wife. Her loss would be a major tragedy for all who knew her. All that was transparent and unarguable. But for Maggs, still young and prone to uncompromising judgements, it was unbearable, mainly because of the effect on Drew. Maggs loved Drew, even while she was cheerfully married to Den and utterly loyal to Karen. And Drew, needless to say, loved Maggs.

Which left little or no space for Thea Osborne.

Hyacinth House looked untidy and self-conscious with its swathes of police tape around the gateway. Thank goodness, Thea thought, there was no reason for them to actually go into the garden with their fingertip searches. The verge outside was already much too close. The reverberations from the day before were loud and intrusive – the limp body of the child, the ravaged features of his mother, still all too vivid to Thea's mind.

She parked further away than before, and attached the lead to the dog's collar. Experience had taught her that Hepzie could stick her nose in just a little too efficiently at times, and find things that might be best left undiscovered.

She hadn't intended to come back so soon – it was still not midday – but after the verbal assault from Maggs, all she wanted was to crawl into a quiet corner and lick her wounds. She was having a very nasty time, she thought miserably. Everything was out to get her, nobody liked her, she had nothing to do for the next twelve days and she had not developed any sort of affection for the house. Even

Blake-next-door, who would have been better than nothing, had gone off. Everything was actually *his* fault, she thought unreasonably. If he hadn't been going away this week, he could have watched over Vonny's house and there'd have been no need for a sitter.

On a Monday, it seemed, very few people had time or inclination to loiter outside, despite – or maybe because of – the fact of a brutal murder in their midst. One or two neighbours had come to stare at Hyacinth House for an hour or so the previous afternoon, before dispersing, presumably to discuss in hushed and fearful tones the few facts they had managed to glean, and then getting on with their lives. Thea had watched the police keeping them at a distance, and wondered how many had actually managed to identify the dead body before it was covered up with one of the white police tents that reminded her of medieval warfare, for some reason. Whatever the locals believed about Gudrun and her son, Thea was never going to learn about it. They were not going to tell her, even if she found the courage to go and sit with some of them in the Snowshill Arms.

She made herself a mug of strong coffee and nibbled at the sandwich she had prepared earlier, only to find swallowing difficult. She was so churned up by the encounter in Broad Campden that her throat had ceased to function. It felt as if her whole upper body was full of slowly congealing cement, as the psychic wounds quietly bled. Normally she would have found ways of recovering her balance quite quickly, finding arguments in her own defence, devising small revenges for the harm done to her.

This time, there was nothing of any consolation. Maggs was right in all essential points, and she, Thea, should sever every link with Drew. She had nothing to offer him but complications and divided loyalties. His business must be in difficulties already, if he was spending most of his time at Karen's bedside. His children must be terrified at the uncertainties surrounding them. He was such a nice man, so well intentioned and good-humoured, it wasn't fair to do anything to make his life even harder. Maggs was right. Hadn't he once told her that Maggs was *always* right?

She could perhaps send him a warning text – *Seen Maggs at grave. Realised I'm superfluous.* Something like that would surely be permissible. But then she heard the self-pitying appeal to him for reassurances, and scrapped the idea. There was nothing she could do that wouldn't make her even more guilty as charged by Maggs. She wanted to talk to Drew, that was the truth of it. Not only about Broad Campden and Karen and Maggs, but about the events in Snowshill and her role in them. Again, Maggs had been right. Thea knew only too well that she had the power to engage Drew's attention, merely by uttering the word 'murder'. And knowing that meant she couldn't do it. And that made her very unhappy.

She wandered out into the garden, only to see someone standing at the front gate. Identification took a few moments and then came as a surprise. 'Hello – Ruby, isn't it? Are you all right?'

It was a pertinent question. The graceful teenager had transformed into a tense pale figure with large eyes and hunched shoulders. She seemed ten years older than the day before.

'It was Stevie, wasn't it? Somebody killed Stevie.'

It seemed churlish to the point of cruelty to pretend ignorance. 'I'm afraid so,' Thea nodded. 'Yesterday afternoon.'

'The police came. They asked us where we were, how well we know Gudrun – whether we saw anything. But they wouldn't tell us what had happened. Just fobbed us off, like little children. Mum was furious.'

'It's a terrible thing to happen.'

'It's a terrible thing somebody *did*,' the girl corrected. 'It didn't just *happen*. He wasn't run over, was he? It wasn't an *accident*.'

'No,' Thea acknowledged. 'It seems not.' She was acutely aware of the events of the previous day, the anger directed against the boy, the exasperation at his behaviour that mother and daughter had manifested. She had a feeling that Ruby was thinking exactly the same thing.

'Everybody knew we were his main victims. It was always *our* garden he ran wild in, *our* fences he broke, *our* cat he tormented. They'll be thinking horrible things about us.'

'Oh, no,' said Thea instinctively. 'Everyone knows the difference between finding someone a nuisance and . . . well . . .'

'Killing them,' finished the girl flatly.

'Right.'

'They asked us a lot about Gudrun,' Ruby repeated with a tentative little frown. She obviously wanted to say a lot more, but couldn't find the words.

'They need to get a full picture,' Thea explained, conscious of a desire to avert the oncoming hypotheses or accusations. 'Family background – that sort of thing.'

'What family? She's like us – Mum and me. Just the two of them.'

'Mm . . . ?' was all Thea permitted herself by way of encouragement.

'Absent fathers. I mean – nobody has any idea who Stevie's father is . . . was. Same as me. Anonymous donor, is all Mum tells me when I ask her.'

Thea had wondered from time to time how that would feel; how a deliberately fatherless child would react when it got old enough to demand information. Did the mystery leave a gaping hole that could never be filled, or was it readily pushed into a file marked *irrelevant*? Both, probably, she'd concluded, depending on the character of the person concerned.

'And me, in a way,' she offered. 'I mean – my daughter and I were left on our own as well, when my husband was killed.'

'That's not the same, is it?' said Ruby, with a flicker of sarcasm. 'Stevie and I – we never knew anything at all about our fathers.'

Stevie and I hung in the air as a phrase resonating with unintended significance, until Thea felt her phone buzzing in her pocket and made her apologies. 'Come over any time, if you'd like to talk,' she said rashly.

'Don't worry,' said the girl. 'You've told me all I needed to know.'

* * *

The phone had been alerting her to a text message, and she had been immediately convinced that it must be from Drew. But she was wrong.

Thnx for msg. Feeling a bit better now. Starting to get angry. Hope that's a good sign. Love Jess. xxx

Well, that was something, Thea supposed. Her daughter was bouncing back from her broken heart, and in the process setting her mother a good example. No use in stewing over past mistakes, or yearning for what you couldn't have. If anger helped the process, then it definitely was a good thing and perhaps she could shelve any worry about Jess for the time being.

She could not stop thinking about the murdered boy. He had been out of control, destructive, perhaps even sadistic, but for all anybody knew, he could well have turned out to be a model character – a valiant soldier, an efficient butcher, a conscientious gamekeeper. There were plenty of roles in society that called for steady nerves and an ability to be cruel where necessary. However outrageous his behaviour, it was impossible to fully believe that that could have given anyone cause to actually kill him.

Gladwin turned up at half past three, and without even asking, Thea made strong tea and found an unopened pack of flapjack in the bread box. 'I bought it on Friday, before I came here. Seems a lifetime ago now,' she said.

'There's a mystery,' Gladwin announced portentously.

'Um . . . yes, I suppose there is,' frowned Thea.

'No. I mean a *new* mystery. We can't get anybody to tell

us who Stevie's father is – was . . . whichever. His mother just clams up and shakes her head. Not that she's said more than twenty words to us since it happened. None of the local people will say anything either, although I'm sure they know.'

'I get the impression they really don't know. I was talking to Ruby across the road, earlier on, and she implied that it was the same for her and Stevie – neither of them ever knew a father.'

'It happens, of course – but I'm not sure I'm convinced by *two* of them in one small village.'

'Then it must be the vicar, or Gudrun's brother, or something dreadful like that.' The possibility of flippancy when Gladwin was around did much to improve her mood.

'Don't,' begged the detective.

'Clara Beauchamp told me he was a mistake,' Thea offered. 'I suppose that implies that she knows who the father was. And Ruby's mother used an anonymous donor.'

'We spoke to the Beauchamp woman this morning. She says she has no real idea of Stevie's parentage. Just heard some story about Gudrun turning back at the door of the abortion clinic, and the whole village thinking she did quite the wrong thing.'

'Well, it's not Blake-next-door,' said Thea absently.

'Why isn't it?'

'His hair's too dark. The boy was almost white-blond. That couldn't happen genetically, surely.'

Gladwin raised a hand. 'Don't get into genetics again. Remember Temple Guiting,' she warned. 'Besides, you're not necessarily right. If Blake Grossman had a fair-haired parent, it could happen.'

'Have you found where he is?'

'He's not responding to our efforts to contact him,' said Gladwin, absently.

'He went away for a few days. I'm not sure where. His girlfriend's in Palestine, and he's Jewish. Doesn't that mean he's unlikely to have a fair-haired parent?'

'Not really. Some Jews are very fair. But why are we talking about him? Did he even live here ten years ago, when Stevie must have been conceived?'

'I have no idea.'

'Who else have you met?'

'Mark Parker. *He's* fair. It could be him, although he's umpteen years younger than Gudrun. She's over fifty and he's thirty. I imagine she could be quite magnetic if she tried. Somebody a boy could learn the basics from.'

'More like the embellishments, I'd have said. The basics come naturally.'

'True,' Thea giggled. 'There must be a hundred possible men, though. Aren't there any clues?'

'She twitched a bit when we asked about money.'

'You think the father gave her some maintenance? The bank would have the details, surely?'

'She hasn't got a bank, just a post office account that doesn't do electronic transfers. She lived very much like a peasant – if we're allowed to say that. Grew her own food, wove her own blankets, mended her own fences. The house is rather nice – simple, fairly clean, like something from the 1930s.'

'As different as possible from this place, then,' said Thea ruefully. 'You've seen the clutter.'

Gladwin nodded. 'Are you meant to be keeping it dusted?'

'She said I didn't need to, but I suppose I will. There's not much to do, after all. She's got two cats, which pretty much sort themselves out.'

Gladwin asked the inevitable question. 'So why pay you to be here at all?'

Thea shrugged. 'Scared of burglars, I guess, or intruders who'd break the things. She does seem very timid. Did I tell you she just chickened out when she saw where Victor was living? Rushed off to gather her courage and tried again next day. *He* thought she was lost, when he phoned me.'

Gladwin frowned more deeply. 'I don't think I'm fully understanding all this. Can you start again from the beginning?'

Thea recounted everything she had gleaned from Yvonne, ending with a laugh. 'I don't know why we're wasting time on her. She's got nothing to do with anything.'

'She has, though,' Gladwin corrected. 'A body was dumped outside her house. You're her house-sitter, and you met the dead child and his mother the same day.'

'Yes, but she was *away*.'

'So she says. We can check road cameras for her car, maybe. Just to make sure she was where she said she was.' Her voice was slow and thoughtful, her eyes flickering from side to side, as she followed ideas and connections.

'You don't want to think it was Gudrun, do you?' Thea challenged. 'You're grasping at any other straw you can think of.'

135

'I'm just being thorough,' Gladwin sighed. 'There's a chance the unknown father wants the kid out of the way for some reason. Or it might be he was some kind of psychopath and Gudrun was scared Stevie would grow up to be like him, and did the only thing she could to prevent it.'

'That's impossible,' argued Thea. 'It doesn't fit at all with how she is.'

Gladwin was holding a small screen on which she made a note with a plastic pointer. Thea recognised it from an earlier encounter. At that time, only a year or so ago, it had seemed futuristic and slightly ostentatious. Now it was barely worthy of remark. 'Mm,' the detective said vaguely. 'But I'm still going to check any sightings of Mrs Parker's car.'

Thea said nothing, accepting her ambivalent position in relation to the police force. Gladwin had become a friend, which led to a greater sharing of her suspicions than was strictly professional, but Thea had no direct influence over her. Nor would she have wanted to. She did, however, feel free to express her own ideas. 'I still can't see how it could possibly work that Yvonne had anything whatsoever to do with it.'

'We'll have to see. I can think of one or two scenarios that would implicate her. If Stevie was in the habit of slashing her roses, and probably other invasions as well, she might have planned to dispose of the little swine, and worked it all out meticulously, giving herself an alibi and everything.'

The phrase *little swine* made Thea wince. You really

shouldn't speak ill of the dead, who could not defend themselves or set the record straight. It led to a fleeting thought about Drew and his graves and his absolute decency in all matters involving the bodies he buried.

'No, I don't think so,' she said mildly. 'Vonny Parker just hasn't got what it would take for all that. And whatever Stevie did to the flowers, it couldn't possibly be bad enough to make her want to *kill* him. Besides, I gather he made far more mess of the garden across the road. That Janice is a lot taller and stronger than Yvonne.'

Gladwin drained her tea and doodled on her electronic pad. 'There are too many gaps,' she complained. 'As usual. Presumably Stevie never got to see his dad, even if he knew who he was. If there'd been visits, the neighbours would know about it. You know what villages are like.'

'I'm not sure about this one. From what I've seen of the Cotswolds, people don't snoop on each other as much as you might think. And they might have met on neutral ground, in a leisure centre somewhere or a park.'

'We'll have to speak to the school, see if he said anything in class. It would have to be the holidays, of course.'

'Medea,' said Thea softly. 'Isn't that the story of the mother who kills her children and makes them into a stew to feed to their unfaithful father?' She shuddered. 'The most gruesome story of them all, by a long way.'

'Does that mean you've come around to thinking it was Gudrun, then, after all?'

'No, not really. It's just that I guess we shouldn't underestimate what people are capable of, especially if they're feeling wronged,' said Thea, thinking of Maggs.

'I've forgotten Gudrun's surname,' she added, out of the blue. 'Not that it matters, I suppose.'

'Horsfall. Without an *e*. Good old Anglo-Saxon name, I suppose.'

'Probably descended from Hengist and Horsa.'

'Were they Saxons?'

'If I remember rightly, yes they were.'

'Pity,' said Gladwin. 'It would fit better if they were Vikings. Gudrun's one of the most Viking women I've met for a long time.'

Neither of them laughed.

Chapter Ten

Monday afternoon drifted to a close, with the feeding of the cats the only real task. Both animals were considerably more approachable by this time, and permitted a few moments of fondling on Thea's part. Their dense coats were sleek and warm and slightly dusty, from a day spent on a sunny window ledge in the main bedroom upstairs. They spent their nights on Yvonne's bed, curled together, as far as Thea knew – the cat flap in the back door only allowed them free range in the daytime. Hepzie ignored them, thanks to a judicious separation in feeding stations on Thea's part. She shut the dog out in the hall with her feeding bowl, and let the cats have the freedom of the kitchen.

She had no firm plans for the rest of the day. She could find more information on Snowshill and decide whether or not to visit the Manor. She even contemplated the alarming idea of walking up to the pub and buying herself a glass of wine, in the hope of falling into conversation with one or two locals. Now that the news was out that a local child had been murdered, there was likely to be plenty of discussion on the subject. If she could cleverly elicit the identity of young Stevie's father, that would earn her a big gold star from DS Gladwin, and make her feel her time wasn't being wasted.

But she couldn't face it. She might be expected to account for herself, to describe the discovery of the child's body, to risk being identified as the house-sitter who had found herself in the midst of a number of violent crimes whilst homeowners were away. She felt shy at such a prospect, reluctant to put herself in a situation where people knew more about her than she realised.

She opted to call her daughter for an update on the state of her emotions.

Jessica answered quickly, breathlessly. 'Oh, Mum – it's you,' she said, covering the disappointment well.

'You sound much better,' Thea said.

'Do I?'

'Aren't you?'

'Not really. He's texting me, really nasty stuff. And he's putting things on Facebook about me. I'm trying to ignore it, as I'm sure you'd advise, but it's not easy.'

'Good God! Can't you report him? It must be completely against regulations.'

'He's not breaking any laws. It's not specific, just general abuse. God, Mum, how could I ever have thought I loved him? What sort of fool have I been?'

The outburst had tears in it, and Thea's heart swelled with helpless rage. 'He's trying to make himself feel better, I suppose,' she said, knowing this was far from what her daughter wanted to hear.

'What do you mean? You're not *defending* him, are you?'

'Of course I'm not. But he's not a total monster. He must have some reason for behaving like this.'

'He says I showed him up in front of his friends, made him look stupid. It was *one time*, when he didn't know who Lloyd George was, and I teased him about it. He never did history, apparently. I mean – there are millions of things I don't know that he does. He surely must realise that.'

'Fragile male ego,' murmured Thea.

'What about *my* ego? He's mouthing off about me to all my friends, he dumped me without having the decency to face me in person, and now I'm starting to think all men must be the same, and I'll never find one I can trust.'

'It's good that you're angry about it. You know he's got his own problems, really – whatever they might be. Nothing to do with you, except you're too good for him, and he's finally come to that conclusion. It's not your problem.'

'But I have to *work* with him.'

'Ah. Well, yes, that's going to be difficult, I can see.'

'And don't say it was always going to be a bad idea to take up with somebody from work. I never *meet* anybody anywhere else. What choice do I have?'

'Maybe he'll ask for a transfer, or get promoted or something.'

'Maybe he'll be given the boot. The way I'm feeling, that would suit me very nicely. Except it's never going to happen. He's quite a good detective, apparently. But not enough to make inspector for a good few years yet.'

'All you can do is brave it out, then. Stay dignified and do a good job. You know what they say?'

'What?'

'The best revenge is to live a good life. Show him you're better off without him.'

'Right,' said Jessica doubtfully. 'Except, I'm not sure the others are going to see it that way. They all think he's wonderful, and that I must be a cow to have made him act like this.'

'They'll soon realise. Nobody really approves of malicious postings. They always rebound on the person writing them, in the end.'

'I hope so. Anyway – how's it going with you?'

'Fine,' said Thea bravely, knowing from the question that Jess had no idea about events in Snowshill, and determined not to compound her worries by mentioning it. 'Now go and have a nice hot bath and read a soppy book, and then sleep tight.'

Jessica laughed feebly. 'It's not even seven o'clock yet.'

'So watch a DVD for a bit first.'

'Yeah. I might do that. Thanks for calling, Mum.'

After that, it was easy for Thea to follow something approaching her own advice. She took the dog out into the garden, staying well clear of the flower bed where the hornet had attacked her, and listened for sounds of life. A plane flew high overhead, a solitary bird sang in a tree across the road, and no traffic passed. She focused on her breathing, and small details of her surroundings. Death had left no long-term physical trace. The grass went on growing, the stone walls would stand for centuries to come. Nothing, in the long run, actually mattered. It was a mantra she had adopted after Carl had died, finding it both a consolation and grounds for despair. And it wasn't true. It *did* matter every time a life was cut short. It couldn't help but matter, whatever words a person might repeat to herself.

There was not a breath of wind to stir the treetops. The stillness began to feel ominous, something waiting to attack, some wickedness biding its time. 'Come on, Heps,' she said. 'Let's go and find a radio. There must be one somewhere.'

Chapter Eleven

In North Staverton, earlier that same day, Den Cooper went directly to see his friend Drew Slocombe after he and Maggs got back from Broad Campden. He had been doing the same thing for the past month, two or three times a week, aware that his employer in Bradbourne was on the brink of losing patience with him as a result. Today he had not gone in at all, setting out with Maggs for Drew's new burial ground before nine that morning. But an irritated employer was a price he had no hesitation in paying, given the circumstances. Drew was struggling, his health threatened, his children silent with worry. The fear about Karen was like a deep trough into which they were all inexorably sinking.

Karen herself seemed to Den to have given up. In the years since her original injury, she had very slowly faded away, becoming physically smaller and weaker, and mentally detached. Personality seeped out of her: reactions slowing, emotions evaporating. Doctors scanned and tested her damaged brain and professed themselves at a loss. It could only be shock, they insisted – something intangible and unreachable had happened, which ought to rectify itself merely through the therapeutic influence of daily life. Her physical brain was fine – as far as they could see.

Except it wasn't. Something deep inside had failed, or burst or blocked in a vital spot and Karen had lapsed into deep unconsciousness. She could breathe without mechanical assistance, and her skin reacted to pain by flinching, but she seemed deaf and blind and infinitely remote from the people who needed her.

Maggs refused to regard any of this as hopeless. She avidly collected stories of people who had emerged from far deeper comas than this, to live many normal years. She pointed to Karen's response to pain as proof that she was still functioning, and would wake up in her own time. Where the men and the children adopted quiet stoicism as their coping strategy, Maggs went wild. She shouted and argued, spent hours at Karen's bedside talking to her in an endless urgent monologue and fiercely defended Drew from any needless bother.

Which was obviously why she had been so awful to that poor woman in the Broad Campden field. They had not discussed it during the drive back. Instead, Maggs had aired her thoughts about the floundering plans for the second burial ground. 'He won't be able to keep it going,' she said. 'I told him all along it was too much. I never understood what he thought he was doing.'

'Expansion would have been good business sense,' Den observed. 'Especially as it fell in his lap, more or less. He'd have been daft to refuse it. Besides, you were all for it, a few months ago.'

'Well, things have changed since then. He'll have to give it up. He can barely keep North Staverton afloat as it is.'

Den knew better than to argue. Maggs based all her assumptions on the expectation that Karen would survive, and be in need of long-term care. If – when – she died, things would look quite different and Drew might well be glad of the distraction involved in setting up a second strand to his business.

Drew's home and office were all part of the same building in the quiet little backwater that was North Staverton. He had been there for seven years or so, filling his land with graves, until the Peaceful Repose cemetery had begun to look as settled and permanent as any churchyard. The graves were not arranged in straight lines. The plot itself was an odd shape, with sections devoted to animal graves and ashes plots, the paths between them running in curves, adding to a sense of freedom to use the space as imagination dictated. There were few rules at Peaceful Repose. No sooner had Drew decided to put a limit on memorial trees or stones than Maggs or a persistent customer persuaded him to change or abandon it. There were quick-growing silver birches, one or two patches of graceful bamboo, a lot of spring bulbs and a riot of flowering shrubs. In total there were two hundred and ten graves, which over the seven-year period had yielded Drew, Maggs and Karen a very meagre income indeed. Karen had worked as a teacher, originally, but stopped when Timmy was born. She had saved money by growing vegetables and scarcely ever buying clothes. She had been part of a collective that ran market stalls and celebrated a lifestyle that depended as little as possible on money.

Drew had been in demand as a secular officiant at funerals in crematoria, creating personal and meaningful ceremonies as people shook themselves free of the church-based rituals that had less and less significance for them. He gave talks, and signed people up for prepaid burials. He also buried them on their own land, now and then – which had happened with Greta Simmonds in Broad Campden, and led to a situation which Maggs at least regarded as unsustainable and troublesome, given the appearance of Thea Osborne on the scene. All these activities raised additional income, but it still amounted to all too little.

Den found his friend in the office, idly sorting through a small stack of papers. 'Hi,' he said, from the open doorway. 'Nice day again.'

'Oh, hello. What time is it?'

'Two-fifteen. Have you eaten?'

Drew shook his head. 'Somebody phoned. Maggs has gone to see them. We've got a burial tomorrow.'

'Yes, I know. Mr Anderson. Half past two.'

'Right.'

'Kids okay?'

'Not really. Timmy wet the bed again. Steph got into a fight yesterday with a girl in the park, who said Karen was going to die. I can't believe how vile children can be, how they seem to actually *want* to hurt each other.'

'They're just testing the boundaries, to see what happens. They have to work out what the consequences are of various behaviours.' Den had taken a course on child development not long ago, thinking he might turn to teaching as a career move. 'They don't mean it maliciously.'

'I think they do,' Drew disagreed.

'Oh, well.' Den had no wish to argue. 'It's good that Steph reacted.'

'It would have got her into trouble, though, if it had happened at school. They won't tolerate any violence these days.'

'Where did Maggs go? Who was it that phoned?'

'The hospice. Somebody wants to make arrangements. She won't be very long.'

'She lost it this morning – did she tell you? In your Broad Campden field.'

'What? Did you go with her? Did anybody tell me that? Why weren't you at work?'

'Come on, mate, keep up. I don't work Mondays any more. It's gone down to a four-day week. The writing's on the wall, we can all see it. I'll be lucky to hang on till Christmas.'

'Oh, God! What'll you do then?'

'Something'll turn up. I can get some experience in a school somewhere and sign up for teacher training. Except I've missed the boat, according to Maggs. Too many out-of-work bankers deciding they want to teach, all of a sudden. We'll get by,' he finished easily. 'It's the same for everybody, and with Maggs alongside, we're never going to starve.'

'What did you mean about her losing it?'

'That house-sitter woman was there when we arrived. With her spaniel. I know Maggs should have minded her own business, but you probably know how she feels about her.'

Drew stared at him. 'No. I've no idea. Why does she feel *anything*? What's Thea to do with her?'

Den trod carefully. The emotional links between all those involved were complex and delicate. 'She thinks you're vulnerable to people like that. She feels she has to defend you from them.'

'Oh!' The undertaker forced a laugh. 'Silly girl.'

'I know. It was pretty much out of order. I felt sorry for what's-her-name. She was pretty shaken.'

'*Thea*. She's called Thea. I haven't seen her for ages now.'

'She said you asked her to go and check the grave.'

'I sent her a text. She's staying somewhere close by. Snowshill, or something like that.'

'Snowshill? Where that kid was killed at the weekend?'

Drew stared harder. 'Kid?'

'A boy was strangled. It was on the news just now. Sounds to me as if the mother did it. Very nasty.'

'Is Thea involved, do you think?' Drew's eagerness would have done nothing to allay Maggs's worries, if she'd been there to witness it.

'I have absolutely no idea. Why would she be?'

'She tends to turn up when that sort of thing happens. Like at Broad Campden. She got me off the hook there, Den. I don't know where I'd have been without her.'

'And you went to see her, with the kids, in Cranham. That seems to be the bit that Maggs can't stomach.'

'Maggs is overstepping the mark.' Drew's energy was reviving by the moment. 'Thea's a good friend, a clever woman who . . . well, who can be very good company,' he finished lamely.

'And she's pretty,' Den observed mildly. 'I can see there's definitely something about her.'

'Am I banned from seeing her, then?'

'If Maggs has her way, yes you are,' said Den candidly. 'And Maggs generally does get her way.'

'She needn't worry. I'm not going anywhere, am I? How can I, when the hospital could call at any moment? I'm nailed to this room, like Christ on the cross. I'm even starting to think I know how he must have felt.'

'I can see it's crucifying you, anyway,' summarised Den. 'You've lost half a stone at least since June, and you look as if you haven't slept for a month, either.'

Drew shrugged. 'Anyone would be the same. It's the not knowing that's such a killer. It's a cliché, I realise that, but when the future's just a massive grey void, you don't feel like putting much effort into the present.'

'Your kids have a future. You need to focus on that.'

'Without a mother? What sort of future is that?'

'Come on – listen to yourself. You've been the most hands-on dad I've ever seen, especially with Stephanie. They're not babies any more. You'd cope. You've got me and Maggs to help.'

Both men were fully aware that the prospect of Karen's absence was assumed as hard fact in this exchange. In the past few days a shift had taken place, leaving only Maggs resisting the irreversible process by which Karen was being lost to them.

Drew focused his gaze on a mat on the floor. 'She was such an amazing girl when I met her. All that hair, and bright beautiful eyes. She was so quick and funny and *good*. She was my *mate*, for life. When it looked as if we might never manage to have kids, I thought – well, that's okay. Nobody in their right mind could ask for more than Karen anyway. She always knew the right line to take, always had such a *zest*. That stuff with the farmers' market, just before she was injured – she was *fabulous* with all that. Everybody loved her.'

'I know. I remember.'

'I was never worthy of her, never really understood what she saw in me. She knew there were times when Maggs had to steer me back on track, when I went astray. But now Maggs has got it wrong. Even she can't put everything right this time. And she doesn't have to be fierce with poor Thea. Things are different now. We've all got other things to learn, other ways of surviving. Maggs is living in the past.' He shook his head in defeat. 'Which is a great shame.'

'Sorry, mate, but I think it's you that's wrong, not Maggs. She's making sure we all remember what we've got to hang on to. If we're ever going to face the future, we need to keep the past in mind, to show us what matters. She's the consistent figure through all this. Even if it doesn't work with you, it'll be a lifeline for the kids. Somebody has to keep the old Karen alive for them, give them that foundation and security.'

Drew rallied again. '*I* can do that. And Karen's mother, up to a point. We both can and will do it. But it won't help them if I crucify myself, will it? I have to be normal and functional, and try to remain my usual self.'

'I think that's what Maggs and I are both trying to say,' said Den with a smile. 'And we'll get there, if we all pull together.'

Drew did his best to answer the smile, before asking, 'But what did Maggs say to her, exactly?'

'I don't remember exactly, but it was pretty strong. It seems she's been working herself up for quite a while and it all came spilling out. She hadn't expected your lady to be quite so attractive, I suppose. She really is a looker, isn't she?'

'She's seven years older than me. Her daughter's twenty-two. Nearly as old as Maggs, in fact. She's a widow and she's daft about dogs.'

Den was unmoved. 'So?'

'So there's nothing for Maggs to get angry about, and no reason in the world to abuse poor Thea. What am I going to say to her now?'

Den tilted his head. 'You have to say something?'

'Of course I do. If there's been a murder near where she's staying, and if she went to look at the grave like I asked, and if she wants somebody to talk to—'

'Oh dear,' said Den. 'Oh dear, oh dear.'

'Shut up,' said Drew.

When Maggs got back from the hospice, Drew forced himself to confront her without delay. 'Den was here a little while ago. He said you'd been rude to my friend Thea. What was all that about?'

Maggs lifted her chin and met his eye in a very direct gaze. 'What do you think?'

'I think you need to back off a bit, and let me live my own life. You're not my mother. It was out of order.'

'Den said the same thing, but I just flipped when I

saw her. I know you, Drew, don't pretend I don't. What about that time with Genevieve Slater? You'd have done something terrible then if I hadn't stopped you.'

'That was seven years ago and anyway I wouldn't have. You exaggerate your influence. You're worrying about nothing. Can't you see how damaging it is, you thinking that sort of thing about me? You're crossing a line.'

'I was thinking of Karen,' she said, no longer meeting his eye.

'I know, and I absolutely understand that you want the best for all of us. But you can't control everything, however much you want to. We've all got to take it a day at a time, and keep things as normal as possible for the children.'

'Yes!' she said loudly. 'That's exactly it. If you go off with that woman, it won't be normal, will it?'

He sighed. 'Maggs, you're all wrong. I can see how scary that idea must be – but it isn't going to happen. It never was going to happen. There's no question of it.'

'Good. Because you're married, and Karen's going to get better, and that's all there is to it.'

'Right,' he said, with another great sigh. Maggs was still so young, he reminded himself, although their long acquaintance often made him forget her youth. She had been seventeen when he first met her, not quite nineteen when they set up Peaceful Repose together. Her entire adult life had been spent in his company, and he had watched as she and Den Cooper found each other and quickly recognised how well they fitted together. Cooper had been a police sergeant at the time, but within a few months had resigned from the force, and taken a succession of low-paid jobs – some of them effectively voluntary – in the caring services. Impossibly tall, he carried an air of calm reliability that made him useful in a wide range of situations. He grew up in mid Devon, slowly identifying where his own strengths and weaknesses lay as he found himself dealing with cases of murder that entangled him emotionally as well as professionally. He could not extricate himself from the sadness of people's lives, the unnecessary suffering they inflicted on themselves and each other, the cunning and malice they nursed within themselves, often for years. When he met Drew, he was introduced to a new way of seeing death that calmed and reassured him and made him see that he was no longer fit for police work.

Drew felt responsible for the austere life that Maggs and Den were forced to live. Their income was risibly small, thanks to him. Maggs owned almost half of the business, which meant nothing in terms of bread on her table. Den had spent years trying to decide where he ought best to direct his efforts, and even now, the idea of teaching felt lukewarm and tentative. He might enjoy much of the studying, but would struggle with the written work. Nobody felt confident that he would finally land a permanent full-time post, with pensions and holidays and sick pay and promotion. And like Drew, he was not so very far from his fortieth birthday – a time when all good men should feel themselves finally grown up.

Maggs had always insisted that she never wanted children, a position nobody argued with while she was still only in her mid twenties. Time enough, they all thought, for her to change her mind. But Den was a different matter. It was easy to visualise him with a baby over his shoulder, or calmly talking a toddler down from a terrifying tantrum. For Den not to have his own children struck his friends as a waste.

When Maggs had gone, Drew accessed the BBC news website and tracked down the story about the Snowshill murder. A boy, nine years old, had been found dead outside a house in the village. Neighbours had suggested he was a child out of control, capable of malicious acts of destruction, and if ASBOs hadn't been abolished, he would undoubtedly have received one by the age of eight. He lived with his mother in a cottage close by and was her only child.

'Poor woman!' moaned Drew. 'I wonder if Thea has met her yet.' There was no doubt in his mind that Thea Osborne, house-sitter and compulsive amateur detective, would have got herself involved in some way. And he, Drew Slocombe, found himself wishing he were free to go there immediately and find out more. Because he was another compulsive solver of mysteries, and here was one he already found deeply intriguing. But he was not free, and that evening, he would again take his place at his wife's silent bedside, while their grandmother sat in his house with his children.

Chapter Twelve

Monday evening found Thea with a suddenly friendly cat on her lap in the bizarre living room, as the daylight disappeared. Hepzie rumbled jealously beside her, but the cat – Jennings, she thought – smugly kept its place, purring defiantly. She had spent some minutes working out the various features of the television, and now had it tuned, perhaps oddly, to Radio Three, which played *Così Fan Tutte* softly to her. Yvonne's only radio was in her bedroom, she had discovered when she searched.

Her thoughts returned compulsively to the hour on the previous afternoon before she found Stevie's body. Why had she not heard anything? If she had only had the good timing to look out of the front window at the right moment, she might have seen the killer depositing the body beyond the wall. A car must have drawn up, bundled the little boy out and then driven off again. Didn't everybody subconsciously note the sounds of such a happening? If Thea didn't, then her dog surely should have done.

It had to have happened while she was speaking to

Jocelyn, as she and Gladwin had already concluded. What an irony, that the impulse to phone her sister should have come at precisely the wrong moment. She might otherwise have been in the garden, in a spot ideal for witnessing events out in the road.

Except, she realised, the boy would still have been dead – killed at some other spot, and brought to Hyacinth House for some grim reason that was still obscure. And if the killer had had the least suspicion that someone was watching from the house, the body would surely have been dumped somewhere else. She could have done nothing to prevent it, however irrationally an inner voice insisted she might have.

Outside, Snowshill continued to be beautiful and serene. If there were ghosts of ancient travellers and mad collectors hovering there, they manifested no horror or outrage at the crime just perpetrated. No doubt they had seen such things before – the monks who sheltered the voyagers would have heard terrible tales from the wider world. Charles Paget Wade must have witnessed violence and misery in the slave plantations of the West Indies. But had anybody ever before been murdered in this tiny jewel of a village? As far as her computer could inform her, they had not.

Hepzie heard the garden gate before she did, which was unusual. Thea was slow to get up, not wanting to dislodge the cat. But then she heard the footsteps and knew she must move. Looking out of the front window, she could see a woman standing on the doorstep, waiting, unmoving. It wasn't difficult to recognise Gudrun Horsfall.

For twenty seconds she dithered indecisively. Did she want to admit the woman and vicariously endure the anguish of her loss? Was she feeling strong enough to offer a shoulder for Gudrun to cry on? She had no choice, of course. Her car was there in full view, the dog had yapped revealingly when the knock sounded. Silently, she went and opened the door.

'They let me out, you see.' The defiance in the words was pathetically outweighed by the ravaged face. 'Couldn't make me say I'd killed my own boy.' Tears glittered in the light from the hall, and thickened the woman's voice.

'Oh, gosh, come in and sit down.' It was obvious, of course, that Gudrun would want to sit with the woman who had found her child and witnessed her collapse. Thea Osborne, if anyone, must be certain of her guiltlessness. Which only made Thea feel a sharp pang of shame at the way she had allowed Gladwin to shake her confidence. 'You poor thing,' she added.

'I can't go home, not with it so empty. They said I could have that policewoman with me as long as I liked, but she's no company. She treats me as if I'm a wild animal. Hardly says anything. One night of having her around was more than enough.'

'You were at home last night?'

Gudrun nodded. 'Been answering questions all morning, mind. They don't mean to be cruel. I understand that.'

'They want to get to the truth.'

'Funny how I can't feel that it matters. You see those people on telly, baying for the blood of their kids' killers, as if that'll make things all right. I don't get it myself. It's not

158

going to bring him back, is it?' She slumped into silence for a few moments, before going on, 'It was washing line – did you know? A length off somebody's washing line.'

'Was it? I thought it was just some odd sort of string.'

'No, it was washing line. Doesn't rot in the rain, see. Plastic. Strong. You can't break it. The sort those whirligig things have. They told me that, and I said I'd never had one. I've got a string across the back, with a long stick to hold it up in the middle.'

The old-fashioned arrangement almost made Thea smile. She had only seen such a line in photographs, as far as she could recall.

'I suppose most people round here have the whirligig sort. "Rotary", that's the word for them.'

'Yeah. Rotary.'

'Gudrun – who is Stevie's father? Does he know what's happened? Is he going to be upset?' Were these cruel and intrusive questions, she wondered uneasily? Or was it the most natural and obvious thing to ask?

'No father,' was the short reply. 'Stevie's mine, all mine. I stole him,' she added, with a quick flash of pride. 'I wanted him and I got him. Easy.'

'You mean . . .' Of course she didn't mean it as it sounded. But what exactly *did* she mean?

'I won't say. Too late for all that now. Didn't turn out as I wanted, anyhow, not really. Serves me right, according to some. Taking what wasn't rightly mine, going against nature. There'll be plenty saying that today, when they hear what's happened. Someone taking him away from me again, just to teach me a lesson.'

'No!' Thea cried out involuntarily against the notion of such a ghastly way to get at someone. 'Who could hate you as much as that?'

'Stevie annoyed a lot of folk around here. He *was* a bad boy, I won't deny it. You saw for yourself. But I'd have brought him round. The teachers were just saying, at the end of term, how he was turning a corner, growing up a bit, listening to them a bit more.'

'And nobody would deliberately kill him, just for being a bad boy. That's ridiculous.'

'Somebody did,' said Gudrun, unarguably.

'Do you want to stay here for the night? I'm sure Yvonne wouldn't mind, if she knew. We needn't even tell her, come to that. She's not home until the end of next week.'

Gudrun tried to form a brave face, tried to get out of the soft chair, but sank back. 'Maybe just the one night,' she accepted weakly. 'Now it's getting dark. I'll be better in the morning.'

'Are there any animals that need you at home?' The cottage seemed a natural environment for chickens, goats, dogs, cats, but she couldn't recall seeing anything by way of livestock.

A painful expression flooded Gudrun's face, and she shook her head. 'Stevie didn't get on too well with creatures,' she muttered. 'Wasn't really safe . . .'

Thea turned away to hide the horrified look she couldn't avoid. If that boy was so out of control and violent that he would harm or terrorise animals, then maybe . . . well, maybe things were a lot worse than she had yet grasped.

'Gudrun – you know I asked whether there was

something the matter with him? I know it was rude of me, and I was angry – but what you just said. Well, it doesn't sound very good, does it? What exactly did the school say about him? There must have been reports or statements or whatever they call them.'

She tossed her head as if to shake away the whole business and clear herself some mental space. 'They never said he wasn't right. They talked about his behaviour being *unacceptable*. That's the favourite word these days. And then they *did* accept it, daft idiots. Couldn't do anything else. In the old days, they'd have taken a stick to him and taught him better.'

'But you never—? How did you keep him in order?'

'I never hit him, if that's what you mean. Shouted, bribed, nagged. Usual stuff. Worked well enough, mostly. Him and me – we were *together*, just us.' She dissolved into inarticulate gasps, the tidal wave of loss and grief submerging her. She struggled back to the surface long enough to add, 'It was only outside he was bad. Sweet as pie when we were indoors.' The defiance melted away as she added, 'Well, mostly, he was. So long as he had something to do.' The gasps turned to sobs and Thea's heart contracted with the pity of it all. She waited for the storm to subside before speaking again.

'It must have been difficult, all on your own. Didn't the father ever help? With money, at least?'

Gudrun's upper lip curled in a sneer. 'He tried to force me to have an abortion. Shocked rigid he was when I told him. Said he couldn't go through all that again.'

'Again? What does that mean?'

161

Gudrun shrugged. 'Seems I wasn't the first. Never asked him for names. It wasn't difficult to guess, but I never said anything. Never heard that it got out, either. Men like that – they ought to be castrated, for everybody's sake.'

'So . . . he washed his hands of you?'

'No!' Her head came up, and she met Thea's gaze with reddened eyes. 'It was me – I told him to forget all about it, that I'd got what I wanted from him and he could go back to his wife.'

'Ah.'

'Not that he'd ever left her. They don't, do they?'

'Were you in love with him?' It sounded crass, even in her own ears. She smiled awkwardly. 'Sorry – that's a daft question.'

'We were good in bed, that's all. I was over forty and wanted a kid. He never thought to do anything to prevent it and I let him think I was taking care of all that. Easy. It was so easy, I thought it must be meant.'

'But it wasn't easy for long?'

'Everybody thought I'd been on the game, making a business of it. I was a looker then, in spite of my age. Men fancied me. They thought I'd got caught, and decided to go through with it because it was my last chance. Not far wrong, either. Except I didn't go to bed with just anybody. Do you know' – again the proud look as her eyes met Thea's – 'I've only slept with four men in my whole life. I married at nineteen, the first boy I ever had anything to do with. He ran off in the end, don't know where he went to. Never even got a proper divorce, as far as I know. Then I took up with a couple of older blokes for a bit, nothing very definite. Tried to make me go and live with them, wanting somebody to cook for them, mainly. First one, then the other, and now I can hardly remember which was which.' She spoke flatly, reciting her history as if reading from a page. 'Never got pregnant in all that time – thought there must be a blockage or something. Always did like babies, though.'

'And his wife never found out? Stevie's father's wife, I mean.'

'Seemingly not.' A watery smile flickered over Gudrun's mouth.

'And did Stevie ever meet his dad?'

The woman shook her head ambiguously, leaving Thea none the wiser. It was more a warning not to pursue such questions than a specific reply.

But there was more she wanted to know. 'How did you manage for money?'

Gudrun blinked. 'Hasn't anybody told you? I was a competitive swimmer – youngest in the national team – and got a bronze medal at the Olympics when I was still in my teens.'

Thea focused on the muscular shoulders and thought she could still see the powerful athlete Gudrun had been. 'Gosh!' she said. 'I had no idea. So you went professional?'

'Not exactly. There were a lot of ways of earning some cash as spin-offs, and then I taught for a bit. People wrote stuff about me and I got a share of the proceeds. Then I broke my shoulder and got a lot of compensation. It'll last me out if I'm careful.'

'That was before you had Stevie?'

The reminder came as a visible blow to the bereaved mother who had for a minute forgotten her loss.

'Ten years before. I'd got a few little jobs since then, but my confidence was gone. I didn't dare dive again, not even from the side. My arm's always going to be stiff.'

'So you bought your little cottage and dropped out?'

'Something like that,' agreed Gudrun thickly. 'It was my cousin's before me, and I got left a quarter share of it when he died. I bought the others out. Didn't leave me with much, but I grew up around here and it's home. I can't stay here now, though. Not now they've taken my boy away from me.'

It was far too early to ask her about any plans for the future. Instead, Thea led her up the stairs, and without a qualm offered her the use of Yvonne Parker's bedroom, knowing from her own experience that sleep would be a capricious disrupted luxury in these first days of horror. The fact of the bedroom's rightful ownership seemed a minor unimportant detail. The niceties of home ownership and authorisation had ceased to apply in this most terrible crisis. Gudrun needed a haven where nobody would find her or bother her.

She crawled onto the bed fully clothed and closed her eyes. 'Thank you,' she said.

The agony of the present moment was all-consuming, the temporary distraction of Thea's questions barely scratching the surface. But she wasn't quite ready to fall silent and leave the woman alone. 'Who exactly do you think it was?' she asked from the doorway.

Gudrun flapped her hand vaguely towards the window and the road outside. 'Them. The people he annoyed. Out there. They ridded themselves of a nuisance, as if he was a fox or a badger they didn't like.'

'No!' The suggestion of ancient remedies for a timeless problem brought a stabbing sense of fear to Thea. Fear and horror. It was simply not possible that a respectable property-owning community could take such a step. She shook the idea away as ridiculous. 'No, that isn't possible. You think they conspired to do it?' She put a hand to her own throat. 'In cold blood, to kill a child they all knew? Absolutely impossible.'

'Somebody did it,' Gudrun murmured. 'We saw him there, dead. And he didn't strangle himself, did he?'

At some point during the past hour Thea had become completely convinced of something immensely important: Gudrun Horsfall had certainly not killed her own child.

She went downstairs quietly, her mind blank. Gudrun's agony was beyond words, the coming days of endurance likely to be made worse by police suspicions. A sense of doing the most that anybody could, by giving the woman a bed and a listening ear, did little to satisfy her, but it was something.

Her phone warbled as she pottered around the kitchen idly tidying up, the bright screen telling her it was Drew. A pity, in a way, that technology insisted on spoiling almost every surprise in life, good or bad. 'Hello,' she said, unable to conceal a certain wariness.

'It's Drew.'

'Yes. How are you? I mean, how's Karen?' She forced her thoughts onto him and his troubles, sitting down at the table, speaking softly.

'Much the same. Listen, Den's just told me how awful Maggs was to you this morning. I've spoken to her about it, if that's any comfort.'

'Well . . .' There didn't seem to be anything she could say, apart from an insincere assurance that she hadn't minded. She felt a flash of embarrassment.

'I'm afraid I can't tell you she's sorry. We're all under strain here. That's the best I can offer as an excuse.'

'She meant well, I suppose. She's obviously terribly fond of you. And Karen. Especially Karen.'

'We are very close. It's a family, really, the four of us. Six, with the children. But I wanted to ask you about the murder. Den told me a little boy was killed in the village you're in. Is that right?'

'I found the body,' she said, with a sad little laugh. 'Again. I'm afraid I'm very much involved.'

'No!'

'It was rather horrible.'

'Obviously. A child is the worst.'

'Yes. It's completely different.'

'Had you seen him before? When he was alive?'

'Actually, yes. He wasn't a very nice kid, which somehow makes it worse. Well – maybe not exactly *worse*, but you can't help worrying when there's ill will floating around. I don't think anybody liked him, except for his mother.'

'Den says she must be the one who did it.'

'Wait a minute. Let me shut the door.' She went to push the door closed, hoping there were no peculiar sound-carrying crevices up to the main bedroom. When she spoke again, it was in little more than a whisper, despite the need for emphasis. 'No! No, she wasn't. I'm convinced of that.'

'Why are you whispering?'

'Because she's here, in the mistress of the house's bed.' She snickered at her own description of Yvonne. 'She arrived an hour or so ago, and couldn't face going home. Her house is very near here.'

Drew kept to the main point. 'So who did it?'

'Somebody in the village who'd had enough of him, I suppose. Just saw red and tied a length of washing line round his neck to shut him up. Then they dumped his body outside this house, behind my car. I expect it was just a horrible coincidence that I happened to be here.'

'Was he an only child?'

'Sadly, yes.'

'Poor woman.'

'That's pretty much it, yes. Makes me realise how precious Jessica is. Who, by the way, is also unhappy just now. That beastly Paul dumped her.'

'Did he? Just as well, in the long run, I imagine. We didn't really like him, did we?'

Thea closed her eyes for a moment, savouring the surge of pleasure the *we* evoked in her. Here was somebody who understood, who had shared enough time with her to know what she thought and what he could say to her. *Dear Drew*, she sighed inwardly. What a good friend he was.

'No, but she did, and it came as a complete shock. He sent her a text.'

'I thought he had a cruel streak. Probably never occurred to him that it would hurt so much more than telling her properly.'

167

'I don't think she'll take long to realise what she's escaped. But it's a pity they work together. It makes everything much more embarrassing for her.'

'We are a sad lot these days, aren't we?' he said, audibly losing interest in the Snowshill murder. 'I don't know how much longer I can go on like I am. I can't be away from the phone, in case they call about Karen. Even if I go out with the mobile, I have to stay within a few miles of the hospital. And the kids need me even more now they're not at school. Luckily Karen's mother has come here for a bit. I'd be totally sunk otherwise. As it is, the days fly past with nothing done, nothing changed. I'm in no state to officiate at funerals. I turned down two last week.'

'I heard Maggs and Den talking about it. I got the impression he thinks there isn't much hope left, but she was insisting Karen might yet recover.' Was there another person in the world to whom she could speak in this way? Not her mother, certainly. Possibly her sister Jocelyn. But Drew deserved unvarnished remarks. He even invited them, in some way.

'Nobody knows one way or the other. Maggs is setting us an example, being so positive, I suppose. I know I shouldn't give up, but I can't see how it can turn out happily, now. When she was injured originally, she was only unconscious for a day or two. This has been weeks and weeks, and I can't see anything of the real Karen there any more. I feel as if she's already gone far beyond recall. I think the children feel it, as well.'

'She's young, though. That must give her a better chance

than some. And they still haven't precisely identified the cause of the coma, have they?'

'They assume there's a bleed somewhere deep in the brain, but it doesn't show on the scans. It's been happening slowly but surely over the past three years, like a dripping tap, draining away her energy and personality. Bullets do appalling things to soft tissue over a wide area. I think some incurable shock was inflicted at the time, and it's finally caught up with her. Such an awful waste. She had so much to offer, before all this.' His voice was tightly controlled, and she had an impression that he had been searching for a chance to say these things.

'Don't give up,' she urged him. 'Maggs is right. There has to be some hope, or how can you bear it?'

He made a wordless sound, close to a moan. 'Hope's so *exhausting*. People don't realise. And it's like a cage, or a prison cell. I'm getting worn out with hoping.'

'Oh, Drew,' she soothed helplessly.

'It's nice to talk to you. And I wish I could come and help you cope with this dreadful murder. I suppose the police are all over you, if you found the body?'

She snorted, remembering Drew's hapless encounter with the police in Broad Campden. 'Not quite. It's my friend Gladwin, thank goodness. She and I get on extremely well. She's blessedly unprofessional when she's with me. Says the most outrageous things. But she's amazingly good at the job, for all that.'

'Always gets her man, eh.'

'Pretty much, yes. And she's sane and decent and energetic. You'd never guess she was a top detective.'

'I must meet her sometime,' said Drew forlornly. Then he seemed to rally. 'Tell me about the suspects,' he invited.

'Blimey! How long have you got?'

'I don't know. If there's an incoming call I'll have to go. The little light'll flash at me if that happens. So fire away.'

She told him everything, from the first sighting of Stevie on Saturday. She told him about Blake Grossman and his bisected garden; Mark Parker and his sister; Janice and Ruby across the road; Clara Beauchamp and – for good measure – Charles Paget Wade, who was possibly a local ghost. 'And hornets,' she concluded. 'There's a hornets' nest in the roof.'

'Janice and Ruby,' he said. 'They sound interesting. If I've got it right, they'd have means, motive and opportunity galore.'

'That's true. But they're very nice ordinary women. I can just imagine Janice strangling the boy in a fit of fury, but not dumping the body and keeping quiet. She'd call the police and own up.'

'People panic. And she'd have to go to prison, even if she confessed. Nobody wants that.'

'Funny how it always keeps coming back to a woman having done it.'

'It's because it generally is the mother,' he said. 'Although I can see how that doesn't really fit in this case. Why would she move the body?'

'Good question.'

They talked for forty minutes, before Drew seemed to realise the time and decided he had gone on too long. 'Thanks for all that,' he said. 'You've distracted me very effectively.

170

It's just what I needed – something else to think about.'

'Any time,' she said lightly.

The house phone rang next, just after nine, and a male voice barked, 'That the house-sitter again?'

'Yes, this is Thea Osborne. Can I help you?'

'Victor Parker. Vonny not back, I suppose?'

'No.' She wanted to add *Lost her again, then?* but controlled the urge. She could also have told him that Yvonne had expressed an intention to go to France to join her sister, but did not. If he didn't know, then she must assume his wife – ex-wife – didn't want him to.

'The woman must be mad, that's all I can say. She was here for half a day and then disappeared off somewhere before we'd had a chance to settle anything. The thing is, she left her car just up the road here, so I can't work out what's happened.'

'Are you sure? I mean, sure it's her car? That sounds very strange.'

'Of course I'm sure. I bought the bloody thing five years ago. I told her it was time she got another one, and she said she couldn't afford it. Pleading poverty, as if I'd swallow that nonsense.'

'Well, perhaps she didn't want to risk losing the space, if she's popped into the West End or something.'

'Gone to a movie or something, you think?' His tone was less forceful as he gave this his brief consideration. 'Has she said that was what she'd do? The car's been there since yesterday, though. I don't know where she spent the night.'

Thea made an impatient sound. 'Mr Parker, I hardly know her. I certainly don't keep track of her movements. If you think she's come to some sort of harm, then you'd better report it to the police. Otherwise, I don't think I can help you.' Was she being excessively discreet, she wondered? Should she just tell him the woman was probably on her way to France by now? 'Did you part on bad terms?' she asked.

'Not really. Not that I noticed. She just went off without a word. Now I've got Belinda raging at me, for good measure.'

'Your daughter,' Thea noted, with a flash of pride. 'She phoned me as well. And Mark came here this morning.' She might choose to protect Yvonne from him, but she didn't see why she should conceal the movements of his children. 'None of you seem to know what the others are doing.'

'That's families for you. Oh, hi, babe. Where've you been?' His voice grew fainter as he greeted someone who had evidently just joined him. Thea hoped, with little grounds, that it was Yvonne, although the *babe* seemed somewhat improbable as a word he might use for his ex-wife.

'Hello?' Thea called, after some seconds in which muttered words were exchanged and the distant sound of a closing door reached her. Victor did not return to the phone. Instead a buzzer went and she heard indistinct voices. Then there was a sudden loud cry, which she was sure came from him, followed by a long silence. Pressing the phone tightly to her ear, she tried to work out what was happening. A door slammed shut, and then another silence filled the universe, until she thought she should just put down the phone and forget the whole thing. But the shrill scream from a female person apparently standing very close to the telephone sent shockwaves through her. Screams, cries, wails of 'Victor! Oh, Victor!' confirmed that something seriously bad must have happened. Repeatedly, she called 'Hello? Hello!' in vain.

At least there weren't any gunshots, she thought as she finally replaced the receiver. Briefly, she lifted it again, hoping somehow that contact had been resumed. All she got was a dialling tone. Moments later, she called Gladwin on her mobile and reported something very disturbing taking place in a Crouch End apartment.

'Do you know the address?' the detective superintendent asked her.

'Um . . . no, but it must be here somewhere. Hold on a sec.'

She went out to the spacious hallway containing an oak bureau, the top of which was crowded with a collection of glass *millefiori* paperweights. When she tried to pull down the flap, it resisted. Locked, she realised. Beneath the flap were two drawers, the upper of which came open easily. Inside she discovered neatly stacked notebooks, perhaps twenty in total, all with pretty art nouveau covers as far as she could see. The lower drawer was less tidy, the contents a motley assortment of brochures, leaflets, catalogues and other papers.

She retrieved the phone from the kitchen window sill and reported her failure. 'I don't know where else to try,' she said helplessly. 'Where do people generally keep their ex-husband's address?'

Gladwin gave an impatient snort for reply.

'Sorry. But you'll find him easily enough. Victor Parker in Crouch End.'

The next snort was almost angry. 'Thea – we'll have to involve the Met in this, if you think there's been violence. Can you backtrack and just see if you might have got it wrong, before we do that? Couldn't it just have been a bit of a domestic? After all, they've been separated for years, with quite some acrimony, from the sound of it. A bit of shouting isn't so surprising, is it?'

'I don't know that it was Yvonne. It probably wasn't her. He called somebody "babe". Then I think he answered the door, after the babe person came in. It must have been a man, who attacked Victor.' She racked her brains for the right sequence of events. 'Yes, that was definitely how it was. You didn't hear that scream,' said Thea urgently. 'I *know* something awful happened. And I never said it was Yvonne there. He called me to say he'd lost her again.'

'Okay,' Gladwin sighed as if the whole story was well beyond her area of interest. 'Look, go and do 1471 on the phone and see if you can get his number.'

Again, Thea put down the BlackBerry and did as she was told. 'It's a mobile number,' she reported back and recited it.

'Have you tried calling it again?'

'No,' said Thea. 'I don't really think it's for me to do it.'

'Well, if he's hurt, it'll be reported soon enough, I imagine. The screaming person will call for help. I will of course make some enquiries, but I am rather occupied.' She spoke with restraint, but Thea could hear stress and impatience in her voice. 'And I can't see this has anything to do with the case,' she added. 'The man hasn't lived in Snowshill for five years. What can he possibly have to do with anything?'

'I'm sure he hasn't, but other things can go wrong at the same time.'

'Look – if the house is full of other flats and bedsits, whatever, somebody on the spot will have heard the screams. It'll be all in hand. If you had the address, it'd be different. As it is, there's hardly anything to go on – do you see?'

'Sort of,' said Thea grudgingly. 'But I *know*—'

'Okay. Just take a breath. I wanted to call you, as it happens, to say you might want to be a bit careful.'

'Why?'

'Mark Parker – you say he drove from somewhere in Wales early this morning?'

'Ri-i-ight,' ventured Thea cautiously. 'That's what he said.'

'He didn't. We traced his car, and it's on the cameras in Evesham on Sunday evening. He stayed in a small hotel there.'

'Oh, Lord. You think he came over here and killed Stevie?' She thought about it. 'It doesn't strike me as very likely. Why on earth would he?'

'Who knows? As I feel sure I've said to you before, the *why* is generally the very last question to be answered.'

'And it's the most important one,' Thea insisted. 'Without having a reason, the whole thing becomes far too frightening.'

'Calm down,' Gladwin pleaded. 'I'm just trying to explain that a scream in Crouch End doesn't exactly factor in here, the way the investigation's going.'

'No. I understand what you're saying. If it's a problem at all, it's *my* problem, not yours. You've got to establish who was in this area on Sunday afternoon, how and why they killed Stevie and dumped his body here, and to do that you've got to check a whole mass of facts. But you do think the Parkers might be involved – the son, at least. You've just made the connection yourself.'

'I suppose I have, and I admit it's perfectly possible that the fight in London – whatever it was – has some relevance on some level. We ought to check Parker Senior's whereabouts for Sunday, of course. And we seem to have lost sight of Gudrun Horsfall.'

'She's here,' said Thea unthinkingly. 'Asleep upstairs. That's if the phone hasn't woken her up.'

'My God, Thea! Why the hell is she there with you?'

'She couldn't face going back to her own house. She needs somewhere safe and undisturbed.'

'Well, be careful. We don't know what she might be capable of. She could be quite dangerous.'

'I don't think so.'

'Some forces would have kept her in custody, if only until her psychological state has been assessed. It's only my chief who thinks she's okay to be released.'

'Well, you know exactly where she is now. And she's no danger to anybody, believe me.'

'I'd really like to,' said Gladwin glumly. 'I guess I should be pleased it's you. I know you're reliable and sensible, and I should definitely take your concerns about the London chap seriously. We'll get somebody to find his address and call round there to make sure he's all right. I'm sorry to dither about it. It's been a hell of a day.'

'I know. It must seem ages since we first found Stevie, but it's only been a day and a bit.'

'That's true. But speed is crucial in this sort of case. People can get a long way in twenty-four hours. We've spent about half that time thinking it was bound to be the mother who did it, and a whole lot more trying to discover the identity of the father.'

'Poor woman,' sighed Thea. 'What must she be feeling? Maybe I should go and see if she's awake and wanting anything. She seems happy to talk to me.'

'I can trust you not to say too much.' It wasn't quite a question, but the worry was there, just the same. Thea's special status had quickly become clear to Gladwin a year earlier, in Temple Guiting, when she was in a relationship with another detective superintendent – but Gladwin knew better than to take it for granted. 'You won't get carried away, will you?'

'I can see it's delicate. Officially I might even have killed him myself. He certainly made me very cross.'

'That's the trouble,' the detective burst out. 'He made *everybody* cross – including his mother. But there's a gulf a mile wide between that and actually throttling the little beast. If that wasn't so, there'd hardly be any small boys alive in the world, would there?'

The truth of this gave Thea little comfort. Somehow it was less appalling to imagine somebody at the end of their tether, driven out of control by the invasions or transgressions of the delinquent child, grabbing whatever came to hand and wrapping it around his neck to restrain or silence him, than to accept the notion that it had been coldly planned in advance.

'I suppose so,' she said. 'Is there anything else I ought to know?'

Gladwin exploded a quick laugh. 'I think *I'm* meant to ask you that. But no, that's plenty for now. I'm sure we'll speak again soon.'

When the house phone rang again, fifteen minutes later in an evening that felt as if it ought to be winding down, Thea began to feel harassed. She had been on the brink of taking a large mug of tea up to her guest.

'It's me,' said a soft female voice. 'Mrs Parker.'

It seemed an odd way to introduce herself, when Thea had assumed they were on first-name terms. 'Oh . . . what a relief. Is Victor all right? Was that you screaming? Are you still at his flat?'

'Screaming? Why would I be screaming? What are you talking about?'

'He phoned me, and then something happened. Where are you now?'

'St Pancras Station. I'm catching the Eurostar in a few minutes. It's very noisy – can you hear me?'

'Perfectly.' All Thea could hear was vague engine noises and some muffled voices. 'So when did you last see Victor?'

'Yesterday. I went back to the hotel for another night. I still don't understand—'

Thea struggled with a growing confusion. 'He said your car's still in his street.'

'What? I'm sorry, I missed that.'

Still Thea could hear no serious background noise. But she caught herself up, and decided it was not for her to cross-question the woman. 'Don't worry about it,' she shouted. 'Why did you phone me?'

'Mark – my son – called just now and said he'd met you. He was in a panic about something, silly boy. They think I'm incapable of doing a single thing without their assistance.'

Thea bit her tongue and tried to think clearly. At least there were some things that were plainly no longer secret.

'You do know that little Stevie Horsfall has been killed, don't you?' she said.

'Who?'

'The little boy from the cottage, a quarter of a mile from this house. Fair-haired. His mother's called Gudrun.' She found herself shouting, and therefore liable to be overheard by Gudrun herself upstairs.

'Oh. Not killed, surely? Was he run over or something?'

'No, he was not run over—'

But Yvonne interrupted. 'Oh – they're letting us through now. I've got to go. I just wanted to confirm with you that I'll be out of the country until Friday of next week. Are the cats all right?'

'The cats are fine,' said Thea defeatedly. 'But isn't it a bit late to be setting out for France—?'

But again Yvonne seemed not to hear her. 'Bye, then,' she trilled and disconnected the phone.

The woman's voice had grown stronger in the course of the conversation, but there remained a timid little-girl

179

quality to it, as if she was being immensely brave to be travelling all the way to France on her own, having found somewhere to leave her car. There had been no response to Thea's alarming news, both of Victor and Stevie. Just a slightly peculiar reference to Mark. She had met this kind of woman before – selfishly obsessed with her own frailties and calamities, unable to admit that others had problems too. She would be consumed with anxiety about finding her seat on the train, getting out at the right station, meeting up with her sister. It would be after midnight, surely, before she reached Avignon, allowing for the hour's time difference. Thea doubted whether there were trains so late at night. Yvonne would stay in Paris, then, before going on next morning. Again, she felt exasperation at the complexities of the woman's movements and the inadequacy of the information she gave. It was clearly typical of Yvonne to be vague and distracted. Perhaps she thought nobody could be sufficiently interested to listen to a full account. It could be diffidence that kept her disclosures brief and confusing. But she had sounded reasonably cheerful, the meeting with Victor on Sunday apparently not too traumatic.

On a whim, she pressed 1471 and noted the mobile number that came up. Sure enough, it was the one Yvonne had given her before she left. *Why wouldn't it be?* she asked herself. It was even possible to explain the mystery of the woman's car. She could have decided to leave it where it was in Crouch End, given the difficulty in finding spaces anywhere in London. Then she could have got a taxi to St Pancras from there, quite reasonably.

For all Thea knew, there was even a direct bus.

None of which went any way towards explaining what had just happened to Victor Parker, or who the screaming female with him had been.

Chapter Thirteen

Drew spent the early part of Monday evening at the hospital, watching his wife slowly disappear. Her eyes were closed, and did not flicker in response to the monologue he was painfully reciting. He told her about the children, and how he had decided it was better not to bring them in for the time being, although he wasn't sure that was the right line to take. He told her that Maggs had complete faith that all would be well and they would come through this and be a normal family again. He said he hoped this was so, and would be able to believe it if only she would waggle a finger or blink an eye to reassure him. He repeated several times that many people had said she could hear him, that hearing survived when other senses closed down, that he knew of cases where this had been so, even though incredible to those observing the patient. He tried to tell a joke whereby he compared her to one of the corpses in his little cool room, at Peaceful Repose, and how he had sometimes talked to them, with a similar level of non-response. 'That sounds a bit awful,

I suppose,' he added, with a rueful frown. 'If you can hear, and if you wake up and remember, feel free to tell me off about it.'

He watched closely for a minute muscular reaction, a kink of a lip, a tightening of the jaw. Nothing. She lay there, breathing, her heart beating, a living body with no discernible spirit. He lapsed into silence, thinking about personality and souls and brains and blood. If ever there was a moment for some consoling piece of supernatural intervention, this must be it. He glanced up at the ceiling, remembering tales of out-of-body experiences, where the anima, or whatever it might be, floated above the body, looking down on proceedings in the physical world. Was Karen up there somewhere? Could she give some sign, like swinging the emergency cord that dangled down, within her reach? Could she cast a shadow somehow, in the bright white room? Could she emit her own special scent, that he would unerringly recognise for the rest of his life?

Nothing.

His wife was not ever going to come back. The stranger lying there no longer cared about him, could no longer argue or challenge or tease or satisfy. Desolation swept through him like never before. He was alone in a hard dark place, and would never again find comfort. His children would carry the scar of this early loss for ever. Timmy, his accidental son, who he never quite managed to adore as he should, would grow up withdrawn and resentful. Drew suspected that Timmy knew, at some level, that he was not as precious to his father as his sister was. It was a shameful fact, which Drew had tried hard to rectify, especially in recent months, but it remained stubbornly true, just the same.

In the first days of Karen's coma, it had felt almost exactly the same as when she had originally been injured, three years before. His thoughts and feelings had flooded back, as if he had travelled back in time and was living those same hours again. She had recovered then, and so he assumed that she would do the same this time. She would stir and smile and say something witty. She would look round at her assembled family and take up the business of living, perhaps shakily and intermittently, but she would return to her old self, just as they needed her to do.

But after all these weeks, this assumption had withered and died. It was not at all the same this time. There would be no jokes, no connections made, no awareness of Drew or Steph or Timmy as people with their own wishes and needs. Karen had become useless in the most profound and unalterable ways.

She had always shielded him from the essential loneliness of his work. She had helped him to feel normal, by being so very normal herself. She had been sociable, cheerful, energetic, bridging the gap between Drew and the rest of the world. Now he had Maggs and Den, who were themselves somewhat awkward in society, for different reasons. Maggs was of mixed race, adopted, clever, and highly unusual in her choice of career. She liked people as a general rule, but found all too many individuals disappointing. They found her, Drew suspected, a bit too strong to handle at times. She could be far too outspoken, as poor Thea had discovered to her cost.

Den was almost freakishly tall, inclined to melancholy and preferring his own company to that of most others. 'What a bunch we are!' Drew said aloud. 'Without you, my sweet, we're going to be a seriously peculiar lot. Come on, Kaz!' he almost shouted. 'Wake up, and do us all a favour.'

Nothing.

He got up blindly, pushing his chair back noisily and covering his mouth and nose with one hand. Why that moment rather than any other brought an end to his vigil, he had no idea. But it did. He'd had enough. Without any obvious drama, with no discernible trigger, he had given up on his wife. He was wasting himself sitting at her inert body, watching so intently for a signal that she might one day return to him. Some men might wait years, lovingly tending the hollow shell, but he wasn't going to. Karen was gone. In many ways, she had been gone for a long time, and now the final fading days had arrived, and it was pointless to cling to hope that she would or could come back. She had made all the effort a person could, in the years since her injury, clinging to ordinary existence for the sake of her children, perhaps. Now it was over. Anybody could see that. Even her breathing had lost its rhythm, catching every minute or so, pausing, stumbling, resuming slowly. The monitors had begun to show blips and plateaux that had not been there a week earlier.

He blundered out into the corridor, hoping to avoid meeting anybody. A nurse somewhere was watching the monitors on a screen; somebody would come and replace the drips and catheters once in a while. Over the entire department

185

there was an air of failure, even guilt that they had somehow let a young mother slip through their fingers. There was no question of turning anything off, nothing so theatrical as that. No moment of semi-murder of the semi-animate thing that had been Karen Slocombe. Nor could they withhold the fluids from the drips without a solemn conference involving everyone concerned. To starve and dehydrate even the shell of a person risked a final cruelty that everybody flinched from, although it happened often enough. Maggs would never permit it. The prospect of her protests was unthinkable. Drew himself could never live with the guilt, however irrational it might be. Guilt was an old friend, it was true, but he had wrestled with it since Karen's decline and almost persuaded himself that he could in no way be blamed. He had followed his own strict ethics almost without deviation, assisted now and then by Maggs. Now, search as he might, he could find nothing with which to reproach himself.

As far as Drew was concerned, the precise timing and means of Karen's death had lost much of their relevance. He had tipped over from hope to acceptance, without meaning or wanting to. It had simply happened, as he sat there, and he had no doubt that it was a permanent state.

He walked down the corridor, his eyes on his shoes and the shiny floor. The place was quiet, the patients mostly settled for the night. When he got home the children would be asleep, and his mother-in-law would be in her customary nest on the sofa, the television murmuring companionably. Her loss was as acute as his, in its way, even though she had never been particularly attentive to Karen since she had married Drew. He could see guilt clear in her eyes, and a desperate regret that she had let the relationship drift. Her passionate overprotectiveness of the children was her attempt at atonement for her neglect. He had almost given up trying to reassure her, to persuade her that Karen had been fully in agreement with the way it had happened. She had promised to remain at North Staverton for the entire school holiday, making it possible for Drew and Maggs to continue with their business, at least to some extent. But now, he vowed to himself, he wouldn't ask her to do it any more. The collective martyrdom could cease – Den with his prolonged lunch breaks, Maggs with her round-the-clock attention, the children with their limbo status arousing the natural hostility of their schoolfellows. It had all gone on for too long.

Tomorrow he was going to face the rest of his life. He was still a father and an undertaker, if no longer a husband.

Thea finally went to bed at eleven, feeling utterly drained by worry and puzzlement. Urgent questions swarmed in her mind, concerning murder and violence and the probable demise of poor Karen Slocombe. There was nothing joyful or consoling to hold on to; only a gnawing sense of obligation to an uncomfortable number of people. Gudrun, Victor, Jessica, Gladwin and Yvonne all had expectations of her. Not to mention Drew, who had so eagerly latched onto the Snowshill murder.

Victor seemed to be the most urgent. It had definitely sounded as if the man had been dealt a blow, a guess that seemed to be confirmed by the woman who had screamed. Perhaps the woman had attacked him, giving a war cry as she did so, for good measure? The few garbled hints that Thea had gleaned about him suggested the existence of a number of women in his life. Yvonne had left her car close to the place where he lived, and then made her way to St Pancras to catch the train to France. Hazily, Thea supposed that you had to check in at least half an hour before departure, which meant she must have been at the station at the time of the phone call from Victor. Her obvious impatient bewilderment at Thea's question about the scream reinforced the impression that she neither knew nor cared what might have befallen her ex-husband.

She tried to visualise his dwelling, from the description Yvonne had given. A small scruffy flat in a house that had been converted to multiple occupancy was how it had sounded. Was it conceivable that a man in his fifties or more with some sort of respectable profession or business would live like that? Mark, his son, had tried to explain it, with scant success. Had Victor managed to set something up as a deliberate deception for his wife, a way of persuading her that he was living in poverty, so she would abandon all claim to money from him to pay for Belinda's wedding? Stranger things had certainly happened, but it sounded very unconvincing as Thea tried it out; this, however, didn't stop her from further flights of fancy. Did the other flats contain drug addicts and mentally ill people? Had one of them burst into Victor's room at random and attacked him?

She finally fell asleep thinking, inevitably, about

Gudrun and her little boy. Perhaps she had, after all, killed him, as everybody still seemed to think. Had she belatedly understood that she must pay a price for what she had done when she 'stole' him, and paid it massively, in a grand and desperate gesture?

Chapter Fourteen

The mobile rang as Thea was having breakfast on Tuesday morning. It was Gladwin with a breathless update on the Crouch End mystery. 'We can't find anybody named Victor Parker living in N6 or N8,' she reported. 'We think he's the same Victor William Parker who runs a company named Handyman Holdings, registered to an address in Kensington, and we'll ask the Met to send somebody over there tomorrow, to enquire after his health. Okay? Go for a walk and don't think about it any more.'

'Yvonne called me from St Pancras last night,' Thea remembered to say. 'She was about to get on the Eurostar, apparently, going to see her sister.'

'Right.' Gladwin's attention was partial. 'So?'

'I don't know. She was just checking in, I suppose. She didn't seem to have heard about Stevie, or to care very much when I told her.'

'Er . . . Thea . . . be careful what you say to people, all right? I mean, I've been telling you things I really shouldn't, if I'm to stick to the rules. You know why – you've been more than

190

helpful in the past and I regard you as an unofficial ally. But don't stir up the mud if you can help it. It's always complicated working out who knows what and when, but it can be very useful to catch them out in contradictions over that sort of thing. If the Parker woman didn't know, then where has she been for two days? It's taken top billing on most of the national news bulletins since yesterday. Not to mention the papers.'

'She's hopelessly vague. I think she left her car near Victor's place on Sunday, and went back to the place she stayed in on Saturday night. Then she went off to France without telling him, and he called me, and then something happened.' In spite of herself, her voice rose, with the frustration of not being able to establish just what *had* happened to the man. 'But that's still a fearful muddle, isn't it? The car part seems odd, for a start.'

'It does, and we'll do what we can to check it all out. But I can't get any sense that this connects to Stevie Horsfall. The only thing is the fact he was left outside Hyacinth House, and you know how that goes. A house-sitter's in charge, who knows nothing about the people and their history. In effect, the place is empty, and therefore a good spot to dump a body. Even if they know who you are and how you've caught people out before, they're going to think this time you won't have a clue.'

'And they'd be right.'

'Don't despair. We've got about a thousand people working on this – all stops are pulled out when the victim's a child. We'll get our killer, probably sooner rather than later.'

Thea had little choice but to let it go at that.

* * *

Drew woke to Tuesday with a sense of foreboding. He and Maggs had a funeral to conduct that afternoon. Mr Anderson was to be buried next to his sister – or as close as they could get him. The bodies would in fact spend eternity lying head-to-head. 'That's rather nice,' said Angela, daughter of the sister, niece of Mr Anderson. 'They always did talk a lot. She talked far more to Uncle Tim than she ever did to my dad.' Dad was apparently living somewhere in Thailand, his every need being served by a child bride. Angela was more than eager to tell Drew the disgusting details, with much bitterness. 'She's about half my age,' she spat. Drew tried his best not to imagine it. Once in a while he found himself wishing people were not quite so free with their family secrets when talking to him.

But it wasn't the funeral that produced his unease. It was nothing to do with Peaceful Repose. The morning would not be busy. Everything was ready for the burial – the grave dug, the coffin closed. Drew was to conduct the brief ceremony at half past four, giving a short eulogy that Angela had written for him. If it rained, as seemed highly likely, they would stand there getting wet for perhaps ten minutes. Ten or twelve people were expected. 'We're all terribly sad,' admitted Angela. 'The world is never going to be the same without him.'

This was what Drew liked to hear. Sometimes he found traditional British stoicism rather irritating.

Maggs would expect him to go to the hospital. She would get on with the business in his absence, answering the phone, making promises with some circumspection, while at the same time doing her best to avoid losing custom. She was yet to show any sign of exhaustion or impatience. Although he hadn't asked her, he felt sure she would stoutly guarantee to carry on like this for years, if that's what it took to get Karen back. The thought depressed him almost more than any of his other gloomy musings.

The office and his house depressed him. His *children* depressed him. The weather was grey and chilly. There was nothing to look forward to. He had nowhere to go and nobody to listen to him.

Except one.

His fingers activated the little buttons of their own accord, his will entirely disengaged from the procedure.

She asked no questions whatsoever, which in itself was a warm relief beyond all logic. Except she did say, after a minute or two of chat about nothing much, 'Do you know Crouch End at all?'

'Um . . . London. North-ish. On a hill. Vaguely upmarket.'

'I'm going there today and thought you might fancy coming with me. A sort of therapy, if you like.'

'I've got a funeral.'

'Damn.'

'It's not until four-thirty this afternoon. It's nine now. How long would your expedition take?'

'If we got a train and then a taxi, probably four hours or so. Maybe a bit more.'

'I can't afford taxis.'

'Neither can I. But what the hell.'

'Is this dangerous and illegal?'

'Probably.'

193

'Thank God. I can get to Paddington by about ten-thirty, I expect.'

'So can I. There's a train that goes from Moreton quite soon. See you under the clock.'

'Is there a clock?'

'Bound to be. Yes – a big one on platform one. Or there was. A lovely thing. Huge.'

'Thank you, Thea. I think you might just have saved me from going mad. Although I guess most people would say that doing this with you is a clear sign of insanity.'

'I know. It's absolutely bonkers. We're not going to find anything, you know. Not so much as a wild goose.'

'Who cares?'

'See you, then.'

He drove to his nearest main-line station, which took fifteen minutes. The ticket was considerably cheaper than he'd anticipated – apparently last-minute journeys were back in favour, for some reason. Maybe the train people were eager to fill a lot of empty seats. He sat next to the window, with a space beside him, thinking that he would for ever associate Thea Osborne with trains and stations, after their Broad Campden adventure. He permitted himself to forget his lost wife, his motherless children, and rerun the crazy conversation he had just enjoyed with Thea, savouring the easy friendship, the natural way they understood each other. There was nothing at all wrong with it. Maggs could not be allowed to sully it with her blundering assumptions. He and Thea were mature adults with considerable life experience. They knew exactly what they were doing, and where the boundaries lay.

* * *

He was there first, the clock easily located. Standing beneath it was difficult, though, with people swarming past on their way to the taxi rank or a train or the Ladies. He resisted the urge to call Thea on her mobile, preferring the old-fashioned suspense of waiting for her to appear. He scanned the faces as they turned onto the wide platform, all of them intent on their destination, pulling wheeled suitcases or humping heavy rucksacks. Small children escaped their parents' grasp and chased after pigeons. One or two dogs trotted confidently on their leads, proclaiming their relaxed familiarity with this place of noise and bustle and endless pairs of legs, smelling of an intoxicating variety of experience and encounter. Dogs! Would Thea bring her spaniel? Could she leave it behind, not knowing for sure how long she'd be gone? Surely she wouldn't bring it. But abandoning it was the equivalent of his irresponsible desertion of his post, without any certainty of being back in time for Mr Anderson's funeral. Whatever happened, they both had to retrace their steps within an hour or two.

It was ten-forty when he saw her, minus the dog. She was so small – he had forgotten how short and slender she was. Her hair had grown an inch or so since he had last seen her in Cranham. She was lovely. Anybody would think so. It was a plain objective fact.

Their eyes met and both smiled broadly, conspiratorially, amused by the adventure.

'Taxis are just through here,' he said.

'Come on, then. I'll explain as we go.'

'What have you done with Hepzie?'

'Shut her in and told her to hope for the best. I'm a cruel and heartless mother.'

'And I'm a feckless father.'

'Actually, I asked Janice, the woman across the road, to let her out if I'm not back by four.' She proceeded to give an account of the hurried visit to the secluded house, where Janice had come to the door looking strained and preoccupied. She had not been unduly eager to take any responsibility for Thea's dog.

'Was that a good idea – to tell her you were away for the day?' Drew asked.

'Why wouldn't it be?'

'If she killed the boy, she might have sinister intentions. Is Hepzie safe with her?'

'Stop it. I'll be back before tea, anyway, and no harm done, I'm sure. Do you think she killed the boy?' she added belatedly.

'I don't know. I was thinking about her and her daughter, on the train. There's a parallel, isn't there, with the mother of the boy who was killed? I mean – two sets of single mothers, and no sign of a father in either case.'

'It's more or less the norm, Drew. Not a bit unusual, anyway.'

'I know. Even so . . . Gosh, do you really think we'll get back in time? If I miss the funeral, I'll never forgive myself.'

'Of course we will. Stop panicking. We've got ages.'

He failed in his attempt to do as instructed. 'No, but if I miss the funeral, I may as well never go back. My life will be over, its purpose lost for all time.'

'Don't be silly. I'd have thought that was quite far down your list of priorities just now.'

'Displacement,' he muttered. 'Isn't that what they call it? And it's very cruel of you to remind me.'

'I know.' She patted his hand. 'Sorry. But I did hear cries and screams last night, and this *is* important as well. Don't think about what's back at home.'

Eight or ten people waited in front of them for taxis. It seemed like a lot, but the cars rolled in steadily, and within four or five minutes they were on the back seat of a cab, heading north.

'Cries and screams?' he repeated, wide-eyed. 'Are you going to explain?'

'Victor Parker, ex-husband of the woman I'm house-sitting for, phoned me last night. In the middle of the call, he was suddenly attacked by somebody. Then, a minute later, a woman screamed. I think she was in another room, and a third person came in and bashed him or something. Gladwin says they can't find the address because there's nothing in Crouch End registered in his name.'

'Wow. What does this have to do with the murder in Snowshill?'

'Nothing whatsoever, probably, although it seems more and more unlikely that there's no connection, every time I think it through. I hoped you might have some ideas.'

'I might if I get a chance to get to grips with it.' He glanced at his watch. 'How well do you know London?' he asked her.

'Not well at all. I've been to Madame Tussauds and Hyde Park and Leicester Square. We came a few times when Jess was little and rode about on buses and went to Hamleys. It scares me a bit.'

'I've been on the London Eye,' he boasted. 'In 2003. It wasn't very good weather, so we couldn't see much. How far is it to Crouch End?'

'Not far,' she said evasively. 'We need to look for Vonny's car, you see,' she elaborated. 'She left it in Victor's street, so if we find it, we'll know more or less where his house is.'

'Do you know its number? The car, I mean.'

She nodded. 'It took me half an hour early this morning to find it, but I got there eventually. I thought I'd have to break into her bureau, but in the end I found the key to it. All the car stuff was in a little cubbyhole.'

'So we walk the streets until we find it?'

Thea produced an *A–Z* map of London. 'It's not a very big area. If we start in the bottom right-hand corner and do a street each at a time, we should manage it fairly quickly.'

'Then what?'

'We look for a house that's got several names on the doorbell, in that street, and see if there's a V. Parker.'

'Heavens, Thea,' he protested, suddenly alarmed. 'This is awfully silly.'

'I know it is. But I don't like the feeling I've got that the Parkers have been playing with me. It's making me cross. Mark lied about where he was at the weekend, according to the police, and the way Yvonne keeps phoning me is weird. It's as if I'm being used somehow.'

It seemed a long way in the taxi and he kept a firm

eye on his watch. 'It'll be at least half past eleven before we get started. I need to get the train back that leaves at ten to three. I suppose it might just work.' His insides were starting to cramp, with icy surges flowing through him at the very real prospect that he would fail to show up for a funeral in his own burial ground. Such a thing was unthinkable.

'What if you had to be at the hospital, for Karen? You'd have to miss the funeral then.'

That was true. Maggs would assume exactly that, if he failed to materialise. She would enlist the assistance of any able-bodied mourners to lower the coffin into the grave and deliver the eulogy herself. She would explain about Mrs Slocombe and the unavoidable absence of Drew, with profuse apologies. It probably wouldn't matter. Nobody was indispensable. 'I expect everything would be fine,' he said uncomfortably.

'No, it wouldn't be fine,' Thea disagreed. 'But it would not be the end of the world. It never is the end of the world, even if it feels like it.'

'Karen would love all this,' he said, feeling an oddly positive kick of emotion at being able to say her name. 'She was quite involved in this kind of thing before Stephanie was born.'

'Happy memories,' said Thea easily.

'Nothing stays the same. I should know that better than most. I actually *say* it to my customers sometimes. You can't rely on any sort of continuity.'

'Right. It's the source of all our sadness. Loss, letting go, everything changing.'

'Shifting sands. But it's not entirely sad. I quite like letting go,' he confessed. 'Most of the time. I just didn't bargain for letting go of the person I chose to spend my whole life with.'

Thea winced. 'No,' she murmured. 'It's a bugger.'

'Where are we?' He changed the subject with a determined little shake.

'Tufnell Park,' she read from an underground station portico, as they passed.

'Never heard of it,' he laughed. 'I wonder who Tufnell was.'

'Not much sign of a park, either.'

They were moving more quickly, along a straight street with scanty traffic. At a large junction they took a road that passed under a high bridge. 'This is all very handsome, isn't it?' Drew remarked. 'North London is another world. I ought to explore it sometime.'

'Where in Crouch End do you want, lady?' asked the Sikh driver.

'The middle,' she said vaguely. 'Wait a minute.' She opened her *A-Z.* 'How about Coolhurst Road. That seems fairly central. At the northern end.'

The taxi turned right at the next traffic lights, the surroundings suddenly green and airy. Drew had time to register a sign saying 'Shepherd's Hill' before the vehicle drew up at the kerbside and the driver pointed out Coolhurst Road on the right. Thea peered at her map. 'Thank you,' she said. 'This is perfect.'

As they stood together on the pavement, she showed him where they were. He quickly counted twelve streets that appeared to be the core of Crouch End, and groaned. 'It's going to take *ages*,' he protested.

'Not if we're organised. It's a green car, which is fairly unusual, for a start. Here's the registration number. We can see it's not along here, anyway. Now you go to the other side, and we'll meet at the bottom.'

The plan worked approximately as Thea had anticipated, with Drew finding himself quickly scanning all the parked cars in sight, and muttering *red, white, grey, red, silver, green* . . . The green one had nothing like the number he had memorised, and he carried on. It took a surprisingly short time before the entire street had been examined. Together they turned right, into Avenue Road which they scanned as before, then retraced their steps, planning to investigate Crescent, Clifton and Coleridge, moving at a brisk trot. When he finally identified a green Peugeot with the right combination of letters and numbers, he stood stock-still, unable to believe his eyes. Thea was nowhere to be seen, having turned into a smaller side street a minute earlier. As if worried that the car would disappear if he let it out of his sight, he stood glued to the pavement until she reappeared.

'Here it is!' he called, self-conscious in the quiet and obviously affluent neighbourhood. Crouch End was clean and tidy, and fresh paint was much in evidence. He looked around for signs of multiple occupancy and failed to find them.

Thea rushed to his side and stared at the car. 'Gosh!' she panted. 'It really is the one. How weird!'

'You didn't think we'd find it?'

'Not really. I mean . . . I didn't know. What's that on the

windscreen? Has she been fined for leaving it here?'

'It's a resident's permit,' Drew ascertained. 'They've all got them.'

Thea frowned thoughtfully. 'Victor must have given it to her. So . . . where does he live?'

'These places don't look scruffy to me,' he said superfluously. 'Didn't you say Yvonne thought it was rather sordid?'

'She did – but you're right.' On both sides of the street were large expensive houses, set comfortably back from the traffic, with front porches and mullioned windows. 'But some of them could be divided up, I suppose.'

'Maybe. But we can't go up to them and look for names,' he objected. 'We'll be arrested. Some of them probably have their own cameras.'

'It's not as posh as *that*,' she disagreed. 'But it's nothing like Yvonne described. Either she's parked much further away than I thought, or she isn't very good at describing places.' She rubbed her forehead, trying to recall Yvonne's exact words and failing.

Drew shook his head in bewilderment. 'It's not terribly handy for St Pancras, either, is it?'

'Presumably it seemed sensible to leave the car here, having got the permit.' She lifted her shoulders. 'I suppose it must make some kind of sense. Victor's just staying for a bit, while he finds another house, according to Mark. Aren't people *complicated*,' she complained. 'I don't feel I understand the first thing about the Parker family.'

'Does it matter?' he asked mildly. 'I mean, *why* does it? There's no sign of anybody being attacked, no police

202

tape or anything. What you heard can't have been as bad as you thought.'

'I guess that must be right. Oh well, we can at least tell Gladwin the car's here. She'll know what to do next – if anything.'

'You mean, just go home now?' It seemed very much a let-down, for the adventure to be over so quickly.

'I suppose so. We can have some lunch maybe, first.'

He gazed along the street, trying to imagine the lives behind the closed doors. 'It really is not the sort of area where you'd expect to hear a scream,' he said. 'If it was as loud as you say, wouldn't people react?'

'Probably not.' She remembered another scream, heard during her very first house-sitting commission, which she had ignored.

'But it's all so *respectable*,' he persisted, illogically. 'Nice middle-class people with children and dogs.'

'Don't stereotype. There are probably rich drug dealers and Arabs and Russians living all along this street, fighting amongst themselves the whole time. Maybe Victor dabbles in something nasty.'

'Now who's stereotyping?' he said. 'You're worse than me.'

'But my stereotype's a lot more exciting than yours.'

'I'm going to find out which one of us is right,' he said, and before she could stop him, he had approached a girl of Hispanic appearance pushing a baby buggy, who had emerged from one of the houses. 'Excuse me,' he smiled. 'But we're looking for a Mr Victor Parker, who lives in this street. We seem to have got the house number wrong. Do you know him?'

'Mr Victor?' responded the girl readily, with a strong accent. 'Oh, yes, he live over there.' She pointed to a substantial house across the street.

'You know him?' The notion of London as a collection of hermetically sealed families, never engaging with their neighbours, quickly evaporated.

'His . . . girlfriend. I know her. And also the cook where I live is sister to the cleaning woman at Mr Victor's.' She indicated the house immediately behind them. 'We know many people here.' She smiled sunnily, proud of her assimilation into the new world of London serving classes.

'Have you seen him yesterday or today?' Thea was quick to catch up and throw in her own question.

The girl shook her head. In the buggy a large fair-headed toddler kicked its heels impatiently. 'Not since . . . I think, Sunday.'

'And he has a girlfriend?' Thea pursued. 'Does she live with him?'

'Oh, yes. Since a month ago, perhaps. Mariella, from Manila. I am her friend,' she boasted. 'She is so happy to find Victor.'

I bet she is, thought Thea sourly. 'Has he had a visitor? An English lady?'

The girl smiled and shook her head. 'I think not. Mariella not like that! She would—' The girl mimed clawing with both hands, Yvonne's vulnerable cheeks almost visible as the jealous concubine attacked.

'Oh dear!' said Drew, with a laugh. 'Like that, is it?' He looked at Thea. 'What now?'

They both stood staring at the house in which Victor

Parker apparently lived. 'We should make sure he's all right,' said Thea. 'Having got this far.'

Drew refrained from another glance at his watch only with extreme difficulty. 'Ring his doorbell, you mean?'

'Why not?'

'Um . . . what will we say to him? Or his girlfriend? Won't he think it very odd?'

'We'll think of something. Come on.' Thea marched up the path, which seemed more like Snowshill than London, with its borders of flowering shrubs and tidy front hedge. 'See – it says "Parker",' she triumphed. 'Bingo!'

Nobody answered the door to them. They had not heard a distant ring or buzz – 'But we wouldn't if he's got a flat on the second floor,' Drew pointed out. 'The walls are too solid.'

'Why isn't there an entry phone thingy?' Thea grumbled. 'I bet all the other houses in the street have one.'

'We'll have to go,' Drew burst out worriedly. 'It's five past one. We might get stuck in traffic.'

'There's loads of time yet,' she assured him. 'But we do seem to have done what we came for. We could probably even get a bus, if we knew where they went from.'

'No, please. Let's find a taxi again.'

She nodded accommodatingly. 'I'll phone Gladwin on the way.'

She extracted her phone and keyed the detective's number. It was obvious that she only got a recording, from the way she spoke. 'It's me, Thea. We've found Victor Parker's address. He's not answering the door.' She recited the street name and the house number, and ended the call.

'Okay. Now we dash down to Hornsey Lane and find another taxi,' she decreed. 'We'll be home before the carriage turns back into a pumpkin, no problem. You might even catch the ten to two.'

He gave her a look designed to quell such inane optimism.

Chapter Fifteen

Mr Anderson's funeral began promptly as scheduled, Drew in his respectable dark clothes, his hair brushed and his manner calm. Angela, niece of the deceased, watched with impressive equanimity as the coffin was lowered by Maggs, Drew and two middle-aged nephews. The eulogy that Drew delivered included his usual references to the inevitability of death and the sadness that accompanied it; the importance of remembering the person who had gone. He said nothing about heaven or God, but did mention the spirit of the dead man, surviving perhaps in the hearts of those who loved him, merging into the great sea of all who had lived in the past. He felt the wording of this final thought needed some further work, but he liked to include it. His aim was to acknowledge the real significance of every life that had ever been, without descending into unconvincing platitudes about a life to come, or any unrealistic prospect that Mr Anderson would be meaningfully reunited with his family and friends at any stage in the future.

Throughout the ceremony, flickering images of the inert Karen and the mischievous Thea intruded themselves. He had permitted himself to think about them both in the train back from London, as honestly and directly as he could. It had been like opening a curtained window to let in light and cool air, as well as flying biting things. There would be no escape from the anguish of losing Karen. Childish adventures with Thea would do nothing to assuage the grief, at least in the first weeks and months.

All of which coloured the tone of his little speech at the graveside. He made no effort to soften or deny the sharpness of the loss, the gap in the fabric of things that the nice old man would leave. He found some of the more distant friends eyeing him doubtfully, as he confronted the realities without mercy.

Angela, however, seemed grateful. She shook his hand, and then pressed Maggs's shoulder in a gesture of real warmth. 'You're both doing a brilliant service,' she said. 'This is exactly how all funerals should be.'

'We think so,' said Drew simply. Angela was easy, compared to the account he was going to have to give of himself to Maggs.

Because Maggs had discovered that he had not in fact been at his wife's bedside all morning, thanks to the station parking sticker he had left on the window of his car, and which she had spotted at twenty paces, the moment he drove in at five minutes past four.

Thea, too, had plenty of time to think on the train home. The mystery of Victor Parker was not even half solved, she

208

realised. She and Drew had been childishly irresponsible in not sticking around until the police arrived and broke down the door of the flat. The timing had been ridiculous, with Drew so worried about his irritating funeral. They had behaved in a fashion that would embarrass the Famous Five, let alone two grown-up twenty-first-century people.

But the whole matter of Victor and Yvonne Parker had all along felt secondary to the far more awful and urgent murder of Stevie Horsfall. That was the mystery she really should be solving, and any unconscious hope that there would turn out to be a connection between the two had been thwarted by the need to rush back to Snowshill before any facts could be unearthed.

Gudrun's confession to having 'stolen' her child was still niggling at her. Many women dreamt of such a theft, of course, knowing how easy it was to seduce a man into careless sex. But Thea had never actually met an example of it being followed through. Men were more wary than they were given credit for; single mothers liked to have some regular financial assistance from the father of their child; and some of them had the foresight to realise that the child itself was eventually going to want to know at least something of the story. Mostly, anyone in that position these days – and perhaps even ten years ago – chose to go a more official route, and take themselves to a clinic where fatherhood was a bureaucratic and sanitised procedure, sanctioned by paperwork, and paid for with money. All that one had to deal with was a small phial of semen. The man himself never comprised part of the picture.

And was there not some sneaking suggestion of malice in what Gudrun had done? She had deliberately deceived the hapless man. He had imagined a no-strings liaison, grateful for his luck, doubtless treated to a suitably sensual experience, and been robbed of something profoundly visceral. And Gudrun had felt no remorse, no qualms about it, still almost boasting of her achievement ten years later, when the resulting child was dead, having brought her a great deal less fulfilment and satisfaction than she must surely have wished for in the first place.

Her mind whirled constantly with the burgeoning mysteries. As she drove hurriedly from the station in Moreton to rescue her imprisoned spaniel, she considered the other characters she had encountered: Blake Grossman and his absent Eloise, for a start. He could easily have fabricated his conveniently vague overseas trip, and come softly back on Sunday afternoon to slaughter the boy. Just as likely – which was to say, not likely at all – Janice and Ruby had together killed him in their rage about the garden. Most probable, it seemed, was a scenario where a passing stranger, a man with mental problems perhaps, had seen red as a result of some outrageous misdemeanour from the boy. Grabbed him, garotted him and thrown his body on the nearest patch of grass behind a car, then driven off over the hills and far away. Just another summer tourist, unnoticed in the general pilgrimage to and from the famous Manor.

But then the oddness of Mark and Belinda Parker, who had grown up in Snowshill, and knew at least some of the present inhabitants, came to mind. And that brought her back to Victor, and the pressing need to establish where and how he was.

And what *about* Mark Parker? He seemed an increasingly large figure in the picture, a rogue element who had wantonly lied to her on Monday morning. She admitted to herself that she had entertained a sneaking hope that she might encounter him in Crouch End, thus proving somehow that he was the silent attacker of his father the previous day. Why or how would become apparent when she challenged him. Stupid idea, of course. It was enough of a triumph that they had found Yvonne's car and established that Victor Parker did in fact live where Yvonne had said he did.

She approached Hyacinth House with churning emotions, wishing she could just collect her dog and go back to her own little house. Hyacinth House was tainted with misery now, after housing Gudrun for the night. The guest had appeared in the kitchen at eight o'clock that morning, looking crumpled but self-possessed. 'I never knew it was possible to sleep for so long,' she said.

'You must be awfully hungry and thirsty.' Thea had produced toast and tea, which the woman consumed absently.

'I'll go in a minute. They might be looking for me,' the woman said.

Thea did not enquire who *they* might be. She assumed it could only be the police. 'No, they won't,' she said. 'I told them you were here.'

Gudrun's sunken eyes met hers with a flash of anger. 'You reported me?' she accused.

211

'In a way, I did,' Thea agreed. 'Does it matter?'

'Not really.' Gudrun's shoulders slumped. 'I'll have to get used to it, won't I?'

Thea understood that *it* meant a whole great mass of stuff far beyond the attention of the police. 'Will you be all right?' she asked gently.

'I'll have to be, won't I?' said Gudrun with a stoicism that Drew Slocombe would have found admirable.

She had not heard anything from Gladwin since leaving the message from outside Victor's house, but assumed that she would, before long. There was no sign of Janice, from across the road, who had agreed to rescue the spaniel if Thea hadn't got back by four o'clock. In the absence of any further excitement, she decided to reward her patient dog by taking it for a walk.

Snowshill was quiet. The pub appeared to be having a rest, the Manor behind its protective wall ignoring the village as usual. A few cars passed on the upper road, and a black dog pottered illegally across the churchyard. 'How did that get in there?' muttered Thea. For reply, the animal leapt effortlessly onto the boundary wall and then loped away without a backward glance. 'Long legs,' said Thea to Hepzie. 'I bet you couldn't jump that high.' In fact, the spaniel was a competent jumper, given the incentive.

They circled the church, with Hepzie on the lead, before Thea decided to walk along the road out of the village and investigate the Manor grounds, as far as she was permitted with a dog. The road had no verge or pavement, but offered no real danger from the traffic. They passed a small car park, and at the last moment, Thea noticed a small gate leading from it, with a sign announcing that this was a footpath to the Manor.

'Come on, then,' she said. 'This looks like a better way.'

It was a ludicrously long walk in the wrong direction, considering that the manor house was behind them. The National Trust in its wisdom had opted to send visitors several hundred yards out of the centre of Snowshill, whether on foot or driving, before admitting them to the grounds. They then had to walk all the way back, leaving their cars in a tastefully tree-dotted area – five hundred yards according to a note on a board she'd seen. By then, hardly anybody realised that they were in fact back where they started, literally next door to the Snowshill Arms where they might well have had their lunch. The walk of nearly half a mile was probably good for them, but the nannying implications were irritating.

No Dogs it said, as she found the entrance, including shop, café and toilets.

'Surprise, surprise,' said Thea in resignation.

A vehicle slowed alongside her as she emerged from the same small gate into the same small car park, fifteen or twenty minutes after leaving it. 'Hello again,' came a female voice. She pulled into the entrance to the park, leaving the road clear.

It was Clara Beauchamp in a chunky red Subaru, looking down from the driver's window. 'I'm searching for my dog. He's run off again, after some bitch somewhere, I suppose.'

Thea had been thinking about murdered children and

dying wives, and barely focused on the woman speaking to her. 'Oh dear,' she said.

'I don't suppose you've seen him? Black. Long legs. Floppy ears. He's part collie and part saluki. Runs like the wind.'

'Oh! Actually, yes. He was in the churchyard about half an hour ago. He seemed to know where he was going.'

'So he might, but there are people around here who disapprove of loose dogs.'

Thea had very painful experience of the risks that such animals ran when they escaped their confines, and nodded sympathetically. 'Maybe he's home again by now.'

'Let's hope so. How are you getting on, anyway?'

'Well enough, considering.' She remembered that she and Clara had discussed young Stevie Horsfall only an hour or so before she found his body. Clara's dislike of the boy had become one facet of the whole business, representative of the general attitude of the village towards him. 'It's so awful about poor Gudrun. She's utterly heartbroken.' The word seemed too weak for the torment the woman was enduring, but Thea had a resistance to the overused 'devastated' and could not bring herself to utter it.

'I know. Everyone feels terrible about it. And of course, we're all eyeing each other, wondering if it was somebody local who finally flipped. I think almost everyone has threatened to kill the bloody kid at some point – including his mother. But you never really mean it, do you?' She shuddered, and added, 'Just imagine actually *doing* it. It's hard enough to put a dying lamb out of its misery, let alone a strapping great boy like

Stevie. He'd kick and scratch. You really would have to mean business.'

Thea's eyes widened at this straightforward talk. Even she had not allowed her imagination to go into quite such harrowing detail. 'He didn't really look as if he'd struggled,' she said carelessly. 'His clothes weren't messed up, or anything.'

'Really?' Clara leaned avidly towards her, as far as the car window would allow. 'You do surprise me.' Quite which detail she meant was obscure.

'You knew it was me who found the body, I assume?'

'I did hear something,' said Clara warily.

'But you haven't seen Gudrun?'

'Me? God, no, of course not. It only happened two days ago. Besides, what would I say to her? I can't pretend I didn't loathe the little beast.'

'You could say you're sorry for her pain.'

A look close to exasperation crossed Clara's face, and Thea felt a sudden pang of acute loneliness. People were so prone to reacting badly to comments like that, and yet she had taken this woman for an exception. Hadn't she herself started it, with her talk of kicking and scratching? 'She wouldn't believe me,' she said simply, thereby somewhat redeeming herself in Thea's eyes.

'Oh. Didn't *anybody* like him?'

'Not to my knowledge. There was a teacher, I believe, when he was seven or eight, who made a bit of progress with him. If you ask me, it's karma.'

'What?' Clara Beauchamp was the archetypal Cotswolds character: rich, confident, impatient, doggy, horsy, healthy

215

and educated. Words like 'karma' did not fit the stereotype at all. 'How do you mean?'

'Well, as I told you on Sunday, the kid never should have been born. She was too old, too peculiar, to be entrusted with a child. It was never going to work out.'

'She told me she stole him,' Thea remembered. 'Funny word to use.'

'Right. That's what she always says. Waylaid some drunk in Cirencester one night and had her wicked way with him, to get a kid, is one version of the story. Dishonest, I call that.'

'Brave, though, if that's really what happened. Plenty of women dream of doing it, but not many go through with it, do they?'

'Don't ask me. People like Gudrun Horsfall are closed books to me. It's all a bit *sordid*, don't you think?'

'The way you tell it, yes. But that wasn't quite the picture I got. And men – well, they don't often turn it down, do they? They probably rather like to think they've got unknown offspring scattered around the countryside.'

'Like my dog,' laughed Clara. 'But the pigeons come back to roost in the end. We had an irate woman turn up with a boxful of mongrel pups, a year or two ago. Her bitch was a prize breeding golden retriever, and we'd cost her thousands in lost income, or so she said.'

'She should keep her dog indoors, then,' said Thea, thinking she could never have managed it herself. If Hepzie hadn't been spayed, there would probably have been three or four unplanned litters by this time. Besides, she had only recently come across a mismatched litter of pups in Cranham, and had a sneaking liking for such disobedience on the part of the dogs. They might be 'slave animals' as some would say, but they did get their own way sometimes.

'She says she did, and Boris jumped in through a window. Anyway, we digress.'

'Yes,' Thea agreed reluctantly. She would far rather discuss dogs than the wretched Gudrun. So she chose another subject. 'How well do you know Yvonne?'

'Vonny? Oh, not very. She works all the time, never seems to have a minute to spare. Teaching must be grim, don't you think? All that bloody paperwork. She strikes me as a bit lonely, no real friends that I know of.'

'Have you seen all the stuff she's got in the house?'

'A couple of times, yes. Very old-fashioned way to carry on. Must be worth a bit, I imagine.'

'I doubt it, actually. It's mostly just cheap knick-knacks. It's as if she can't bear to see a clear surface. The garden's the same.'

'Don't go psychological on me,' begged Clara. 'We've all got our quirks.'

'You seemed to know where she's gone and why, when we talked before. Did you know Victor?'

Clara rolled her eyes. 'Yes, I knew Victor. Self-important little braggart was Victor. Vonny's much better off without him. Did they get Belinda's wedding sorted out, then?'

Thea shrugged her ignorance. 'Their son came here yesterday morning, saying something about his mother, worried that she'd gone missing. She doesn't seem to have kept him and his sister very well informed.'

'Oh, Mark. Take no notice of him. He's as daft as Gudrun. Seems to think he's Oscar Wilde most of the time.'

'Oh – is that who he was being? I never did manage to work it out.'

Clara laughed cheerfully. 'Well, better go and catch that damned dog before he gets himself shot. Who'd have them, eh?' She eyed Thea's docile spaniel with something like envy. 'Though yours seems okay.'

Thea bent down and stroked the soft mottled head of her pet. 'Yes, she's very good,' she said. 'Although she's had her moments.'

Gladwin still hadn't called back by the end of Tuesday afternoon, an omission that Thea felt was slightly insulting. Not that she could say with any real justification that Victor Parker was actually of any significance to the Gloucestershire police in their quest for the killer of Stevie Horsfall. Even so, she did think she had grounds for insisting that somebody check up on the violence she had heard, having presented the gift of the London address where it had presumably happened.

There was a growing accumulation of anomalies surrounding Victor and his family which ought surely to be of interest to the police. Perhaps other things were developing quickly in the investigations, with DNA analysis under way or key witnesses providing hard evidence of somebody's guilt. She assumed she would only hear about it afterwards, if so. That should, by rights, come as a relief, but instead she felt unfairly sidelined.

* * *

It was time to feed the cats when she got back, and then find something for her own supper. Julius and Jennings were waiting for her and she gave them their Felix on the kitchen floor. Hepzie stood back, making much of her own obedience, liquid eyes bulging with the effort, one or two soft squeaks emerging from her throat. 'Okay,' Thea told her. 'Yours is coming.' She filled the bowl they always carried with them, mixing the meat and milk and biscuit to just the right tempting consistency, and gave it to the dog. The simple satisfaction of providing for domestic pets never palled. There was something reassuring about their dependence. While you had a dog, you had to get out of bed in the morning. You could not sink into depression or ME or general inertia. You owed it to your animal to continue to function. Farmers, of course, took this to crazy extremes, with hundreds of beasts just waiting to die if you neglected them for a moment. Everybody knew that farmers got up at 5 a.m. because otherwise they would never get everything done.

It was a cloudy evening, the light outside uninviting. Indoors the usual obstructions to any sense of relaxation presented themselves. She could phone Jessica; watch television; read a book; send texts to Drew. None of these options felt right. Jess would probably prefer to make the call at a time of her own choosing. Television was seldom very engaging. Books were for bedtime and Drew was off-limits.

Passing through the hallway, heading for the kitchen, her eye fell on the bureau tucked in beside the foot of the stairs. She remembered the drawer she had hurriedly pulled open when looking for Victor's address, which had been full of notebooks. It wouldn't hurt to have a quick look to see what they were. The drawer wasn't locked, the bureau not hidden away in a bedroom. It was undoubtedly an intrusion, but no harm would be done by it. At least, no further harm – she had already discovered the key to the bureau flap on a hook by the telephone and opened it to search for Yvonne's car documents. That was intrusive by many people's standards. Now she would merely be compounding a felony already committed. Besides, she would put everything back exactly as it was, and Yvonne would never know. Was there a house-sitter in the land who would resist just having a little peep?

The packed desk drawer called to her, once everything was finished in the kitchen. She had no sense of solving mysteries or unearthing secrets. She merely wanted to take a closer look at the contents of the books. 'Lesson plans, probably,' she muttered to herself. 'Or account books.'

The covers of the notebooks had been the initial attraction. Brightly coloured swirly designs suggested bright and interesting material inside as well. Carefully, Thea removed the top left book, ascertaining that there were three more in the pile, with another five similar piles – twenty in total. Perhaps they were unpublished novels, or poems. She could well imagine Yvonne Parker writing reams and reams of bad poetry.

The first page revealed a diary. *10th March 2000. My forty-fifth birthday. Victor gave me a bracelet. Mark gave me a clock. Belinda gave me a pair of slippers. I went to work as usual, and bought a cake for the staffroom. None of the children knew about my birthday, of course. Young Isaac Simpson played up again and I sent him to the head. Victor and I went to the pub in the evening and had steak.*

Hmm, thought Thea. *Just as you'd expect. A dull woman with a dull life.* The slippers were almost ludicrously dull. Isaac Simpson would be into his twenties by now and probably couldn't speak a word of French. She flipped through the book, the handwriting consistently small and neat, some entries extending to half a page, but never more. There was something for every single day, as far as she could tell. The final page read: *19ᵗʰ December. Bought the turkey, fresh from Mr Gordon. Finished the last of the cards, just in time. Term ends tomorrow, thank goodness. Victor's mother phoned from Lerwick, saying the weather's lovely there. Pouring with rain here. Belinda's boyfriend dumped her last week, she's just told us. Mark's results abysmal. Victor shouted at him. Had a letter from Mary saying Daniel's left her.*

Poor Belinda and poor Mary, thought Thea. Unkind men on all sides, it seemed. The scanty lines with their near-complete absence of emotion nonetheless managed to conjure ordinary family life. So ordinary, in fact, that there was very little sense of transgression in reading them. It was simply a record of daily events, with potentially useful details such as Victor's mother being alive and apparently well in Lerwick, that particular December.

She put the book back, just as she had found it, and selected the top one from the adjacent pile, thinking there had to be a more stimulating way to spend an evening.

9ᵗʰ Feb 2006. Letter came for Victor, with a printed

letterhead. He wouldn't let me see it, but it's obviously very bad news. I thought he was going to be sick or cry or something. Looks as if it might be something medical.

Flood in the girls' toilets at school. Lexie Jones slipped and bruised her hip.

Had estimate for new boiler – £2475.

This came halfway into the new notebook. Did Victor have gonorrhoea or something, Thea wondered wildly? Did they get the new boiler? 2006 was surely close to the date when Victor left home. Had it been connected somehow to this letter? Did Yvonne find it, discovering something terrible about her husband in it, and kick him out of the house?

The suddenly interesting entry nudged her conscience. She really ought not to be prying into secrets. It was none of her business, by any reckoning. If the roles were reversed and she learnt that Yvonne had been reading her diaries – not that she had any – or emails, she wouldn't like it. It was an indecent thing to do. Firmly she replaced the book and closed the drawer. Intimate as the position of a house-sitter might be, given the freedom of somebody's house and trusted with their cats and keys, the boundaries were clear. You definitely did not read people's personal diaries containing suspicions about their husband's state of health.

The warbling of her mobile came to her rescue. She wouldn't think any more about Yvonne and the volumes of her daily life. 'Mum?' Jessica's voice was thick with emotion. Thea's heart lurched.

'What's the matter?' she demanded.

'Paul. He's been attacked.'

'Attacked?' The word summoned ferocious mad dogs, or a horde of cartoon savages with spears tearing into the man's body. 'How? What happened?'

'A bunch of BNP morons, or something. Nobody seems to know for sure. They stamped on him. His pelvis is shattered.' The words came in breathless jerks.

'My God!' She had no notion of what to say or how to feel. 'Have you seen him?'

'No. It was *racist*, Mum. They did it because he's black. He's probably going to be crippled, for nothing more than his skin colour.' Sobs clouded the last words.

'He won't be crippled,' Thea assured her recklessly. 'It'll heal up.' But already she could visualise the crushed kidneys and testicles, the complex pelvic area never fully functioning again.

Jessica rallied enough to voice her rage. 'It'll be on the news, any minute now. The whole of the north-west is going to be doing overtime until they catch the bastards. They're not going to do it to anyone else.'

Thea could almost hear the vengeful macho comments from Jessica's colleagues, closing ranks in the face of this attack on one of their own. At the same time she heard Drew saying *We didn't like him much, did we?* For a flickering second she accused herself of bringing this damage on Paul by her own ill-wishing. 'They won't get away with it,' she said, as firmly as she could. 'What a horrible thing to do. At least it sounds as if all his friends will rally round.'

'They might.'

Thea heard doubt. Did Paul Middleman *have* friends, she wondered? Would it be left to Jessica to nurse him

223

through a long convalescence? She knew better than to ask.

'And what about you, Mum?' Jessica asked valiantly. 'What's going on there?'

'Quite a lot, as it happens. I suppose you've seen Snowshill on the news?'

'What?'

It struck Thea that she was closely connected to two major headlines in a single week, which seemed excessive to the point of embarrassment. 'Never mind,' she said. 'Let's just say I'm seeing quite a bit of Sonia Gladwin again.'

'Oh, *Mum*!' Jessica reproached.

'It's not my fault. Things happen. I went to London today,' she added, for no good reason.

'Shopping?'

'Of course not. Playing detective with Drew, actually.'

'With Gladwin's blessing, I hope?'

'More or less. Anyway, darling, it's ghastly about poor Paul. Nobody deserves that.'

There was a soft snort before Jessica opted to quell any indignation. 'No,' she agreed. 'Not even Paul deserves to be crippled by a bunch of ignorant racists.'

Except, thought Thea, perhaps they weren't so much ignorant racists as people who knew Middleman for what he was. But even then, he hadn't deserved it. Of course he hadn't.

'So Gladwin's letting you in again, is she?' Jessica reverted to her mother's news, her voice thoughtful. 'She's not supposed to, you know. What was it this time?'

'A little boy was killed.'

Jessica breathed an exhalation of distress and concern.

'So can't you just butt out this time and leave it to the cops?'

'Not really. It was me who found his body.'

'*What?* You didn't, did you? A child's body? That must have been horrendous.'

'Yes.' She pushed back the memory of just how horrendous it had been. 'Poor little chap.'

'Who did it?'

'Somebody local, probably. Gladwin hasn't ruled out his mother. He was a bit of a tearaway. Nobody seems to have liked him.'

'Not even his mother?'

'Oh yes. She loved him.'

'So she couldn't have killed him, could she?'

'I hope not,' said Thea.

Chapter Sixteen

Gladwin finally phoned at nine. 'This is becoming a habit,' said Thea. 'Shouldn't you be at home with your family?'

'I am, but I can still make phone calls. I don't regard calling you as work, either.'

'How nice. What am I, then?'

'Don't ask me. I've been wondering how to describe you in my report.'

Thea laughed. 'I'm an anomaly. I quite like that.'

'So – what did you want to tell me about the Parker man? All I got was an address.'

'And did you tell the London police? Have they been to check?'

There was a small silence, into which Thea read a cooling of the initial friendly words. 'Sorry. That sounds as if I'm telling you how to do your job, doesn't it? But I can't just let it go. I heard something horrible happening. I know I did.'

'You went to London today – is that right?'

'Oh, yes. Drew and I went to Crouch End to look for

226

him and we found Yvonne's car and a South American childminder who said Victor lives there with a girlfriend. She hadn't seen him since Sunday.'

'And was that unusual?'

'I don't know. Probably not,' Thea admitted.

'And he lives there with a woman – is that right? So wouldn't she report any trouble? Listen, Thea, I did pass on the address to the Met, and suggested they have a look, or at least make a phone call. But you must see that it's not going to be high on their list.'

'The woman screamed,' Thea repeated doggedly. 'And nobody came back to the phone.'

'Yes, I believe you. But things like that happen all the time, with no harm done. People hit each other more than we like to think. Even in Crouch End. It will all have been patched up by bedtime. I'm amazed you went to the bother of going all the way to London. It seems crazy. And who's Drew? Is that the name? Drew who?'

'Drew Slocombe. He was involved in that murder a few months ago in Broad Campden. He's my friend,' she added childishly. 'He's an undertaker. I told you before.'

'So you did. I'm not sure I believe in him, though. People don't have undertakers for friends. Although I suppose *you* might, come to think of it.'

Thea finished the story, despite a growing understanding that Gladwin really wasn't very interested. 'Anyway, we found the car. She said she left it in a quiet street before going off on the Eurostar, and there it was. With a resident's permit and everything.'

'Whose child does the South American person mind?'

'Oh, I don't know. That isn't relevant.'

'But there's no Victor Parker registered in Crouch End. I told you.'

'I guess your London colleagues didn't look hard enough. Maybe they just fobbed you off and never even tried.'

'They wouldn't dare,' said Gladwin without conviction. 'Anyway – I think we might forget the Parkers now. Listen to me, Thea. I should have told you before all this Parker stuff diverted me. We're charging Gudrun Horsfall with the murder of Stevie. There's new evidence, which I can't really reveal. It's very damning, I'm afraid. The CPS are going to accept it as enough for a prosecution, I think.'

'Oh no!' The shock and grief came like a physical blow. 'You can't. She *can't* have killed him. I won't believe it. You must tell me what the evidence is. I might be able to explain. It must be a mistake.' She was gabbling mindlessly, desperate to change the collective opinion of the police. 'I mean – she's his *mother*. Her DNA would be all over him, and his on her. So it can't be that. *What* evidence could there be? Her footprints, and fingerprints as well, were at the scene here, because I went to fetch her and she picked him up.'

'It's something in her house, that's all I can say.'

Thea's thoughts raced over all the possibilities. Things knocked over? Something about the washing line? Bodily fluids? Everything she could think of was easily explained away by the fact that Gudrun and Stevie lived there together.

'Please tell me,' she begged. 'What harm can it do?'

'It would spell the end of my career if it got out that I'd disclosed something like that to you.'

'It won't get out. I won't tell anybody.'

'You absolutely mustn't. Not even your undertaker. If you do, I'll never speak to you again.'

'Trust me.'

'Did you notice his feet?'

'What? Stevie's? No, I don't think so. They were practically under my car.'

'He was only wearing one shoe.'

'Oh-h-h.' The thought took no time at all to form. 'And the missing one is at the house? Shit.'

'Exactly. Explain that if you can. It was just inside the back door. I expect you can picture it.'

'Yes,' Thea admitted, running the scene where the murderous mother lifted the heavy inert child, his feet dangling awkwardly, perhaps getting wedged in the door somehow, a shoe coming loose, unnoticed. Then she carried him up the lane and round to the front of Hyacinth House, and dropped him behind Thea's car, before running home and sitting in the kitchen to await whatever came next. 'You think he was dead an hour or more before she moved him?'

'About that.'

'So you're not looking for anybody else?'

'Witnesses. She must have carried him in broad daylight, about four hundred yards.'

'If only I hadn't been on the phone.'

'Right.'

'Um . . . she might have brought him across the field, behind this house. It slopes downhill, so nobody overlooks it. She could have risked coming through the gate at the end of the garden without me seeing her and maybe heaved him over Yvonne's front wall. She's probably strong enough to do that, even with her bad shoulder.'

'Bad shoulder?'

'You surely must know about that. She gave up her swimming because of it, and it's never really been right, apparently.'

'Hmm.'

'You didn't know?'

'No.'

'You should probably check it out, then.'

'Yes. Thanks.'

Thea could hear that the detective wanted to leave it there, but she wasn't ready to endure the rest of a lonely evening without giving voice to some further feelings. 'It's horrible!' she burst out. 'I don't see how she could possibly have done it. She'll make an awful witness,' she realised, with a further sinking of her spirits. 'I can't bear for it to be true.'

'Well, we have to go with the evidence,' said Gladwin, slightly stiffly. 'That's how it works.'

'It's wrong,' persisted Thea. 'I just know it's wrong.'

'We'll have to see, then, won't we?' came the deeply unsatisfactory reply.

The news seemed to put a stop on all productive thought. All Thea could manage was a repetitious internal protest against the horror of deliberate infanticide. Even though inadequate incompetent women occasionally abused and starved their wretched children, barely knowing what they did, it remained a vanishingly rare event. She had met Gudrun Horsfall, spoken to her, felt she had some slight rapport with her. She had complained to her about her son, as one mother to another, before he died, without meaning anything very much by it. The following day, the boy was killed and Thea would have sacrificed a lot to have her own words unsaid. Had she been the final straw, the last inescapable demonstration that the boy was incorrigible? If a stranger, who knew nothing of the history, found him objectionable, then perhaps, even to his mother's hitherto rose-tinted eyes, he really was a hopeless case.

Still she worried at the actual details of how it could have happened. She had been right there, only yards away. How could she have been so unobservant, so unsuspecting of the horror unfolding just beyond the window? If she had listened properly, she might have heard the screams of the dying boy in the cottage beyond the field. Perhaps Gudrun had begun by reproaching him, cuffing his head, chasing him up the stairs and down again, grabbing at him, enraged beyond all reason by his insolence and quicksilver movements. Would she seize the length of washing line at random, wrap it around the infuriating little throat and pull it tight? Would she? Would any mother ever be capable of that? And if so, would she achieve some tiny vestige of atonement by confessing it all, in the end?

She sat quietly in the restless living room, the dog on her lap, thinking dark thoughts about the evil that people were capable of. The monsters who had stamped on Paul Middleman's pelvis; the person who had shot Karen Slocombe three years ago; all the cunning malicious murderers she had heard Phil Hollis describe and actually encountered herself now and then. Even Stevie, who had thrown stones at harmless defenceless cows, had corrupt tendencies, it seemed. Somehow he had become brutalised, had opted to inflict pain and damage as his source of diversion, in this place of calm beauty. Shaking her head at her own naive assumptions, she had to concede that it was very far from unusual for a boy to be like that. Hadn't they pulled the wings off flies and tied things to the tails of cats for centuries past? Had Stevie really been so much worse than the average underoccupied ten-year-old?

And then there was Drew, who had been so glad to play truant and desert his family and business for a few hours. Whatever bit of irrelevant nonsense they might have indulged in on their brief trip to London, she hoped it had done him good. He would just have got back in time for the funeral, assuming the train behaved itself. The children would cheerfully greet him, supper would be consumed, and probably a visit to Karen's bedside during the evening. She could not expect him to contact her, with so much going on. Their findings concerning Victor Parker were impressive in one sense, but completely unimportant in another. It had been a Famous Five kind of expedition, a defiant challenge to constraints laid on them by others, more than anything else. They had done it because they had realised it was possible, and they were the sort of people who took action against all logic. It made them feel special, different, refusing to succumb to ordinary pressures. She hoped it had done Drew some good, in the midst of his anguish over Karen.

The realities of the Parkers and their marriage remained obscure, and would probably continue to do so. Curiosity had been piqued by the two staccato phone calls from Victor, and the very different ones from Yvonne. They had both opted to involve her, by making those calls, and she had risen to the call beyond anything either of them could reasonably have expected.

Nothing more happened that evening to disturb her meditations. She slowly got ready for bed, taking the dog out, making sure the cats were in their rightful place and the cat flap locked. Poor things, she thought, prevented from their natural nocturnal prowlings, for no good reason that she could see. But they seemed resigned to it, presenting themselves unfailingly at nine-thirty or so, and curling on their cushions for the night. They were wonderfully low-maintenance, especially compared to some of the creatures Thea had been asked to care for in the past. One of them was pawing repeatedly at a small space between a cupboard and the wall, in the scullery, perhaps at a small toy or morsel of food, while his brother ignored him. When Thea turned off the light and left them to it, it was with the small consolation that they at least had shown her no malice – unlike the hornet in the garden.

In North Staverton, Drew Slocombe was having a far less peaceful evening. Worse than any jealous wife, Maggs had insisted on a full explanation of why he had been catching a train at ten that morning. Where had he been, why and with whom?

'It's that woman, isn't it?' she had accused. 'Where did you go with her this time?'

'It's not your business,' he repeated, quietly. 'There's nothing whatsoever for you to be concerned about. I got back in time to bury Mr Anderson, I played with my kids and ate supper with them, and tonight it's your turn to go and see Karen – if you want to. I won't be going. I'll stay at home and be a good father. I did want to try to talk to you about Karen, as it happens, but only if we can both be sure it's safe to do so. At the moment I don't feel that at all.'

'Safe? What the hell do you mean, *safe?*'

He closed his eyes, feeling very old. 'It's too serious to risk either of us flying out of control. I suppose you could say it's the most serious thing that will ever happen in my whole life. I'm never going to forget the next few days or weeks, whatever else might occur to rock our sinking boat. Last night I finally understood that Karen isn't going to get better, and I managed to get some way towards accepting it.'

She shook her head impatiently. 'I don't get it. What does this have to do with you going on some mysterious train journey?'

'Nothing directly. It's something to do with my inner state. I can't explain without using silly New Age jargon, unless I can feel that you're with me, that you do understand. And I can't feel that, Maggs. It's not your fault. Karen isn't your wife, Steph and Timmy aren't your children. You're very young. I know you had to watch your Auntie Sharon die, when we were first here, and that was awful, but I don't think it's really prepared you for this.'

'You've given up on Karen?' She glared at him in horrified rage. 'Just like that – given up on her?'

'Not just like anything. It's about as hard as anything can ever be. But yes, I've lost hope for a recovery. She isn't going to get better, I know that. Whatever the doctors might do, however long they keep her heart beating, she's never going to know us again. And I'm not giving up – this is just the first step in a long and ghastly process. Don't say anything, please don't. Go home and talk to Den about it. See if you can put yourself in my place. Just don't shout at me any more, or demand anything of me.' He met her eye, unsmiling, revealing his naked emotion. 'I need you to be kind, Maggs. Don't make me fight you, as well as this horrible thing that's happened to me and my family.'

He had not seen her cry since her beloved Auntie Sharon had died of stomach cancer, the same week that Timmy was born. Now she simply stood there, tears flowing down her dark cheeks, her eyes reddening and her nose a mess. 'I haven't got a hanky,' she choked, wiping a hand across her upper lip, making everything worse.

Drew had learned to keep a supply of tissues to hand at all times, and quickly fetched a box from the kitchen. 'Here,' he said.

'I'm crying for Karen,' she said, a few minutes later. 'Not you or the kids or myself.'

'Go home,' he ordered. 'I'll see you tomorrow.'

During the night, Thea was awoken by a crash from downstairs, followed by a squeal. 'What was that?' she asked her dog, which lay sleeping at the end of the bed.

Fumblingly Thea switched on the bedside lamp, and Hepzie raised her head with no sign of concern.

'We'll have to go and see. That's what I'm being paid for. Come on. You can be my defender.'

Together they went onto the landing, and Thea put on every light she could find as they went downstairs. There were sounds coming from the kitchen. 'It's those cats,' Thea said. 'They must have broken something, and from that squeal, one of them sounds to be hurt.'

She opened the door, and before she could switch another light on, a rushing twofold flurry of fur shot past her legs. Perfectly game for a chase, Hepzie followed. All three animals bounded up the stairs while Thea dithered. In the kitchen she found nothing worse than a saucepan on the floor – presumably the source of the initial crash.

Still muzzy from her deep sleep, she trailed after her charges and tracked them down to the bathroom, where Julius was growling under the basin and both the others stood with swishing tails staring hard at him. Jennings was plainly furiously angry and Hepzie was enthusiastically prepared to assist in any way she could.

'What have you got?' Thea asked Julius. 'Let me see.' Without ceremony, she dragged the cat from its lair. As she did so, a smaller creature dropped from its mouth and scuttled behind the lavatory. 'A mouse! All this fuss for a mouse. Now it's let loose up here and we'll never catch it. Well, it's too late to worry about it now. Back to the kitchen, you two.' She scooped up the disgruntled Jennings and took them both back to quarters. Hepzie remained, sniffing importantly after the rodent.

It took some time to settle down again, but eventually she drifted back to sleep, having quashed her feelings of irritation with the cats, and concluded that the whole adventure had been rather funny in its way. *Light relief*, were the last words she consciously thought before sinking into sleep.

Chapter Seventeen

Wednesday dawned grey again, and Thea retrieved the clothes she had worn the day before from the bathroom where she had carelessly abandoned them. Never especially tidy, she had half intended to put them through the wash that day, and therefore saw no need to fold them or hang them up anywhere. The trousers were the ones she had packed at the last minute, just in case it was too cool for shorts. Which it had been for most of the week. The long-sleeved shirt, however, would not do for another day, so she left it where it lay, to be joined by a few other things that could be washed when the pile was large enough.

The cats drank their morning milk and slunk outside as soon as she opened the back door for them. They ignored her reproaches about the disturbed night. Hepzie too seemed to have forgotten the whole episode, and for a moment Thea wondered whether it had all been a dream. Where had the mouse got to? Had it been injured as the two Burmese fought over it? Was it an outdoor mouse – perhaps a vole or shrew – or one that habitually lived in the house? She had no especial antipathy towards mice; spiders were a great deal worse, in her opinion. She was expected, in her role as house-sitter, to deal with the normal run of rural wildlife and so far she had encountered no serious difficulties. Probably the most intrusively trying creature so far had been a parrot called Ignatius in Lower Slaughter.

After the turbulent events of the previous day, and the wretched news from Gladwin in the evening, she felt a definite stasis that morning. There was nothing she felt constrained to do, nobody she should speak to, not even any great mystery yet to be solved. She would have to remain at Hyacinth House for another nine days, taking the dog out for walks and drives, reading up on local history, hoping for improved weather and some lazy time in the garden. The great wound in the fabric of the village caused by the murder of one of its sons might yet create further trouble, and would certainly remain a talking point for years to come, but if Gladwin's team of investigators had it right, there were very few loose ends still to be teased at. Gudrun would be treated with a mixture of kindness and horrified disdain, interviewed by a dozen different people, all of them urging her to confess and thus save herself the ordeal of a long trial.

It was ten o'clock when a man's voice from the open front door said, 'Still here, then?'

She had virtually forgotten him. *Thursday*, she remembered now. *He said he'd be back on Thursday.* But this was only Wednesday. He'd come back a day early. 'Yes, I'm still here,' she said, standing in the hall beside Yvonne's bureau. 'Weren't you meant to be away until tomorrow?'

'Change of plan,' Blake shrugged. 'I heard about poor little Stevie. What an appalling thing! Eloise is going to be horrified. She always said he was nowhere near as bad as everyone claimed. She was quite the champion when anybody complained about him.'

'How was your trip?'

'Oh – boring, mainly. The whole exercise got changed at the last minute, actually. Very annoying.'

'You didn't go?'

'I didn't go to where I'd originally intended. It was Ankara, as it turned out, when I'd been expecting Damascus. It's a crazy world out there. You've never seen madness until you've been involved in a trade delegation.' He smiled ingenuously, as if describing a minor amendment to a bus timetable.

'So not entirely boring, then?'

'Compared to what's been going on here, definitely boring. Speeches, meetings, trying to stay diplomatic all the time. And the *paperwork*!'

'When did you get in?'

'Landed at Birmingham at seven-thirty. Knackered now, of course, after about three hours' sleep.'

He looked perfectly fresh to her. Shaved, showered, uncrumpled – nobody could ever guess he had just got off an early flight from Turkey.

'Yvonne's in France now, apparently,' she said, for the sake of saying something.

'Right. All square with Victor, then?'

'I have no idea.' *Be wary*, she reminded herself.

'I expect she'll fill me in with everything when she gets back. She usually keeps me informed. I hope she's got better weather than this, anyway. It's freezing!'

'Disappointing,' agreed Thea. 'You'd think we'd learn not to get our hopes up, wouldn't you?'

'Ever optimistic,' he said lightly. 'Still a couple of months to go before the nights start closing in. Of course, I'm off to Dubai in a week or so, all being well. Should be good and hot there.'

'Another trade delegation?'

'More of the same,' he sighed. 'No peace for the wicked.'

'What are you trading? I mean, do you represent one particular company? Or is it more complicated than that?'

A superior little smile reminded her that she was not at all sure she liked this Blake Grossman, since he had been so rude to her the last time she met him. '"Complicated" is hardly the word,' he said. 'Trust me, you really don't want to know.'

He was right, she admitted. He was welcome to his self-important little deals with inscrutable Arabs and Turks. 'I expect I'll see you around, then,' she said, looking over the odd configuration of the two gardens and sighing silently to herself. However much an occupant of Hyacinth House might wish to avoid Blake, it would be virtually impossible, the way things were arranged. Whose idea had it really been, to start with? Which of them did it benefit more? What did the invisible Eloise make of it?

She took a firm hold of the front door, wishing she could break the bad habit of leaving it open so often. She did it in her little house at home, letting the dog come and go as she liked, and she continued to do it in her various house-sits, when the weather and traffic would permit. Blake had not come further than the threshold, but if the door had been closed, she might have given herself more time to think before answering his knock. 'Well, I'd better get on,' she said. 'And you must have things to do.'

He cocked his head and stood his ground. 'You don't want to talk about finding Stevie, then? About fetching his mother before calling the police?'

She repressed a desire to ask him how on earth he knew so much. The papers and TV had given the story some prominence over the past two days, and although she had avoided it all, she could well believe that her own part had been thoroughly aired, despite her refusal to be interviewed. 'No, I don't, thanks,' she said coldly. 'I have friends and family for that sort of thing, if I need it.'

'How's the hornet sting?' he went on to enquire. 'No ill effects?'

She had forgotten all about it. 'Nothing at all, thanks. It itched for a day or two, but it's gone now. And I haven't seen any more of them. I'm not sure there is an active nest in the roof, after all.'

'Oh, it's there,' he assured her. 'They just don't like this weather. Half a day of sun and you'll see I'm right.'

'The first sign of sun and I'll take my dog and go off for a picnic, then,' she said. 'Bye for now, Blake. Thanks for dropping in.'

Except she had not let him in. She had deliberately kept him on the doorstep, for reasons she could not have fully explained. He had made no attempt to push past her or invite himself for coffee, but she was in no doubt at all that he had noted her lack of hospitality.

Barely five minutes after he had finally gone back to his own house, Thea was in the living room, straightening cushions, when through the front window she saw a car draw to a stop next to her own. For the fiftieth time she wished she had been standing in the same spot on Sunday when the little boy's body had been dumped.

A small woman pushed open the driver's door and came to the gateway. Thea went to meet her, and was through the door and halfway down the front path before the visitor had properly entered the garden.

'Hello?' she said, only then wondering if this was another press reporter, following up the story of the murder. 'Can I help you?'

'You're the house-sitter.' It was a statement, not a question. The woman was of Oriental appearance, no taller than Thea herself, with a direct look and lovely skin. On this cool August day – it was 1ˢᵗ August, Thea had vaguely noted at some point during the morning – she wore a sleeveless dusky pink top that emphasised her golden colour. 'I'm Belinda. Can I come in?'

Standing back to give free access to the front door, Thea's thoughts squirmed like a nest of snakes, entangling and hissing. She realised that she had expected something quite different – if not a journalist, then Victor's mysterious girlfriend, or merely a passing tourist being outrageously nosy. 'Belinda,' she said. 'Yvonne's daughter.' Adopted, she remembered. Of course.

'That's right. Mark told me about you, and I decided to

come and see for myself. Plus, I'm worried about my mum. Something rather odd has been happening, apparently.'

The accent was pure middle-class English. Belinda was about thirty, and perfectly self-possessed. She was as different as anyone could imagine from what might be expected of Yvonne's daughter. 'Oh? As far as I know, she's in France with her sister. Isn't that right?' They had moved through the hall and into the living room. Belinda sat on the sofa, with its partly plumped cushions, and ignored the spaniel sniffing her legs.

'I don't know. Auntie Sim – Sylvia, as she is officially – lives on a hilltop near Avignon, with no modern facilities. She certainly doesn't have a phone, and I don't suppose Mum's old thing would work overseas.' She became aware of Thea's frowning confusion and gave an impatient sigh. 'Am I going too fast for you?'

'Not really. I mean – everything's such a muddle, you're just one more factor. And I suppose I assumed that you and Mark—'

'That we came from the same ethnic background?'

'I suppose so.'

'I was born here in England. They didn't trek out to a Chinese orphanage in the mountains and choose me from a thousand abandoned baby girls, if that's what you're thinking. Although I admit I'm sometimes tempted to spin some sort of story like that. As far as I can discover, I'm actually only half Chinese. The paternal half.'

'I was thinking more that Yvonne must have been unusually young to adopt.' She did the sums laboriously. 'Only in her early twenties.'

'So?'

'Well – it just seems unusual.'

'She had undeveloped ovaries. She already knew, by the time she was twenty, that she'd never be able to have children. Physiologically, she's still prepubescent, even now. They gave her hormone treatment to help her appearance, but the organs were never going to function.'

'Gosh! Poor her.' *Too much information,* she inwardly protested. There had been something almost like relish in the rapid explication. She had not noticed anything particularly undeveloped or childlike about Yvonne. 'Well, it must have worked. She seemed quite normal to me.'

Belinda shrugged. 'What's normal?' she asked rhetorically.

'Can I get you some coffee?'

'Okay. Thanks. God – isn't this room *awful*! How can you bear to be in here?'

'I don't come into it much,' Thea admitted with a laugh. 'I'm scared of knocking something over.'

'It's not very *normal*, though, is it?'

A thought – a sudden insight – struck Thea. 'It's the sort of thing teenage girls do, I suppose. Collecting china animals, or candles, or little boxes. Your mum just never stopped.'

'Right! That's exactly right. She's stuck at about fourteen. Makes her a good teacher, of course,' she added ruefully. 'The kids love her. They think she's fun.'

'Let me get the coffee. Is instant all right?'

'Fine,' said Belinda, with an irrepressible little grimace. *Too bad*, thought Thea. *I'm not wasting time doing the real thing. This is far too interesting.*

She was back in four minutes, carrying two mugs and a plate of biscuits on a small tray she had found. 'I gave her that tray,' said Belinda. 'About twenty years ago. I don't think she ever uses it.'

Why would she, thought Thea? *She probably only ever eats in the kitchen.*

'It was dreadful seeing this house on the TV news. Like a nightmare. Were they all camped out like vultures, making you live under siege?'

'Actually, no. Not at all. The police kept it quiet until the middle of Monday, so it was bad then for the rest of that day. But I think they quite soon realised it was too terrible to make a big splash about. Or something.'

Belinda raised her delicate eyebrows in a sceptical question. 'Surely not? The more gruesome the better, as far as they're concerned. I didn't see *you* in the news, though.'

'No. And I still think they were uncomfortable with the story. Plus there was absolutely nothing to see here, apart from some tape and the SOCOs crawling about. They filmed that from all angles and then drifted away. After all, there was no chance that anything else was going to happen here, was there?'

'I guess not.'

'You don't sound sure.'

'I've got a nasty feeling, that's all. You've seen Gudrun, I suppose.'

Thea nodded. 'You know her?'

'I *did*. Very well, actually. She taught me to swim when I was twelve. I was quite good, and she was an inspiration to me.'

'You knew Stevie?'

'Barely even saw him, except at a distance. I'd left home before he was born. I don't think I even knew she had a child for a year or two. She was never around when I came here for Christmas or anything. Not that I come back very often. And even less since my parents split up. I've been rather firmly on my dad's side, to be honest. I can't imagine what Mum thought she was doing, making such a fuss about such a little thing.'

'Why? What did he do?'

'They never told us the full story, but Mark and I worked out that it must have been something to do with telephone sex. Or maybe the Internet. Something got her incandescent and she made it impossible for him to stay. She was such a fool. He was a good husband, a wonderful father. I'm sure she's regretted it ever since. And it's been a financial disaster for both of them.'

'She told me he lives in a cramped little flat in Crouch End. Is that true?' It was an innocent piece of cunning, she assured herself. Just checking for consistency.

Belinda laughed, her mouth wide and eyes damp with merriment. 'God, no, of course not. That's Mariella's place, and it's really rather pleasant. He's there a lot, but he's just between houses. He's trying to buy somewhere in Hampstead Garden Suburb. He's put the offer in.'

It fitted well with Mark's account, Thea noted, with a certain relief. 'Mariella?'

'She's his girlfriend. Filipina. I don't like her at all – she's younger than me – but he seems to be infatuated. I endure her in order not to fall out with him.'

'Does your mother know about her?'

'Must do by now, if she's been to the Crouch End place. We've been trying to keep it from her, up to now. She'll be pretty sick about it, of course. Any wife would be.'

'Even an ex-wife,' Thea nodded. 'The age difference alone makes it pretty hard to take, I imagine.'

'Right. But she cooks like an angel, I'll give her that.'

'I went there,' Thea confessed, with difficulty. She had no idea how she was to explain herself. Even in her own mind, she no longer knew what she thought she was doing. 'We met a nanny from across the road who said they have a cleaning lady.'

Belinda stared furiously at her. 'So what if they do? What in the world did you go there for? What business is it of yours?'

'I had a weird phone call and the police said they couldn't find anybody with your father's name in that part of London, and your mother's car was there, with a resident's permit on it.' She was gabbling, trying to justify herself.

Belinda held up a dainty hand in appeal. 'A weird phone call?'

'From your father. On Monday evening. I went there yesterday. I had another reason as well. It's not quite as crazy as it sounds.'

'But you didn't see Dad?'

'No.'

She frowned, and seemed to be slightly out of breath. 'He's not responding to my calls. *How* was it weird? The phone call, I mean.'

Thea's own heart rate was accelerating as she processed the fresh details, which fitted uncomfortably well with everything she had learnt. *Gudrun,* insisted a little voice. Somehow, all along, she had known there was a link between Hyacinth House and Gudrun Horsfall and her dead child. Nothing Belinda had said quite confirmed this, but she could feel it coming closer. Somewhere everything connected, with Victor Parker at the core of it.

'He cried out, as if he was hurt. And a woman screamed. But nothing's been reported, as far as I know. And now they've charged Gudrun with killing Stevie, the police aren't at all interested in your family. Why would they be?'

'No reason,' said Belinda slowly. 'But something isn't right. I wonder whether my dad is in some sort of trouble.'

'Can you go to London and check?'

'If I have to, yes.'

'I have told the police all this, and given them his address. They don't appear to be taking it at all seriously. If you tell them you're worried, that might galvanise them a bit.'

The grimace returned, with no attempt to hide it this time. 'That seems a bit . . . excessive. I mean – I'm sure he's all right, really.' She picked at her lower lip for a few seconds. 'They arrested Gudrun – is that right? They think she killed the boy?'

'That's right. It was probably on the news, but I can't bear to watch it. It's so horrifying, to imagine how she could ever—'

'Has she been in custody since Sunday, then?'

'Oh, no. I saw her on Monday and Tuesday.' Guiltily she suppressed the information that Gudrun had actually spent Monday night in Belinda's mother's bed. Somehow she did not think the young woman would approve. 'I'm not sure where she was after I saw her yesterday, and I don't know for sure that she's in custody now. Probably she is, for her own protection. As far as I know it was sometime yesterday that they decided there was enough evidence to charge her.'

'So when you heard my dad cry out, Gudrun was free?'

'No, no – she was here, upstairs actually. I wasn't going to tell you. It was one thing after another that evening – first she arrived, then Drew phoned, and then your father. It was around nine by then. Why?' Thea had never for a moment linked Gudrun with Victor, and still wasn't sure that this was Belinda's drift.

'It's only a hunch – but I've had a suspicion for a long time now. I saw Dad once, just before the separation, talking to Stevie. They were out in the field, and Gudrun was there, picking elderflowers. Stevie was only about five at the time. I hadn't long known of his existence and I was curious to see whether he was like her. People had been gossiping in the pub about who his father might be. All sorts of filthy suggestions were flying around, that I didn't like at all. Anyway, I saw Dad put a hand on the boy's shoulder, just lightly, no big deal – but it stayed with me. Something about the image they made together, and then Gudrun looked over at them, and called Stevie away, and Dad came back to the house, and that was it. I couldn't make anything of it, but ever since then there's been a niggling idea at the back of my mind, which I could never quite squash.'

Thea heard that idea, loud and clear. 'You think Stevie might have been his son?' She felt dazzled by the numerous light bulbs going on inside her head. 'My God! That puts the whole thing in a completely different light. Have you ever told anybody?'

'Hold on!' Belinda leant back in the cushions and stared at the ceiling. 'Just hold on. It was only a fleeting idea, that's all. It's probably quite wrong. If Gudrun killed the boy, then that's all there is to it. She must have had a fit of madness or something. Or did it by mistake, trying to restrain him. I never should have said anything. My father has absolutely nothing to do with it. Obviously he hasn't.'

But Thea's mind wouldn't stop. 'But why *now*?' she demanded. 'What's changed to make it happen now, with Yvonne away and Victor between houses? Could it be that Victor asked for contact with his son? Has he threatened to tell Yvonne about it? Yes! That would make sense. At least—' The complications began to run away with her, and she stared frustratedly at her visitor. 'Sorry – I shouldn't talk like this about your parents, should I . . . ?' she tailed off.

'I have no idea what you're trying to suggest. You're making ridiculous stabs in the dark,' Belinda pointed out. 'Just guessing, on no basis at all. But I *do* want to make sure that Dad's all right. That's my main concern. After all, if Gudrun killed her own child, she might be capable of other terrible things. She might have gone to London to tell him Stevie was dead, and—'

Thea tilted her head enquiringly. 'You'd be perfectly justified in phoning the London police and asking them again to go and have a look. After all, it's already on their files, because Gladwin spoke to them again yesterday and passed on his address.'

'Gladwin?'

'The senior detective working on the case. I know her, actually. She's a good person.'

Belinda said nothing to this, but picked at her lip again.

'Do you know Blake-next-door?' Thea asked. 'Or his girlfriend?'

'I've met them a few times. Mum never stops talking about him. He seems very protective of her, listens to her complaining, admires all her dopey things. I sometimes wonder whether he just makes her worse.'

'How do you mean?'

'I think she might meet more people, find new things to do, if he left her alone a bit more. It always sounds a bit *pushy*, somehow, when she talks about him.'

Thea nodded. 'I know exactly what you mean,' she said. 'And what's the deal with the garden? He can't just hand over half his land without some sort of contract, can he? What happens if one of them wants to sell?'

'I know. But she won't be told. Says it suits them both perfectly, and anyway she can't cope with a lot of paperwork.'

'But she's a *teacher*,' Thea protested. 'I thought their whole job was managing paperwork.'

Belinda laughed. 'Ah, but she says it's the same stuff, term after term, and she just ticks the same boxes and hopes for the best. She's been doing it for twenty-odd years now. I guess it does get pretty routine.'

'Maybe,' said Thea doubtfully. 'Do you want another coffee?'

Belinda shook her head and eyed the mug balanced on the arm of the sofa. 'I haven't quite finished this one yet. I ought to be going, I suppose. It's been great talking to you, although I'm not sure we've come to any conclusions. In fact, I'm a lot more worried about my dad now than I was when I arrived. I suppose I could go and see if I can find him, but the *traffic*,' she groaned. 'North London can be awful.'

Thea's knowledge of London geography had scarcely been improved by her visit to Crouch End, but she did recall the basic layout. 'M25 and then straight down into Cricklewood,' she suggested diffidently. 'Isn't that the quickest way?'

'Is that how you went yesterday?'

'No, I used the train. But I did have a quick look at a road map, as well as the *A–Z*, when I was wondering how your mother was going to manage it, on Saturday. It looked reasonably easy, actually.'

'I hate it. Give me the good old A44 every time.'

Thea was reminded of Belinda's brother Mark, and his dubious movements on Sunday. 'You and Mark must use it a lot,' she suggested.

'We probably know every inch of it, between us. He told me he came here on Monday morning, of course. After what he said, I felt I had to come and see you for myself. We've never met a house-sitter before. He thought you must be getting rather bored by now.'

Thea smiled. 'I get used to it.'

Belinda made to get up, putting out a hand to lever herself out of the soft cushions and swiping the coffee mug onto the floor. 'Oh, damn,' she cried. 'Right on the lambskin rug. Quick – get a mop or something.'

The coffee was already spreading and soaking into the wool, but Thea felt little panic. 'It'll be okay,' she soothed. 'I'm sure it won't stain.' She had been aware of a slightly lumpy tissue or hanky in her pocket, as she'd been talking to Belinda, and now she reached in for it, thinking it would work as at least a preliminary cloth to wipe up the worst of the spillage. Belinda's peremptory order to run to the kitchen made her stubbornly resistant to any show of blind obedience. The visitor had made the mess, she knew where the mops and sponges were kept – let her go and find them.

'Here,' she said. 'Use this.' And she handed Belinda Parker a large dead mouse.

Chapter Eighteen

Belinda screamed with far more horrified terror than was necessary, in Thea's view. The soft grey-brown body lay in her hand, tiny feet curled tightly, tail stretched out. Thea's own sense of shocked revulsion had passed in seconds as she realised what must have happened in the night-time bathroom. 'Poor little thing,' she murmured. 'And I've been carrying it around all morning without realising.'

'Take it away! For God's sake – it's *dead*.'

'Surely that's preferable to being alive and running all over us?'

'But it was in your *pocket*.' Belinda was at the farthest edge of the room, her face white, her mouth a rectangle of disgust. 'How *could* you? That's so utterly gross.'

'The cat let it go last night, in the bathroom. It must have been injured, and crawled into my trousers to escape. Poor little thing,' Thea repeated. 'It's only a mouse.'

'I *hate* mice. They're revolting.'

'They're not as bad as hornets,' said Thea with some force. 'Blake says there's a nest in the roof and your mother doesn't want them removed. Compared to the sting of a hornet, a mouse is totally harmless. I'd far rather be bitten by a mouse than stung by a hornet. Besides, this little thing isn't going to hurt anybody.' She stroked the soft warm body, just to make her point, fully aware that she would never have normally shown such solicitude. On her own, she might have indulged a few more shivers of abhorrence at what she'd been carrying so close to her body for the past few hours.

'Throw it away,' Belinda pleaded. 'It's making me feel sick.'

'Okay. It's going. I'm sorry you're so freaked about it. I honestly had no idea it was in there. I thought it was a hanky.'

Somehow they got themselves outside, Belinda shakily conceding that she had made rather a lot of fuss. 'Lucky nothing else got knocked over,' she said. 'I must have flown across the room before I knew what I was doing.'

'Lucky my dog didn't cotton on to what was happening. You'd think she'd have detected a mouse in my pocket, wouldn't you? Useless thing. Although I suppose she just thought I knew what I was doing, and it was none of her business.'

Belinda smiled feebly at this. 'I imagine she's good company.'

'Oh yes,' Thea agreed fervently. 'She's definitely that.' She chirruped at the spaniel, who looked up from where she was sitting on the lawn, and wagged her long tail slowly.

When Belinda's car had finally disappeared from sight, Thea went back into the house, and mopped up the puddle of coffee. The lambskin seemed little the worse for the experience, but she decided to give it a careful wash in the bath, for good measure. It was obvious that Belinda had only taken a few sips of the disappointing instant. Thea found herself wondering whether she'd made a very good impression – being mean with the coffee and bizarrely harbouring a dead mouse in her pocket. Not to mention stirring up alarming visions of Belinda's father being attacked. 'I wonder what else I did wrong,' she muttered to herself as she carried the soggy sheepskin up the stairs.

At Peaceful Repose Burial Ground, Wednesday morning was considerably less eventful than it had been at Snowshill. Drew sat miserably in his office, waiting for the phone to ring. Maggs could barely bring herself to speak to him, and the gap where Karen should be had become a huge aching hole that seemed to grow bigger with every passing hour. He was desperate to talk to her, to explain how wrong Maggs was about almost everything – Thea, the future, Broad Campden, Cranham, the children, and Karen herself. He was equally desperate to understand how it was, there in that black silence inside Karen's head. Did she want permission to sink peacefully into permanent oblivion? Or did she still hope that Drew could magically save her, by the sheer force of his will? Or was all that wanting and hoping long gone, the cells dying and shrivelling and leaving only a husk?

He was an undertaker, for heaven's sake! He should have an instinctive grasp of all this stuff, having been party to so many deaths. He had even been at the bedside of hospice patients, hours before they died, assuring them they would receive the sort of funeral they desired. But they had all *talked* to him. Karen said nothing. And yet she breathed without assistance. Her heart continued to beat and her blood to flow. This prolonged limbo was far beyond his experience or his understanding. It was beyond language, too, despite his argument with Maggs. Mundane decisions about how Karen should be treated seemed to be entirely off the point. He had considered pleading with the doctors to open her head and delve deep into her brain to find the problem, all the time knowing this would be impossible. She would die, once and for all, under their probing scalpels. But at least they would have tried, and her death would be unambiguous. He suspected that the doctors too were tempted to hasten the end under the guise of trying one final time to cure her. Any activity was better than this stasis – even Maggs felt the power of that instinct. But you couldn't say it. The words would not come.

Stephanie had been odd over breakfast, playing with the food and banging her heels on the chair like a toddler. 'Is Mummy coming home soon?' she asked. 'Daddy, *is* she?'

'I don't think so, darling,' he had said, too far gone in hopelessness to offer her a platitude. 'I really don't think she is.'

'You mean she'll *die*?'

'I think so, Steph. We don't know for sure. Maggs thinks she might wake up one day. But I . . .'

Stephanie stared at her uneaten Weetabix. 'I see,' she said. 'Thank you, Daddy.' She looked up and met his eyes steadily. 'It's better to know, isn't it? Even when it's very bad, you do have to know.'

Drew was unsure whether she was merely quoting something she had heard an adult say, or whether she really felt the truth of it for herself. He nodded at her, and forced a smile. Stephanie reached a hand to her younger brother, who stared from face to face with large terrified eyes. 'It's okay, Tim,' she consoled. 'Mummy doesn't hurt. And, you know, everybody dies. We have to understand that.'

There speaks the child of an undertaker, thought Drew ruefully. Stephanie had weathered the death of a hamster with remarkable stoicism. When it came to her own mother, it seemed she took the same line. He felt admiration, concern and envy when he looked at her.

Timmy let out a great howl. 'No!' he wailed. 'Mummy won't die. I won't let Mummy die.' He looked again from sister to father with rage and despair. 'Daddy, you have to wake her up again.'

'Oh, Tim,' sighed Drew. 'I would if I could, but it's just too difficult.'

His little son scowled accusingly at him. 'Just try harder,' he said.

'I *have* tried, Tim. As hard as I could. Mummy has to try as well, but I think it's too late.' He bowed his head, and watched his shaking hands. He felt deathly cold.

'She can have a grave in the field, can't she? She'll be there all the time.'

He stared at the little girl. Not for a single moment had this thought occurred to him. He had not, then, faced the prospect of his wife's dying, not at all. The leap from her not waking up to being dead and buried had been too great. Stephanie was well ahead of him.

'Yes,' he said. Then he pushed back his chair and lunged for the child. 'Oh, Steph,' he sobbed, clutching her tightly to his chest.

She stroked him clumsily on his back, with a hand that was only free from the wrist. 'Don't squash me, Daddy,' she yelped.

'Do daddies cry?' asked Tim wonderingly.

With a vast effort, Drew took control again. 'Yes they do,' he replied. 'As you can see.'

'Maggs can look after us,' Stephanie suggested briskly. 'When you're too busy and Granny has gone back to her farm. We can manage.'

Of course, Drew reminded himself, they had had three years of a semi-absent mother. Karen had been unfocused, forgetful, inattentive ever since her original injury. Stephanie had dealt with this withdrawal by finding a substitute in Maggs, to some extent, and by cementing her already solid relationship with him, her father. Timmy had been the real loser. Timmy's deprivation was enormous and irredeemable. Drew felt very, very sorry for his little son.

Thea was trying to decide where her duties lay regarding the Parker family. The visits from both members of the younger generation felt acutely significant, even though she was unsure of precisely how. They seemed to be checking on her in some way, as if worried by something she might be doing. And she didn't think it was concern for the knick-knacks that motivated them.

Could it be the diaries? Did they know of their existence? It seemed improbable that they would care about jottings made by their mother ten years ago. Neither had even glanced at the bureau, so far as she had noticed. Did they not trust her to actually remain in place, after what had happened on Sunday? Did they . . . ? Her imagination ran dry at that point, and she sighed helplessly. Let Belinda go and find her father. That at least would be one puzzle resolved. In fact, on closer inspection, that now seemed to be the *only* remaining puzzle. Yvonne was in France. Gudrun was in custody. Blake was probably dozing after his early flight and Gladwin was completing all the prodigious paperwork associated with charging a woman with killing her own son.

Belinda's suspicions about Gudrun, Stevie and Victor had certainly been startling. Again, it took some concentrated thought to trace all the threads and conclude that here, finally, was a possible connection between the Horsfalls and the Parkers, beyond the proximity of their two houses. It required her to go over the exact timings of the past four days, just to work out who could have been where and when.

Why am I doing this? she asked herself, after a while. *What's the point?*

To exonerate Gudrun Horsfall, came the unambiguous reply. The police had got the wrong person, despite the stark evidence of Stevie's missing shoe which convinced them that Gudrun was guilty. There could be other explanations for that – the most obvious one being that somebody had deliberately placed the shoe in Gudrun's house to cast suspicion on her.

Ideas could come at lightning speed, sometimes. Or they could take days to form themselves and push their tentative little heads above the surface of the unconscious mind. The shock and horror of Gladwin's announcement that Gudrun was to be charged had paralysed some of Thea's thought processes. It was too big a disaster for her to contemplate, the emotions too excruciatingly raw. The conversation with Clara Beauchamp had been close to unbearable, with the image of the struggling child fighting for his life. It had sent Thea's mind into hiding, where all such imaginings were firmly tucked away.

But now the dam was breaking and a whole lot of suspicions came tumbling through the breach. Somebody had framed Gudrun. Somebody had attacked Victor. Mark, she remembered, had dissembled as to his whereabouts at the weekend. And even Blake had changed his plans, with no credible explanation. Mark and Belinda were worried about something connected with Hyacinth House and their mother. Janice and Ruby generated many questions. And poor little Stevie was irreversibly dead. Thea could no longer just sit tight and let things drift. It wasn't in her nature. She had to do something, and talk to somebody.

And the only candidate for that discussion was Drew Slocombe.

She couldn't just phone him, she decided. It was only the day before that they had indulged in their childish escapade, and as they parted at Paddington, they both acknowledged that it could not mark any deepening of their friendship. It was obvious that he had more than enough to cope with at home, and there was no real reason for further contact, with things as they were.

There were times when house-sitting felt like imprisonment, with the implacable routines of animal feeding making sure she was on duty at given times. And hadn't Yvonne asked her to keep an eye on the cows in the field at the back, as well? She had done no more than cast a quick eye over them since Saturday. If one was lame or sick, would anybody know? Their owner, Yvonne had made clear, was the person ultimately responsible for them, but she had implied that daily monitoring was down to the occupant of Hyacinth House.

Everything seemed to be normal when she went to the gate and looked over into the field. Five handsome beasts lay quietly chewing their cud under a spreading oak tree. Whilst it wasn't possible to scrutinise their legs or gait, the picture of idyllic contentment was quite enough to reassure her. Stevie's stones had only made glancing contact, as far as she had been able to judge. It was the *intention* that she had taken such exception to, the idea that a child could actively wish to inflict pain on an animal.

The theories that had arisen when Gladwin told her about Stevie's shoe re-emerged now: the possibility that Stevie's killer had crossed this field with him, as the quickest way from the Horsfalls' cottage. Looking at it now, she wasn't sure it really would be quicker, unless the killing had taken place in the field itself. Then it would have been easy to use the gate into Yvonne's garden, and past the house into the road beyond. As far as she could tell, there was no matching gate at the further end of the field – no direct access from the cottage.

If she was serious about proving that somebody else, other than his mother, had killed the boy, then details of place and timing became crucial. Both Blake Grossman and Mark Parker could have been lurking around Snowshill at the time Stevie was killed, while maintaining alibis that they were elsewhere entirely. Both knew Gudrun and her boy and it wasn't too hard to imagine motives for killing him. The main problem was that they both seemed too soft and sensitive to do such a thing. Blake less so, after his snappy words on Saturday, but surely the boneless Mark could never do such a thing.

And yet she knew that people could dissemble, hiding their malice and obsessions under bland smiling exteriors. Trust was often found to be misplaced. In recent years she had really liked people who turned out to be killers. The role of a house-sitter was convenient in that respect – the friendships she formed were temporary and provisional. Even when she thought she had found a real chum in Ariadne Fletcher, during her stay at Cold Aston and again in Lower Slaughter, their relationship had soon foundered on the realities of lies and violence. She was very tempted to go home to her old friend Celia and her daughter Jessica and a few other stalwarts, and forget the tribulations of the latest commission in a gorgeous Cotswold village.

But she couldn't forget Drew Slocombe. He was beginning to feel like a constant, despite their geographical separation.

It was 1.15, time for lunch, and she always tried to maintain at least some sort of daily structure designed around meals. Too much free time and too few distractions could lead to very sloppy habits, especially in someone else's house. She made herself a sandwich, with some slightly stale sliced bread and cheese. 'We can go shopping later on,' she told the spaniel. 'There's hardly any food left.'

Ever since Belinda had gone, there had been a growing sense of waiting for a report on what had been found at Victor's flat. How long did it take to drive to Crouch End? She had asked herself the same thing on Saturday, when Yvonne failed to turn up as planned. She went out to her car and brought in the road map, plotting the most obvious route.

Initially, she had assumed that this led down to the M4, then around the M25 to the M1 and down into north London that way. But then she realised that the A44 took you to Oxford, and then the M40 connected to the M25 not far from where the A4 did. And that would almost certainly be quicker. Two hours could do it easily, if there were no hold-ups. And Belinda loved the A44. Whatever her mother might have decided, Belinda would take the latter route, and might well be in Crouch End already. It had been eleven when she left Hyacinth House.

What would she find when she got there? Suddenly it seemed hugely important to know. No further theorising could be fruitfully entertained until Victor's whereabouts were established. Except that theorising came to Thea as naturally as breathing, and the more she tried to curtail it, the more it persisted. For example, if Belinda's idea of his being Stevie's father had any basis in fact, then he might have been in the habit of making secret visits to Gudrun and the boy. He might have done so on Sunday, having only pretended that Yvonne had stayed all morning at his flat. He might have had some reason to want the child out of his life. Financial claims, jealous new girlfriend, family complications . . . but that would give Mark and Belinda motives of their own, as well. Suddenly the very suggestion of Victor's paternity brought oceans of implications, involving just about everybody Thea had met.

She realised she was fitting puzzle pieces together that might well belong to a completely different picture. Poor old Blake, for one. He showed no sign of having any reason to kill Stevie. Unless . . . The more she considered, the more unsure she became about him. A whole list of possible motives came unbidden to her mind. She knew so little of the background history, of how Blake and Yvonne really felt towards each other, where Eloise fitted in, and what any of them truly thought about Gudrun Horsfall. Gudrun was a single woman with an obvious passion for life. She herself admitted to a wholly groundless local reputation as a loose woman, to give it an old-fashioned characterisation. She had also denied it in extreme terms, claiming to have had the most minimal of sex lives. Perhaps she had been lying. Perhaps Blake lusted after her, but saw Gudrun's boy as an impediment.

'This way madness lies,' she muttered to herself, after fifteen steamy minutes spent mentally slandering half a dozen people. 'Where are the *facts*?'

There were very few hard facts. Stevie had lost a shoe, around the time he died. Again the image of him kicking out as he was being strangled forced itself into her mind. Had Gudrun killed him in her own house, then? That was apparently what the case against her would claim. The murder weapon had been cut from a length of washing line, the remainder found in Gudrun's garden shed, despite her firm assertion that she had never owned such a thing. Was that another element in the plot to frame her? Stevie had been essentially out of control, his mother inevitably blamed and criticised for her failure as a parent. Nobody had yet admitted to having liked him. And Gudrun had steadfastly refused to reveal who his father was. Furthermore, Belinda's suspicion on that subject could be wholly illusory, based on a few seconds of biased observation.

The house phone rang at 2.45, just as Thea had finally settled down in the garden, despite the cloudy weather. She had been to Broadway for some supplies, including two books from the bookshop there. The expedition had taken just over an hour – much less than intended, but the sense of restless waiting had not abated, and she felt she was being neglectful in moving out of earshot of Yvonne's phone. Too few people had her mobile number – not Belinda or Blake, anyway.

'It's me. Belinda,' came a strained voice. 'It's just struck me that you'll be wondering what happened.'

'Yes, I was. How thoughtful of you.'

'Not at all. The police will be after you soon, anyway. I'm going to tell them what you did yesterday.' The tone had hardened into something like accusation.

'What do you mean?'

'He's *dead*. That's what I mean. My father – stabbed to death. I *found* him. There's blood everywhere.' For a woman who had screamed at the sight of a mouse, she sounded amazingly calm.

Thea herself was stunned into silence. She tried to think. It could be barely two hours since the woman had made her ghastly discovery, and here she was phoning her mother's house-sitter? 'Where are you now?' she asked.

'At a police station. Waiting to be interviewed. I'm going to tell them all about you,' she repeated.

'That's okay. I've got nothing to hide. I tried to tell them myself, but they didn't seem very interested.'

'You *heard* it, for God's sake. You heard the whole thing as it happened. Dad's mobile is on the floor beside him, with a dead battery.' Hysteria was now audible, and Thea's own heart rate began to accelerate painfully.

'I did my best,' she blustered. 'I told Gladwin and she asked the London people to go and check. But they couldn't find him.'

'You found the house yesterday. Why didn't you try to get in? You just walked away, with nothing accomplished. How do you explain that?'

'You wouldn't understand,' said Thea hopelessly. 'I'm not sure I do myself. I *was* worried about Victor. And then that nanny girl seemed to think there was nothing to worry about, so we just came home again.'

'Who's *we*?'

'Me and my friend Drew. He's not relevant.'

'Everybody's relevant now,' said Belinda darkly. 'This is a terrible murder.'

A double murder, thought Thea, remembering Stevie Horsfall.

Chapter Nineteen

Even as she was speaking to Belinda, her mobile began to ring. 'I expect that's Gladwin now,' she said.

'Who?'

'The local CID superintendent. She'll have heard what's happened. Listen, Belinda – I'm terribly sorry about your father. It's dreadful. Tell the police your end everything I've said. I'll help in any way I can. And your mother – she's going to have to be told as well.'

'Never mind her,' said Belinda hollowly. 'It's Mark that worries me most. This is going to destroy him.' Her voice broke with emotion, as Thea grabbed the mobile and took the call.

'Bye, Belinda. I have to go now,' she said, switching ears like someone in a farcical office comedy. 'Hello?' she said into the mobile.

'Thea? I've just had the Met onto me. About Victor Parker.'

'He's dead. I know,' she said. 'His daughter just called me.'

'This is bad, Thea. For the police, I mean. I have a logged call here to say you heard violence occurring at 9.00pm on Monday while speaking to Mr Victor Parker. Two days later, his daughter finds his body. In the meantime, you actually went to the house in question.'

'But the house isn't registered in his name. He rents a flat in it – or his girlfriend does. How could anybody have found him?'

'You did,' said Gladwin flatly.

But Thea did not respond. *Girlfriend* was echoing in her head. 'Where is she? The woman he was living with? Why didn't she report the attack?'

'What?' said Gladwin.

'She must have been the one who screamed. She must have been in another room when it happened. After the killer had gone, she came out and found him. Why in the world didn't she call the police or an ambulance?'

'Thea, you were on the end of a phone. You couldn't see what was going on. She must have been the one who did it. Do you know her name?'

'I can't remember. Something fancy. Like Floella, but not. Ask Belinda.'

'They'll have done that. It's not my case. Except . . .' she tailed off miserably. 'Thea Osborne, this is a bloody horrible mess, and I can't help thinking I should blame you.'

'Feel free,' Thea invited. 'I have much the same feeling myself. Although I *did*—'

'Yes, yes. You told me you'd heard something. And I told the Met. And they couldn't find him. All nicely logged into the bargain. But he's been lying there for two days, damn it.'

'Nobody reported screams?'

'Nope. Look – you'll be needed for a statement.'

'In London?'

'Probably not. Just don't go anywhere, okay.'

'Don't worry. Belinda says he was stabbed. Is that right?'

'Belinda? The daughter. You know her?'

'Only since this morning. She called in for coffee.'

'God, Thea, it's impossible to keep pace with you. You told her about the cries you heard, right, and she went to investigate?'

'Precisely. I assume she had a key to the flat and just walked in on her dead father.'

'It *must* have been the girlfriend. Do you know where she's from?'

'The Philippines, I think. Somewhere like that.' Gladwin made the wordless *chhssk* of disgust that wives across the land expressed at such relationships.

'I know,' said Thea. 'Apparently it's on the increase.'

'We can talk about that another time. I suspect it's our own fault – we've made too many demands on the poor dears.'

'But she *screamed*. I don't think it was her who killed him.' Regret flickered through her. It would be all too comfortably neat if the girlfriend could be found and prosecuted for killing her sugar daddy. But it simply did not fit with everything she knew.

'At least we know Gudrun didn't do it. She was here with me at the time.'

Gladwin's bewilderment was palpable, even down the phone. 'What? Damn it, Thea – why in heaven's name would she kill him?'

'There's a suggestion that Stevie was Victor's child. You could do a DNA test to prove it either way.'

'We can *ask* her. That might be quicker, and definitely cheaper.'

Thea chuckled, enjoying the detective's wit, as always. 'Maybe she still secretly loved him and paid somebody to go and murder him.'

'Stop it. Nobody does that sort of thing.' Uncertainty now filled her voice. 'This is turning complicated, just when I thought we had it all sewn up. You're not thinking that possibly *Victor* killed the boy, are you? That Gudrun realised, and got him killed in revenge?'

'It did occur to me, about half a minute ago. But you've got the shoe evidence, haven't you? How would that fit in?'

'They could have done it together. A pact to dispose of their impossible kid, who was making their lives unbearable.'

'No,' said Thea emphatically. 'That's going too far.'

'You're right. I think. Although . . . Listen, I'll have to go now. But you have to make a full statement, with every tiny detail of that phone call. The Met are going to want it. Victor Parker was a wealthy businessman, you know. This one has to be big. The papers are going to love it. Anything involving these Asian babes makes great headlines. There'll be columns giving every angle on it. Look at the way you and I are so keen to talk about it. It'll be the same for everyone. They'll assume he met her on the Internet and shipped her over to be a sort of sex slave.'

'He's got a cleaning lady already.'

'How the hell do you know that?'

'I *told* you. I spoke to the nanny from across the street. There's a whole network of them, all related or friendly. I suppose they get jobs for each other. It's like the mid-nineteenth century all over again.' The historian in Thea was beginning to find some fascination in the modern version of the upstairs-downstairs scenario.

'Slow down. Look, there's a message just come through from London about your statement. Can you be here by three-thirty?'

'Barely. You mean Cirencester, I assume?'

'No, of course not. We've set up an incident room in Broadway. Didn't I tell you? We were going to take it all down today, but there've been a few delays. Maybe just as well, as it turns out.'

'Where in Broadway?'

'There's a little school. Turn right and then left. You'll find it.'

'I was in Broadway only an hour or two ago,' Thea complained.

'Sorry,' said Gladwin unapologetically.

The fact of a violent and mysterious murder in London was a lot less viscerally distressing than finding a child's body only yards from the house she was occupying. It was more of an intellectual puzzle than anything else. She examined her conscience and found it to be relatively clear. After all, she had dutifully reported the alarming phone call to the police, and, for good measure, done her best to check for herself that nothing too terrible had happened. Nobody could have done any more. She had even conveyed her worries to Belinda at the first opportunity. It was very much thanks to her that the body had been found – although presumably the cleaning lady would eventually have shown up and made the discovery. She must be very much part-time, Thea concluded, sharing Victor with a number of other clients.

She had to go through the centre of Snowshill to get to Broadway, passing the pub and the church and the Manor and all the lovely little cottages. Within minutes she was passing Broadway's church on her left and turning into the main street that so many tourists found irresistible, but which left Thea rather unmoved. The only part of Broadway she admired was the cul-de-sac at the eastern end of the high street, where the houses were seriously gorgeous and historic.

The road took her round a bend to the left, and to the school where Gladwin was waiting for her.

The interview was recorded, and although everyone was perfectly friendly, with the detective superintendent the same as always, there was a subtle atmosphere of wary reproach. Why, she could hear them wondering, did this woman always know so much? Was she a witch? Or the cleverest possible arch-criminal? What amazing skill did she possess, whereby she landed herself in the midst of one murder investigation after another, all too often identifying the villain ahead of everybody else?

Thea herself had asked these questions many times. In Cranham, the glimmerings of an explanation had begun to emerge. The laws of cause and effect were working in the reverse direction from that which people assumed. The presence of a house-sitter acted as an enabling element in the minds of those plotting a crime. The normal systems were disrupted, leaving a gap for evildoing. It was a realisation that brought some shock with it. Taken to its logical conclusion, it would spell the end of her career before very much longer. The police would start to follow her from in front, as it were, staking out anywhere she was in charge of, in the expectation of a murder. No self-respecting householder was going to stand for that. Even with the positive spin she had managed to put on it – whereby she did at least help to catch the killer and restore order – the stain never quite went away. In Frampton Mansell and Temple Guiting, as well as Cold Aston and Cranham, she had been instrumental in blackening a few characters whom nobody had suspected of anything at all illicit.

And now, in Snowshill, it seemed to be worse than ever before. She was right in the heart of the murders, virtually witnessing them as they took place. Anybody but Gladwin might have harboured serious suspicions as to her culpability.

'Is there anything else?' the DS asked her, after twenty minutes of questions. 'Even if it's only guesses.'

Thea pondered, trying to review the five days since she arrived in Snowshill. Fragmentary images were viewed and dismissed: the long-legged black dog in the churchyard, the ghosts in the Manor and the pub, Janice and Ruby fretting over their garden and the feeling of being under siege, Yvonne's ridiculous clutter, Gudrun winning international swimming races, the surreal dead mouse in her pocket . . . 'No, I don't think so,' she said, before adding, 'You'll speak to Blake Grossman, I suppose? He says he was in Ankara on a trade delegation.'

Gladwin looked away quickly, as if caught off guard by mention of the name. But she instantly recovered, with a wry smile. 'Don't worry. We're speaking to *everybody* – again.'

'Especially Gudrun,' Thea suggested with an unhappy shiver. 'Do you think this throws doubt on whether she really did kill Stevie?'

Gladwin pursed her lips and said nothing.

'I'll never be able to believe it,' Thea said. 'In spite of the evidence, I can't imagine her doing it. You didn't see her when I did. It feels almost criminal to accuse her of such a terrible thing.'

'You'll make a great witness for the defence,' said Gladwin glumly.

'How is she? Is anybody looking after her?'

The DS raised her eyebrows. 'She's in custody, of course. Solitary, for her own good. She obviously isn't happy, but I'm not sure that being in a cell is making it very much worse than it was already. She's shown a few fits of temper, I gather.'

'I'm not surprised. If somebody has killed her only child, you'd expect her to be out for revenge.'

'It's not that sort of temper. It's directed at us, "for being such fools", to use her own words.'

'Poor Gudrun.' Thea's throat was thick with the sympathy she felt. 'I'm tempted to agree with her, to be honest, even if you do think you've got damning evidence against her. I think she was framed.'

Gladwin glanced uneasily at the tape machine, still running. She held up a hand, and dictated, 'Interview terminated at 4.04 p.m.' Then she switched it off. 'Sorry – I should have done that five minutes earlier. That's going to lead to a few awkward questions.'

'Oh?' Thea frowned in puzzlement.

'You mentioned the evidence against Gudrun. You're not supposed to know about that.'

'Oops!'

'It's my own fault. Don't worry – I can swing it . . . probably. You didn't go into any detail, luckily. It depends on how this whole business turns out, of course.'

Thea glanced around at the school hall where they were sitting at a small table, with makeshift screens erected for a degree of privacy. She had seen these ad hoc incident rooms before, set up in any local space large enough to accommodate computers, whiteboards, telephones, and a team of dedicated police officers. Ideally this one would be in Snowshill itself, but nobody was going to expect the National Trust to accede to the use of their precious Manor, and the pub was hardly suitable.

What was happening in Crouch End, she wondered? Maybe there was a similarly empty primary school, although she doubted it. There would be busy holiday clubs and urgent staff meetings, probably throughout the summer holiday. Even in Somerset, Drew had said there was an activity week coming up shortly, which his children were signed up for.

'Can I go now?' she asked.

* * *

Late afternoons had always been Thea's least favourite time of day. The long evening still stretched ahead, with its limited options, the events of the day bringing strands of emotion that had to be processed. Summarising the day so far, the word 'surprise' seemed to be pre-eminent. Surprise that first Blake and then Belinda had come to the door of Hyacinth House, and something bigger and nastier than surprise at Belinda's subsequent discovery in Crouch End.

But there was also surprise at her own responses. The suggestions and implications that perhaps Gudrun was after all innocent of killing her boy brought hope with them, and some flickers of excitement at having a new mystery to think about. It was shameful, surely, to feel anything positive in the face of such dreadful happenings. She ought to be deep in sympathetic misery for the losses endured by the survivors. The trouble was, she realised, that at that precise moment she had no idea which survivors were deserving of her compassion. Somebody had done wicked and terrible things, and it might well be one of the people she had spoken to during the past week.

It was five o'clock when she finally allowed herself to phone Drew, after ten minutes of inner wrangling. It was an unequal contest – of course there was no earthly reason not to update him on the news, after his involvement the previous day. With luck Maggs would have gone home, and so not catch him speaking to his forbidden friend. He might be getting tea for his children, or watching them play outside, or finalising the business of the day. She had only briefly glimpsed his burial ground and the house and office that formed part of the same property, but it was enough to be able to imagine him in a variety of activities.

'Peaceful Repose Burials,' he recited into the phone. Thea tried to put herself in the shoes of a recently bereaved person, looking for a funeral, and could not help feeling that Drew fell somewhere short of the ideal. His tone was flat and automatic, as if he was thinking about something else entirely.

Which he almost certainly was, of course.

'It's me. Thea,' she said. 'Doesn't your phone tell you who's calling?'

'Yes, yes, but I just grabbed it without looking properly. The sun's on the screen, so I can't read it easily.'

'Are you okay?'

'More or less, if living in a perpetual state of limbo can be okay. I had rather an awful conversation with the kids this morning, and we haven't entirely recovered from it yet. And Maggs is falling apart. She found out where I went yesterday and that led to a whole lot of aggravation. It's been like a long line of dominoes knocking each other over. And it's still going on. I have to go to the hospital soon, with all that that involves.'

'I feel as if some of it at least might be sort of my fault,' she suggested.

'Maggs would agree with you.'

'And you?'

'I don't know. I don't think my judgement can be relied on just at the moment. Why did you phone?'

'Victor Parker's dead. He was right there in that house, stabbed to death, as we stood outside talking to that nanny.'

Drew said nothing for several seconds. 'Are you

sure?' he finally managed. 'That seems incredible.'

'I did tell you about hearing him cry out and a woman screaming. I *knew* it was something serious, but somehow talked myself out of getting too concerned. Everything there seemed so ordinary and normal, didn't it?'

'I'm not sure I know what's normal for places like that – but yes, I suppose it did. So you're a kind of witness to *two* murders now.' He almost sounded envious, and Thea gave a short huff of laughter.

'I sort of am, yes. At least I did everything right – contacted the police, as well as actually *going* to London. I think they should regard me as a model citizen. Obviously now there's a massive murder investigation, with the Metropolitan people taking over, and media coverage and all sorts.'

'And a rethink about the little boy in your village,' he said slowly. 'I assume.'

'Right. Although I have a nasty feeling they'll do their best to pin both murders on Gudrun. Then nobody loses face.'

Drew made a low moan. 'I can't.'

'Can't what? What do you mean?'

'I can't get involved. I can't even let you tell me about it any more. There's too much happening here. The children need me, even with Karen's mother here.'

'Is she staying all through the holiday?'

'We don't know. She'll have to be back and forth from North Wales, if so. Her husband's having an awful time without her, or so he says. They're both in pieces over Karen, of course.'

'But she must be quite useful?'

'Oh yes,' he sighed. 'She does free me and Maggs up to get some work done, at least. But the business can't stand a lot more of this. We hardly dare book any funerals at all, in case we won't manage to be here at the right time on the right day. Look at yesterday – I came within a whisker of missing that one.'

'Which had nothing to do with Karen,' she reminded him with a pang of guilt. 'I do see what you mean about me and my problems being one demand too many.'

'"Demand" isn't the right word,' he corrected. 'Not exactly.'

'I think it is,' she argued gently. 'I think it's exactly the right word. Look – call me any time you think I can help. Just to dump on, that sort of thing. Apart from that, I don't really see . . .' She didn't know what she had intended to say, but he understood anyway.

'No,' he said. 'Thanks, Thea. Good luck with your murders.'

Chapter Twenty

Maggs had watched Drew closely all day, while trying not to let him notice she was doing so. Her tearful outburst the previous evening had left her feeling ashamed and resentful in equal measure. And frightened. Peaceful Repose was all the life she knew, and she retained undimmed her high ambitions for it. So what if progress had been so halting since they opened nearly seven years ago? They were still in business, still attracting customers from a wide area, and even an object of some local pride. The Slocombe family had taken her into their midst, from the outset. Drew had always treated her as an equal partner, permitting her into his personal life without question. He had rejoiced when she and Den had got together, having been there from the first moments. His children regarded her as something between an aunt and a big sister, and she cared deeply about their welfare. She worried about Timmy, disapproving of Drew's obvious preference for his daughter.

There had been moments when Maggs had worried

for the Slocombe marriage, especially when Drew became inappropriately entangled with a woman named Genevieve, nearly ten years his senior. Then another, even older, named Roma, had become a close friend. Drew liked women rather too much at times. And they liked him with his open face and ready smile, even if he was an undertaker. They trusted him to accept their emotional turmoil without running away as many men did. They responded eagerly to his perfect mix of competence and sympathy. Maggs had learnt from him in countless ways. Born to be an undertaker herself, seeking out a job in a local funeral director's while still at school, she was already halfway there when she went into the partnership with Drew. He had smoothed her rougher edges, whilst nurturing her unique manner that customers found so appealing. Maggs was not afraid to laugh, to ask the pertinent question, and to answer the uncomfortable ones.

But now it was all collapsing around them. Everything was going wrong at once. Karen might die, leaving the children entirely to Drew's care. He would not be able to continue with the business, if that happened. Already it was losing custom, people being regretfully turned away, which would have been utterly unthinkable six months ago. There was also the new burial ground supposed to be opening in the Cotswolds, which Maggs had initially resisted, but soon come to regard as potentially important to the growth of Peaceful Repose. Drew had talked about moving there with his family, leaving Maggs to run North Staverton on her own. They would have to employ people, at least part-time, and expand their advertising and promotional work. What would happen to all that now?

Since her encounter with the Osborne woman and her seductive little dog, a whole new ocean of worry had threatened to swamp Maggs. The woman was lovely – any man would fall for her at first glance, and Maggs had a horrible feeling that Drew had done just that. He had actually told lies to her and to Karen in the days following his first encounter with her, up there in Broad Campden. The Cotswolds now carried a bright-red danger sign in Maggs's mind. She forced herself to jump ahead to a future without Karen, with Drew moving himself and the kids up to the new cemetery, sharing a house with this woman and forgetting all about Maggs and Den. It seemed all too horribly possible. Even Den, her stalwart husband, carried little conviction when he tried to persuade her that her fears were groundless.

She and Den had finally married earlier that year, in a low-key ceremony that echoed the low-key funerals she believed in so completely. They had spent almost no money on it, apart from a rather startling honeymoon in Syria. 'Just to be different,' she had joked to Drew and others. In fact it had been beyond fabulous. They had seen things hitherto undreamt of and the people had been so magically hospitable that Den had taught himself some basic Arabic during the trip, in an effort to express his admiration for them.

She and Den were different enough already, of course. He was pure Devon, six feet five, tawny-haired and reddish-skinned. She was half black, half white, five feet three and plump. Her adoptive parents had lived in Plymouth for most of their lives, content to marvel at the clever little cuckoo they had bravely introduced into their home. When she asserted her intention to become an undertaker, they had not objected. The family had moved to Somerset and Maggs had forced herself on Daphne Plant, proprietor of a large funeral directing company in Bradbourne.

There were other worries lurking, too. Her father wasn't well, having recently been diagnosed with diabetes. Den was treading water career-wise, and had been for years. And he had starting speaking wistfully about babies.

Maggs had decided from the outset that she never wanted babies. She thought she had made that clear. The discovery that he had not entirely believed her had come as quite a shock.

And so she watched Drew as he plodded through the day, spending long minutes in the office doing nothing, holding his head in his hands. He seemed to her broken in some dreadful incurable way, having lost hope for Karen's recovery. She wanted to make him smile, to remind him that life went on, that he had walked beside people in the same situation many a time, and helped them take their next steps without the loved one who had died.

But Karen had not died – that was the heart of the trouble. She hovered on the brink, but she was still in the world. And Maggs for one continued to believe that she might yet return to them. Whilst forcing herself to listen to Drew's hopelessness, and accept its logic, she still thought he was wrong. Somewhere in another reality, Karen was still fighting and thinking and listening and loving. Behind some horrible thick curtain, she was groping for a way to return, and she needed Drew's steady encouragement to do that. If he gave up on her, then it was as if he had killed her. And if Maggs could see the truth of that, then Stephanie and Timmy probably could as well. And none of them might ever forgive him.

Thea felt trapped and confused by the events of the day. It had taken her hours to remember Yvonne, whose husband was now dead, and who ought to be tracked down in France and informed of the disaster. She had gone off on the Eurostar oblivious of what had been taking place behind her, in the London flat she had so recently visited. Had they settled anything regarding Belinda's wedding? She had sounded reasonably cheerful on the phone, as if something had been resolved and she was free to indulge in a little holiday. Now she would presumably have to be consulted about the funeral of the murdered man, even if they were divorced. She, Belinda and Mark together would be the chief mourners. The exotic girlfriend, however devoted, would be relegated to a distant pew at the back, assuming she ever turned up again and managed to exonerate herself of his murder. Her current whereabouts was just another burning question in the whole bewildering story.

It seemed reasonable to assume that Belinda would be the one to inform her mother and brother as to what had happened. After all, she had gone to the trouble of phoning the house-sitter only a couple of hours after the discovery of the body, sounding to be in full control of herself. So Thea could be excused from any such task. It definitely wasn't down to her, she decided.

The evening was much brighter than the day had been, with the low sun illuminating the garden beautifully. As usual, Thea threw open the front door, wanting to catch the light and air and bring them into the house. Along with them, however, came loud thumping music, which was far less desirable. Blake-next-door must have turned his sound system up to the maximum, something that came as an unwelcome surprise. He surely must know that it would spread across the shared garden and into Hyacinth House. Had he always done it, with Yvonne's blessing? Or was he making some peculiar point, aimed at Thea herself? There was something aggressive, almost malign, in the discordant bass notes and the harsh yowling vocals that accompanied it. It made her think of the awful things men could do if they were somehow turned away from goodness and decency. It conjured words like *hate* and *assault*. She most definitely did not like it.

But was she justified in going over and complaining about it? It was still daylight, so she couldn't possibly claim that it was disturbing her sleep. She couldn't even pretend to be trying to concentrate on anything important. And yet it was an intrusion, a nagging reminder that he was there and that she could not trust him. She should close her door, and perhaps even lock it, because Blake Grossman might be a murderer. But then, *anybody* out there might be a murderer. Somebody had killed Stevie, that much was certain. Just as they'd killed Victor Parker – although that was in London, which could be viewed as a very different country.

She did go to close the door, but met a willowy figure on the threshhold. 'How can you bear it?' Janice demanded angrily. 'We can hear it right across the road. Come with me, and we'll make him turn it off.' Hepzie approached and did her usual annoying scrabble at Janice's lower legs. 'Your dog's all right, I see. I didn't come over yesterday. You were back by four.'

'Yes.'

'So – come on. Let's do it.' She took a step towards Blake's house, but stopped when Thea held her ground.

'Oh . . . I don't know. It's not late, is it? I think he'll turn it down before long.'

Janice looked at her sceptically. 'You don't know him,' she said.

'That's true. Even so – why don't you come into the kitchen and have a drink, or something? If we shut the door, we'll scarcely be able to hear it.'

'Wimp,' Janice accused, with a mitigating smile. 'You're scared of making a fuss.'

'There's been more than enough fuss over the past few days already,' said Thea feelingly. 'I'm not keen to make even more trouble.'

'Isn't it all pretty well resolved now? It said on the news that Gudrun was under arrest. They showed a whole lot of stuff about her swimming career, and hinted that she had a doubtful reputation locally. I imagine you've seen it?'

'No, I couldn't bear to. Did they interview anybody

from the village? There's usually some old codger who says they'd always suspected something sinister.'

'Actually no. Not a one. We're not like that in Snowshill.'

'When the media realise the link with Victor, they'll be trying all over again, I suppose.' She spoke absently, almost to herself, shuddering at the prospect of more reporters and cameras trying to formulate a story ahead of the police investigation. It took a moment to notice Janice's reaction.

'*Victor?* Victor Parker? What link do you mean?'

'Oh, damn. I'm probably not supposed to say anything. As usual.'

'What? You've got to tell me.'

'You knew him, then.'

'We were neighbours for twenty years, for God's sake. Of course I knew him.' Janice checked herself. '*Knew?* Why the past tense?'

'He's dead,' said Thea, not especially gently. 'Somebody killed him on Monday. They've only just found the body.'

Janice folded up like a collapsed string puppet, landing on a kitchen chair by sheer good fortune. 'Jesus!' she gasped. 'That's incredible.' She wiped a large hand across her lower face, rubbing at her mouth. 'It must have been Gudrun, thinking he'd killed their kid.'

'So Stevie really was Victor's?' A thread of excitement quivered inside her. Was everything to be suddenly explained by this woman?

Janice nodded. 'I think Yvonne must have found out, which explains why she forced him to leave.'

Thea considered this for some moments. 'That would

be unbearable – for her and for Gudrun. Wouldn't it? How could they go on living so close together?' She remembered Belinda's disclosure. 'I don't think Yvonne could possibly have known. Did she ever say anything to you about why they separated?'

Janice shook her head. 'I just had to guess, the same as everybody else. I only know it was very sudden.'

'So Victor kept the secret as well. Wasn't that rather noble of him?'

Janice pulled a face. 'Selfish, more like. Worried about his image. "Deny everything" is Victor's motto.'

Again, Thea rummaged through her memory, grasping at snippets of conversation that might be assembled and formed into a coherent picture. 'Hmm . . . ?' she said.

Janice's eyes had somehow elongated, her skin turned grey. 'Dead,' she muttered. 'After all this time spent hating him. I almost feel as if I'd done it myself.'

For a moment, Thea almost thought the same thing. 'I went to his flat yesterday,' she said. 'That's where I was going.'

'But you didn't find him? You said that was today, didn't you? Finding his body, I mean.'

'Right. Belinda.'

Janice inhaled deeply and gripped her big bony hands together. When she spoke, it was with her gaze focused intently on the tabletop. 'He never acknowledged her, not for a second. Just acted as if nothing had happened. He was such a swine!' She looked up at Thea, who was standing close beside her. 'A villain. That's what I called him to myself. Victor the Villain.'

'He was Ruby's father?' Thea hazarded. 'Is that what you're saying?' She hardly needed the slow nod the woman gave in reply. 'And he lived here, right across the road? How was that possible? Didn't Yvonne know? Didn't *Ruby* know?'

'It isn't so unusual. The trick is never to let anybody guess the truth. So you tell some convincing lies. Luckily, I was away a lot at the time, so it was easy to invent a fling with a married businessman in a conference hotel. Happens all the time.'

'Were you living on your own in that big house? How old were you? Under thirty, anyway.'

'Not on my own. My father was still alive. It was his house. He only died last year. Dear old Daddy.' She went misty. 'He was terribly good with Ruby. I was sorry to lie to him, but it was for the best. Hell's teeth – fancy bloody Victor being *dead*. I still can't believe it.'

'So – you knew about Stevie, but Gudrun didn't know about Ruby? That they were brother and sister?'

Janice shook her head. 'I didn't *know* about Stevie. I just guessed. The kid had a look of him. Something about his feet, as well. The toes turned out. Not the kind of thing most people notice.'

'Were there any more, do you think?' Thea asked recklessly. 'Is the village full of little Victors? And I still don't understand why it had to be such a secret.'

Janice squared her shoulders. 'I'm not aware of any more,' she said with dignity. 'The secret was because of Belinda and Mark, primarily. They were both adopted, you see, because Yvonne was sterile. I couldn't do anything

292

to harm them. Besides, I had my pride,' she added.

'Then you think Yvonne found out about Stevie and threw Victor out.'

'That's what I imagined must have happened, yes. But you've made me wonder, now. It was all very sudden and shocking. One moment they were the ideal couple, the next he was driving off with two suitcases and never came back.'

'Didn't Yvonne ever tell anybody what had happened?'

'Not to my knowledge. She dropped some hints about deviant behaviour. One or two people thought she'd found kiddie porn on his computer. She's a teacher – she can't afford to have anything to do with that stuff. But I thought that was just a cover story. It didn't fit with Victor's character. He wouldn't find much joy in cyberbabes, or whatever they call them. He likes the real thing too much.'

'Wouldn't she have confronted Gudrun if she'd found out about Stevie? She doesn't strike me as a very *subtle* person.'

Janice grinned cynically. 'No, she's not. And I must admit I have never heard a single soul even hint that Stevie was Victor's, any more than they did about Ruby. You know – you're the first person I have ever told, in all these years. It's like cracking open a dead shellfish, and letting the rotten stink come out. It's because he's dead, I suppose. The shock has loosened my tongue.'

'Will you tell Ruby now?'

'Oh no. God, no. Nothing's changed, has it? Except I can sleep easier now, knowing he won't ever show up and give away the secret. I've dreaded that ever since she was born.'

'He must have been a very peculiar man.'

'Do you think so?' She pondered briefly. 'No, he wasn't. Just following his primitive urges – sex and money were what drove him. Yvonne had inherited a fair bit from her grandmother when they first married, and he used it to set up his business. He was always very sleek and self-satisfied.'

'Belinda doesn't know exactly why Yvonne threw him out, either,' Thea remembered. 'She guessed it was something sordid like telephone sex. Which fits with the hints you heard.' The small consistency was somehow consoling.

'Right.'

Thea couldn't drop it. There was an important point to be established. 'But you've always assumed they broke up because of the affair with Gudrun? When did you find out about that for sure?'

The tall woman stood up abruptly. 'I didn't,' she said. 'I was never sure. It just slowly dawned on me that it was the obvious explanation. It was the feet, I suppose. I hated that kid,' she finished with a flash of ferocity.

'Did you kill him?' Thea looked at the big hands, the sturdy arms. 'I could understand how you might.'

'No, I didn't. But I wouldn't blame anybody for doing it. Not even his mother.' She cocked her head. 'The music's stopped,' she said. 'I'd better go.'

Thea almost grabbed Janice's arm. 'Must you? It seems—' After such intimate revelations, it felt almost violent for the woman to leave so suddenly.

'I must. It's nearly supper time. Ruby will be wondering where I am.'

Did neither of these women go out to work, Thea wondered belatedly? Or were they running some sort of creative industry in their handsome house? It seemed only too likely that she would never know now. There was a strong sense that Janice was never going to want to see her again.

Yet again, the TV offerings for the evening seemed nothing more than a criminal waste of time. Life was worth more than that, she had realised, when her husband had been killed in his thirties. She owed it to him, if not to herself, to make good use of every passing hour – and watching unfunny comedians or superficial historical reconstructions did not qualify. She could instead make notes about the two murders, at the very least. She could go and have another look at the cows in the field behind the house. She could, came one final daring thought, have another look at those diaries of Yvonne's.

But before she could open the bureau drawer, somebody was knocking tentatively on the firmly closed front door, so quietly that she would never have heard it if she hadn't already been in the hall. She went and opened it, feeling more nervous than if there had been thunderous banging.

A young woman stood there, as exotically un-European as Belinda Parker had been earlier that day. But this one was darker skinned and rounder eyed. 'Yes?' she said. 'Can I help you?'

'You are Yvonne Parker?'

'No, no. I'm her house-sitter. She's in France.'

'Ah. I suppose she knows that her husband is dead?' Tears filled the brown eyes.

'I'm not sure.' Thea frowned warily. 'Who are you?'

The answer came obliquely. 'I was present when he was killed, with a knife. I ran away.' Her accent was musical, with American overtones, the English words obviously coming easily to her. 'I thought I would be killed too, so I ran away.'

Thea had to think for several heartbeats. This was a dramatic turn of events, a totally unexpected development. Distress, danger . . . yes, and a very disturbing set of implications. She stared hard at the beautiful little face. 'But why come here? Why didn't you go to the police when it happened? Who *are* you?' But she already thought she knew who this must be. The Filipina girlfriend.

'I came because I have to understand what it was about. Why is poor Victor dead, when he was such a kind sweet man?'

'Was he?' Thea glanced at her mental image of the Parker patriarch as a selfish, slightly intimidating man, with unwholesome proclivities when it came to choosing female company.

More tears filled the doe-like eyes. 'How will I ever manage without him? I have no visa, no money, nobody to be with. Victor organised it all, he paid my fare. He said he would marry me, and I could stay here for ever.'

'How did you know this address? How did you find this house?'

'I went back later, and took this.' She held up a bulging Filofax, which struck Thea as rather old-fashioned. 'It was in his briefcase. It says "Yvonne. Hyacinth House, Snowshill, Gloucestershire". I found it on the computer, quite easily. There is a train to Moreton-in-Marsh and then a bus.'

'You amaze me.' The girl had even pronounced 'Gloucestershire' almost correctly. Still Thea did not usher the grief-stricken creature into the house. This was, after all, an illegal immigrant, an e-bride of some description. And an ear witness at least to the killing of Victor Parker – as Thea herself was, she remembered. 'I heard it,' she said impulsively. 'He was talking to me on the phone.'

The eyes widened as this information was processed. 'I came home with the food,' she began slowly. 'He was speaking on his mobile. I went into the kitchen with the bags, then I went to the bathroom and closed the door. He was still speaking. I heard nothing. I was there for . . . two, three minutes. Perhaps less. I came out and he was on the floor, blood like a fountain from his chest. He was wearing no clothes.'

'No clothes?'

The girl flushed. 'He liked air on his skin. It was a warm night.'

'You must have heard something. *I* did.' She cast her mind back to the truncated conversation. What had she really heard, before the screams began? Little more than doors opening and closing, and Victor saying, 'Hi, Babe,' before giving a choked cry that might well not have been very loud.

The Filipina simply shook her head.

'How could the attacker get in? Wasn't the door locked?'

'I left the key in the lock. My hands were full of the bags. I intended to go back for it.'

'I heard the buzzer,' Thea remembered. 'Why would the killer press the buzzer, and then just walk right in, anyway?'

The girl had no explanation, but simply shrugged.

Both women were aware that the details of the doors mattered scarcely at all. Thea, however, could not abort her obsessive need to visualise the whole episode. 'You must have been followed,' she said. 'The timing is too coincidental otherwise.'

'I stayed out on Sunday, when Mrs Parker visited. Victor said it would be best.'

'So you never saw her? And she didn't know about you?'

'I know Belinda and Mark,' said the girl defensively. 'Victor said Vonny should be kept in the dark, for her own good.'

'Was it a man or a woman who stabbed him?' she asked swiftly, hoping to catch the girl unawares.

'How can I know? I think a man. A woman – how could a woman do such a thing?' She wept unrestrainedly, her mouth a childlike arch of misery.

Thea was too caught up with the mystery of it all to feel much sympathy. There was still a chance that this was a murderer standing before her. 'Where did you go on Sunday?'

'To my friend in Tufnell Park. She is a nanny with her own flat.'

'Were you a nanny? Before you met Victor?'

'Oh no. A nanny has a visa, a permit to stay here. I am merely a visitor. Three months.' She grimaced miserably. 'Now I have been here eight months.'

'You're in trouble,' said Thea flatly. 'Particularly as you failed to call the police to a dying man. Did you run away leaving him to bleed to death? Don't you think you might have saved his life if you hadn't been such a coward?'

'No, no. Of course I didn't do that. He was dead in seconds. I could not stay – what good would that do?'

'It was two days before he was found. Belinda went there today. How do you think she felt, walking in on her dead father? Probably covered in flies by this time.'

'I put a blanket over him. I am sorry, but it was not my fault at all. I was afraid.'

'But you took the time to pack a bag and take his Filofax.'

The small chin lifted. 'The bag was packed already. We were going away for a little holiday. I went outside, for a moment, and then turned back for the things.'

'You could have killed him yourself,' Thea said carefully. 'Did you think the police would come to that conclusion?'

'Perhaps, yes. I felt I should find his wife and tell her he did not suffer, that he was a good man, very kind. I felt we should be together in our mourning.'

Thea found this sentiment hard to swallow. 'I'm not sure you're right about that. Victor was probably very sensible in keeping you apart. I think it's more likely that you thought you could somehow blackmail her into helping you.'

Emotion swamped the delicate features. Defiance, confusion, pride all jostled for dominance. Thea resisted a temptation to like her. 'But he phoned me and said she never came. He gave up waiting for her.'

'Was that on Saturday or Sunday?'

'Saturday.'

With resignation, Thea accepted that she could not prolong this doorstep conversation any further. Either she should send the girl away, or let her into the house. Neither seemed feasible. Once in, she might never leave again. But if she had no transport, where was she supposed to go? Irritation at being placed in such an impossible dilemma made her speak sharply. 'I still don't understand why you came here. What are you planning to do for the night? Where will you stay? What did you plan to say to Yvonne, for heaven's sake?'

'I see,' said the girl hopelessly. 'You will not understand. You are not a relative, you know nothing about the Parker family. I am sorry to have bothered you.' The delivery was stilted, dignity keeping her chin high. Thea wondered why she had so little pity for the creature's plight. What harm could it do to let her in and give her a bed for the night? Normally, she liked to think, she would have been very much kinder.

'It isn't my house,' she said. 'I can't just invite you in. I don't know for sure who you might be. And people have *died*.'

'People?'

'Yes. Your . . . boyfriend wasn't the first. We're all having to be careful – do you see?' Was she simply being xenophobic, suspicious of this person purely because she was foreign? Or was her caution entirely valid? She remembered that Belinda had said she didn't like her, and wondered whether that was having an influence. On the face of it, here was a pathetic exploited waif, enticed to Britain with all sorts of promises and then expected to devote her life to the service of an ageing businessman with a suspiciously complicated family life. How could it ever be expected to work? How could the girl have been stupid enough to go along with it? Thea had no idea of the economic or social conditions in the Philippines, but she had met one or two exploited girls before and never found a proper answer to these questions.

'You want me to go away, then?' Again, the uplifted chin, with little hint of any reduced self-respect. The girl had a sort of class, Thea acknowledged. Perhaps in her own country she was an aristocrat, assuming she had rights wherever she was in the world. She seemed capable and educated. Why, then, not apply for a proper visa in the approved fashion?

'I'm afraid so,' she said firmly. After all, this was not really a 'girl' at all. She seemed quite self-possessed – with fabulous bones and skin that would preserve her youth for decades – and old enough to take care of herself. And it was, after all, just remotely possible that she was a double murderer. She might have her own excellent reasons for wanting both Stevie and Victor dead, for all Thea knew.

'Is there another bus?'

'I have no idea, but I doubt it. There are B&B places in the village, though. And perhaps the pub offers accommodation.' Appalled at her own lack of charity, she silently thought, *And it's a warm summer night. You can lie under a hedge with the cows.*

'B&B? That means a place to sleep?'

'Bed and breakfast. They probably charge around thirty pounds or so. Of course, it is high season. They might be full.'

'You don't care about me, do you? You have no kindness.'

Thea's mind filled with scenes from films and books – not to mention the countless nativity plays she had seen – where hard-faced women refused entry to obviously needy travellers, out of meanness of spirit or paranoid suspicion or sheer reluctance to put themselves to any trouble. Now she had become one of them, and it stabbed her own sense of who she was. But she held fast to a powerful instinct. 'It's not my house,' she repeated. 'I have no authority to let total strangers in for the night. And when you think about it, it isn't very likely that Yvonne would want you under her roof, is it?'

'If she were here, she would let me in. I am certain of that. Victor always said she was a soft-hearted woman.'

Soft-headed more like, thought Thea, with a small inward grin. 'I'm sorry,' she said again. 'But you really must go now.'

And miraculously, the woman went. She walked with a firm step, a rucksack over one shoulder, and turned towards the village centre. Somebody would take pity on her, Thea assured herself. The pub, probably. And if she told her story, they would think harshly of the unfriendly house-sitter who would not admit her. Or would they? Much depended on the general view of Victor and Yvonne, and quite how a young Asian mistress would be regarded by the respectable citizens of Snowshill. Dimly, she knew that she ought to call

Gladwin and report the appearance of this key witness to whatever had happened to Victor. She was fumbling for her phone when a voice made her forget what she was doing.

'Who in the world was that?' Blake stood at his own front door, watching the departing figure.

Thea regretted lingering outside, instead of going back into the house right away. It was Hepzie's fault – she had pottered off into the vegetation, forcing Thea to wait for her.

'Nobody,' she said. 'Hurry up, Heps. I want to go in.'

'Come on – don't give me that. She was talking to you for ages, but you never let her in.'

'You were watching us?'

'Of course I was,' he said brazenly. 'I was curious.'

'Well go and ask her, if you want to know. Maybe she'll persuade *you* to give her a bed for the night, because she failed miserably with me.'

'Maybe she will,' he said, and to Thea's amazement he trotted down the hill after the vanishing Filipina.

She wanted someone she could trust and speak her mind to. Someone who knew she wasn't a cruel mean-spirited person, but was just being sensibly careful, and following her gut feelings about the importunate female who had pleaded for hospitality. The look Blake Grossman had cast at her, before setting off on his rescue mission, had been harsh enough to hurt. Accusing, contemptuous, angry – a look she did not ever want to see again.

Questions were making her dizzy, their possible answers even more so. Why had that female turned up as she had? What would she have done if Thea had let her into the house? Was she looking for something? Would

Blake really bring her back to stay next door? Was she in fact being pursued by Belinda or Gudrun and cunningly calculated that her best hope was to take the fight to their own home ground? Or had she actually killed Victor, sick of his slobbering attentions? The swirling questions prevented her from taking the obvious course of phoning for DS Gladwin.

What if this foreign girl was perfectly innocent, simply in automatic flight from a scene of horrific violence, bringing her by some unconscious instinct to a place where she thought there might be people who loved Victor as she had done? If so, it had taken her forty-eight hours to cover the ground – and where had she been in the meantime? Where had she slept for the past two nights? How much money did she have on her? How could she possibly hope to exist in Britain without proper papers?

Should she, in short, be feeling sorry for the wretched creature? Would reporting her to the police result in a cruel deportation to some ghastly fate back home?

The living room window was open and she heard voices approaching. As expected, when she went for a look, she saw they came from Blake and the newcomer. He was carrying her rucksack, bending his head towards her in solicitude. As if aware that Thea was watching, he shot a venomous look towards Hyacinth House before escorting the girl through his own front door.

She tried not to mind. He could have no proper idea of her reasons for refusing entry – certainly couldn't make any accurate assessment of her character on the basis of a single act. He didn't know that Victor was dead, that this was his girlfriend come in search of succour or sympathy or revenge. Presumably he was shortly to find out.

Eighty-five miles away, Drew was at breaking point. His mother-in-law had forced him to admit his conviction that there was no longer any hope for Karen's recovery. The resulting reproaches were even worse than Maggs's had been.

'But you *can't* just give up!' she protested. 'What about the children?'

'I told the children this morning. I think they deserve to know the truth.'

'But it isn't the truth, it's just what you think. You can't be sure. You *have* to assume she'll come through it. She's my only child!'

'I'm sorry,' he said. 'I can't help it.'

'But Drew, it's desperately important. You're her next of kin. If you tell the doctors you've abandoned hope, they'll stop treating her. You *owe* it to her to hang on.'

Karen's mother was a robust woman in her mid sixties, who had spent the past twenty years with her husband on a farm in Wales, the pair having become belated bohemians when Karen left home to go to college. They had made approving noises about their daughter's marriage and the arrival of the two children, but kept at a remote distance from the little family. Her mother visited once or twice a year for a single night's stay, but her father never left his farm. Drew's mother-in-law was unsure about the funeral business, despite being unsentimental by nature and quite unsqueamish. Her inspection of Peaceful Repose Burial Ground had been cursory.

When Karen had been injured, three years earlier, she had briefly rallied and spent a week helping Drew with the children. Since then her visits and phone calls had increased somewhat, but she could still hardly be counted as an active member of the family. Karen's father was even worse. He remained at home, claiming to be indispensable and sending stilted messages via his wife.

'I suppose they do love you?' Drew had asked his wife, years before. 'In their own way?'

'I think they feel they've done right by me and now I'm your responsibility. They've always been much more to each other than they have to me. I don't hold it against them at all, although it would have been nicer with a sibling. They've just sort of forgotten about me, somehow. I promise I won't be like that with ours.'

'Good,' he'd smiled. 'Although my parents aren't very much better. Don't they call couples like us "babes in the woods"? Orphans of the storm, or something?'

Now, of course, Karen had broken her promise, and as far as he could tell, forgotten her children completely. And his mother-in-law had shown interest at last, when it was just about too late.

'I suppose Jack and I will have to move down here, then, to help you. He has been talking about selling up and retiring, although I don't quite believe him. He loves that farm, even if it doesn't make any money.'

'Don't do anything rash,' said Drew tightly. 'Let's wait and see, shall we?'

She had rolled her eyes and sucked her teeth and gone off to inflict a totally false jollity on her grandchildren. The sound of her forced laughter, and Timmy's grimly polite rejoinders, was too much.

'I'm going for a bit of a drive,' he called to them. 'I don't know how long I'll be.'

Feeling like a cowboy spurring his horse into a wild dash across the prairie, he accelerated the car down the small country lane, turning northwards when he reached the main road.

Barely ten minutes elapsed before there were shouts and screams from Blake's house. Thea froze, listening helplessly and trying to work out whether murder was going on, and if so who was victim and who the aggressor. Odd words from Blake could be made out, which proved entirely useless for the purpose of interpretation. 'NO!' roared at full blast, was the most frequent, and 'Oh, God!' scarcely any less stentorian. The female screams resolved themselves into something slightly less disconcerting – more like placatory wordless bleats, like a puppy trying to soothe an enraged lion. There was no suggestion of actual physical harm, Thea decided with relief. Perhaps she needn't summon the police, after all.

But she could hardly just ignore it. Blake sounded dangerously angry and out of control. Already doubting his trustworthiness, she began to suspect that he had less than pure motives in taking the Filipina into his house. But she had gone willingly, and was quite old enough to know what she was doing. The last thing Thea felt inclined to do was to stage a dramatic rescue, only to have to eat her own words and offer the little nuisance shelter, after all.

Then a vaguely familiar green Peugeot appeared and parked neatly beside Thea's Fiesta, fitting itself onto the narrow space with effortless ease.

'Good God!' said Thea to her spaniel. 'It's Yvonne.'

Chapter Twenty-One

If Yvonne was back, then did that mean that Thea would have to leave – perhaps that very evening? Obviously she would no longer be required, and she was at a loss to imagine how they would operate together, allocating dog and cats, breakfast toast and troublesome phone calls. Despite the chaos and the sadness and the noise from next door, she found she was reluctant to just gather herself up and go.

And yet Yvonne deserved a friendly greeting, and a patient ear for whatever the explanation might be for her early return. Perhaps she had argued with her sister, or heard about Victor and come rushing back by some miraculously rapid means of transport to console her fatherless offspring. Perhaps she would be nicer to the Filipina woman than Thea had been.

Her confusion as to her role made her slow to go to the door, and before she was properly into the hall, Yvonne had opened it and come into the house. 'Oh, there you are,' she said. 'Good.' She seemed almost ludicrously normal, a smile on her face and a plump red bag over her shoulder.

'Hmm?' said Thea. 'Hello. Did something happen?'

Yvonne laughed ruefully. 'Just a few things, yes. I've had quite a time of it. I'm really sorry to come home sooner than I said. Of course, you must stay tonight, and I'll pay you the full fee. It's not your fault.'

Thea relaxed and smiled. 'Shall I make some coffee or something? Everything's all right here. The cats are fine.' Then she remembered the dog hairs on the sofa and the bed upstairs, and the crumbs on the kitchen table. 'It is a bit messy, though. I was going to do a big clean-up tomorrow.'

'Don't worry about that.'

'At least we haven't broken anything. All your things are just as you left them.'

'Good,' said Yvonne again. 'Coffee would be lovely, actually, if you don't mind doing it. I'll just go upstairs for a minute, and come back when it's ready.'

Only gradually, as the coffee machine gurgled into action, did Yvonne's manner begin to strike Thea as odd. For a start, she obviously knew nothing of what had happened to her husband. She showed no sign whatsoever of distress or shock. For another thing, the dithery woman from Saturday had mutated into somebody a lot more confident and decisive. Perhaps Thea's memory had exaggerated the air of incompetence, or perhaps the relief of getting home after such demanding travels had wrought the change.

The next set of thoughts were not so much confusing as alarming. Would *she* have to break the news about Victor? Should she explain that his lady friend was next door, being yelled at by Blake? Should she try to recount all the events that had taken place since she discovered little Stevie on Sunday afternoon? Would Yvonne want to know about Belinda's visit and Gudrun's arrest? If she, Thea, didn't tell her, then who would? And what on earth had happened to send the darn woman home more than a week sooner than planned?

Take it a step at a time, she advised herself. *Make the coffee, tidy the living room, and wait to see what happens next*. It was only about half past six – there was a long evening ahead, and the calmer it could be kept, the better. In London, the police would be collecting evidence as to who killed Victor Parker, with Belinda presumably still there. But . . . the woman next door with Blake was at least a witness to the essential events of his death, even if she insisted she neither saw nor heard what was going on in the next room, while she spent two minutes on the loo. She should be speaking to the police, not hiding away in a Cotswold village, even if it was the one where the former wife of the victim lived. That, she supposed, must be why Blake was making such a fuss. He was reproaching her for dereliction of duty.

This made the girlfriend seem considerably more vulnerable to Thea than she had at first. In the surprise and bewilderment of her sudden appearance, the real extent of her importance had not been immediately clear. Now, perhaps because of the shouting, Thea started to worry. Blake was too closely connected to the Parkers for comfort. Perhaps his loyalty to Yvonne explained his rage at her replacement. Pouring out the coffee, the fear blossomed and burgeoned until Thea was physically shaking. Because it would be her fault. She had virtually handed the wretched creature over to the untrustworthy man next door. By being so stupidly suspicious and unkind, she might have caused real harm to the girl.

'Coffee's ready!' she called up the stairs. A door opened and closed, and Yvonne replied to say she was coming. Thea watched her walking steadily down the stairs and wondered how to begin to explain her fears for the woman in jeopardy next door.

'Yvonne – would you say that Blake is a reliable person?' she began clumsily. 'He hasn't been here much, so I've hardly spoken to him. I just thought . . . well, he does seem a bit . . . um, moody. Volatile. He seemed nice at first, but then . . .'

Yvonne seemed to give this some serious thought, as she slowly took the coffee and went into the living room with it. 'He's always been all right with me,' she said. 'Why should you worry? You won't ever have to see him again.'

'Well, I might. You see—'

Yvonne waved an impatient hand at her. 'Let's not talk for a bit, all right? I'm exhausted. I need to settle down quietly. If that's awkward for you, I can go upstairs.'

'Gosh, don't be silly! If I'm in the way, then it's for me to go upstairs, or into the kitchen. But, honestly, I do think I should tell you—'

'Please! I'm sure people have been intrusive, with the awful business you told me about – you know, the little boy . . .'

Thea nodded helplessly. Yvonne was obviously incapable of listening to anything unpleasant or upsetting. 'But I really don't want to talk,' she went on. 'Not yet. Do forgive me.'

The conversation with Belinda came back, in which Yvonne's odd hormonal deficiencies had been described. Knowing that, the present behaviour did make some sense. The equivalent of a teenage girl shutting herself in her room rather than listen to sensible lectures from the adults, perhaps. The prospect of conveying the news about Victor felt more and more daunting with every passing minute. *And why should I be the one to do it, anyway?* she wondered mutinously. Eventually the police, or Belinda, or even Mark, would presumably make contact and force Yvonne to hear what they had to say.

But it felt close to ridiculous to be sitting there quietly when a few yards beyond the walls of Hyacinth House there was violence and grief and tragic loss all going on, much of it closely linked to Yvonne herself.

The ban on talking was astonishingly powerful, as well as ludicrous. Even to open her mouth felt unkind and aggressive after such clear pleading for silence. The paradoxical strength of weak individuals had struck Thea before, on occasion. The pathetic *don't hurt me* stance effectively rendered all but the most insensitive quite incapable of action. Yvonne Parker clearly had it off to a fine art, worthy of any languid Victorian lady. And yet she functioned as a schoolteacher, she had reared two children and seemed capable of all the requisite tasks for normal life. She surely couldn't be as feeble as she pretended. Thea could feel a rising surge of impatience, as Yvonne simply sat there, eyes almost closed, and she fidgeted at the imposed hiatus.

'Yvonne – I'm afraid I think this is rather silly,' she said eventually. 'There are important things going on, and you will have to know about them sooner or later. I can't see anything to be gained by postponing it.'

The eyes closed more firmly, and a small sigh escaped from the immobile lips. 'Oh dear,' she murmured, almost inaudibly. 'I do see that this is awkward for you. Perhaps it would be best if I go upstairs after all. And if you could do the usual with the cats, and act as if I wasn't here, we can manage. I'd like you to leave early tomorrow, if you don't mind. I'll send a cheque on to you.'

Again there seemed to be no defence, no way of insisting on being heard. The sheer implacable force of the woman was extraordinary. 'All right,' she said. 'You're the boss.'

'Thank you, dear. Do feel free to carry on with any plans you had for the evening. TV, or a little drive – anything you like. And you'll need to do your packing, of course.' And with that, she got up from the sofa, and without a backward glance went out of the room and up the stairs.

Thea was at a total loss. Angry, frustrated, bemused, she looked at her dog for suggestions. Hepzie had providentially settled on a rug in front of the empty fireplace, rather than jumping on any of the furniture, and was curled up peacefully as if nothing strange was happening. 'It's all right for you,' said Thea crossly. 'Get up. We're going out to look at cows for a bit.'

The dog was always ready for exercise and new smells, so got up willingly enough. They went out quietly and followed the path to the back of the house and the gate into the field. The arrangement was very reminiscent of the first house-sitting commission in Duntisbourne Abbots, two years earlier, she realised. In that case, the field had been a rougher patch of land, sloping downwards to a pond and bordered by hedges. This one sloped upwards and had fences on three sides. Duntisbourne sheep were replaced by Snowshill cows. But the fact of a violent death, leaving shattered relatives behind, was similar.

'It's not the same at all,' Thea muttered aloud. Only the gate, leading from a well-tended garden into a field, was a common factor – and Thea's instinctive resistance to actually going into this field, because of what she had found in the earlier one.

She leaned her forearms on the top bar of the gate and tried to still her turbulent thoughts. If she had had somebody to talk to, she could have aired the legion of questions and half-made connections that were swarming through her head. As it was, it felt almost dangerous to her sanity to give them a free rein. What about Yvonne's car, for one thing? She must have gone to collect it from the street in Crouch End, oblivious of what had happened to Victor. *But wouldn't she have called in on him while she was there?* came a niggling voice. Or had she scuttled rapidly to the vehicle and driven away, hoping not to be seen by him, unaware that he was dead? That would be more in character, Thea judged. In any case, she must have moved it before Belinda discovered Victor's body, or the police would have swooped on it and arrested it as suspicious.

She listened for sounds of further strife in Blake's house, but all seemed quiet. Had they arrived at some sort of understanding? Had he thrown the woman out again? Had she managed to explain to him exactly who she was and why she was there? Should she, Thea, behave responsibly and go to check that all was well? Blake had sounded furiously angry, capable of violence, in the moments before Yvonne had appeared. To confront him now felt like the height of recklessness. The more she thought about it, the more unreliable Blake Grossman seemed. Yvonne had dismissed any hint that he should be mistrusted, and she ought to know. She had spoken warmly of him when Thea had first arrived. And yet she had no choice but to go with her own gut reactions, and they told her that he was not on the side of the angels. He had shown little concern for Stevie's death, which had become, in some clouded way, Thea's rule of thumb for assessing people in recent days.

She felt lost and alone, a small figure in an indifferent landscape. She could, just possibly, have an early night, get up at six the next morning and drive home, leaving Snowshill and its residents to resolve their own foolish problems as best they might. She had no special insights, had witnessed no key events that cast any clarifying light on the terrible things that had happened. They could perfectly well do without her. She could even load up her dog and her bag and go now. As she stared into the field, the other side of the gate, she was tempted to do exactly that.

But there was Gudrun, surely falsely accused. There was the Filipina woman, distraught and adrift with little hope of rescue. There was Belinda, who had seemed rather a nice person, as far as Thea could judge. Above all, there was Yvonne, upstairs in her bedroom, fiercely refusing to be told that people had died and questions really did have to be answered. In spite of her impatience and frustration, Thea felt a degree of responsibility towards the owner of Hyacinth House, whose life seemed so narrow and difficult and frightening that she simply retreated from it when things became threatening.

The summer evening was already closing in, an hour earlier than it had done in June. While the sun had some way still to go, the light was changing and some of the birds were starting to sing their day's-end songs. By the same time tomorrow, she would be back in Witney, in her own dusty silent house, where she still felt as though she lived in a suspended state, three years after losing her husband. She should sell it perhaps and find something in the Cotswolds, now that she knew the area so well. Or she could bank the money and alternate short-term rentals with house-sitting, becoming a real Flying Dutchwoman, with no permanent base. She could spend time abroad, as more and more people did. And if the house-sitting commissions dried up, she might consider some completely new career in a completely new place . . . fantasies began to flit into her mind in which she found a position as live-in matron in a boarding school, or full-time carer for a rich old lady . . .

'Hello?'

She turned lazily, forgetting for a moment where she was and why she might be well advised to remain on guard.

'What are you doing?'

'Nothing,' she told Blake, who stood with his hands on his hips and eyes wide open with indignation.

'That's Vonny's car out there. I've just noticed it.'

'I know.'

'Where is she? I have to speak to her. *We* have to speak to her. The three of us.'

Victor's girlfriend glided up behind Blake, looking sinister in the slanting rays of the sun, which caught her face and turned it to bronze.

'You can't. She's gone to bed. She won't talk to anybody.'

'I'll damn well *make* her,' he said, with a jerky twist of his body, as he turned towards Hyacinth House. 'She can't hide away like that.'

'Why? I mean why don't you leave her alone? What's it to do with you?'

'Oh, shut up, you fool. I thought you were stupid, the first time I saw you, and nothing you've said or done since has changed my mind.'

Nobody since her older brother, thirty years ago, had called her stupid. It was one epithet she could confidently reject. Except . . . there *had* been a few episodes over the past year or so where her behaviour hadn't been entirely sensible. This time, though, she could see no possible justification for the accusation.

He ignored her outraged spluttering and strode to the front door, followed by Nutella. *No, it's Mariella*, Thea suddenly remembered. She should at least do the woman the justice of getting her name right. She wrestled with her powerful urge to stop them, or at least warn Yvonne. 'She'll probably be asleep,' she protested. 'You've no right—'

Blake paused at the door and scowled at Thea. 'I have more right than you,' he said. 'That's for sure.'

'But what are you going to do?' she persisted. 'What do you want with her?'

'Vonny!' called Blake in his powerful bass voice. 'Come out here!'

There was nothing friendly or compassionate in his manner. If he had learned of Victor's death from the girlfriend and felt it incumbent on himself to inform Yvonne, he was going about it in a very unpleasant way. Granted, he knew a lot more than Thea did about the Parker family, but it still seemed unforgivable of him to be so loud and aggressive about it.

As Thea expected, there was no response from Yvonne. 'Stop it!' she ordered him. 'She must be asleep.'

'She's not asleep. She's got to take what's coming to her, and I'm going to make her.'

'You are not. You're to leave this house now, or I'll call the police.'

These words did appear to penetrate his angry brain, and he hesitated, still on the doorstep. Thea seized her chance. 'I will,' she repeated. 'I've got the number of the detective superintendent. She's a friend of mine. She's not going to take kindly to you behaving like this. It's harassment. Whatever grievance you've got against Yvonne can be discussed reasonably when she's feeling better.'

At some point during the past few minutes it had begun to seem as if Blake did not simply want to inform his neighbour of Victor's death, but to enforce some kind of punishment on her, for reasons Thea could not grasp. He was *personally* angry, thanks to something the Filipina must have told him. And she must have told him within moments of entering his house, because he'd been shouting at *her* before Yvonne returned. There was some logical thread to be grasped, but her head was far too jangled and confused to be able to find it.

The little tableau seemed frozen for a few seconds, as Blake appeared to consider his next move, the two women watching him closely. None of them paid attention to another vehicle pulling up a little way along the lane outside the garden gate. Only when a female voice addressed them did they react.

'Is Vonny home already? That's her car, isn't it?'

Clara Beauchamp stood in the little gateway, wearing jodhpurs and a ribbed jersey. She looked sweaty and dishevelled. Thea found herself thinking that this was quite possibly the first person she had seen, in two years, who completely represented the stereotype of a Cotswold resident. 'Is something going on?' Clara added, looking from face to face and resting curiously on that of the foreigner. 'Who's this?'

Nobody replied, but Thea felt some of the tension in Blake drain away. He made a small tutting noise and took a step towards the newcomer. 'Go away, Clara. How do you always manage to show up at the wrong moment?'

Clara shrugged this off. 'Where's Vonny, then? She's not meant to be back yet, is she?'

'Mind your own business.' Blake's voice had resumed its loud tones, the anger returning. 'Just go away.'

'Don't speak to me like that. I know you, Blake Grossman. Always thinking you know best what's good for people, forcing yourself on them, telling them what to do. If Vonny doesn't want to listen to you, then she doesn't have to, poor thing. Never mind telling me to go away – looks as if it's *you* that needs to back off. And who *is* this person?' She pointed a rude finger at Mariella and looked to Thea for an explanation.

'She's come from London. She wanted to see Yvonne, but I sent her away. Blake went after her and took her into his house, and started shouting at her, for some reason. Now they both want to speak to Yvonne.' It sounded rather a masterly summary in her own ears, but Clara seemed bewildered. Obviously she had no idea of what had happened to Victor. The news could hardly have started to spread yet, unless Belinda or perhaps Janice had chosen to phone all and sundry with it.

Suddenly the sound of a bolt being shot into place came from inside the door. Then that of a key turning in the lock.

'She's locked us out!' exclaimed Blake. He gave Thea a savagely accusing look. 'This is your fault. We've lost our chance now.'

'Chance for what?' asked Thea, thinking that Yvonne had probably just done a very sensible thing. She checked to make sure her dog was on the right side of the door, finding it close to her feet, sitting unconcernedly licking its paws.

The atmosphere of conflict dissolved into a group of people standing rather foolishly outside a locked door, each of them deeply confused as to what the others were intending. Blake's anger had comprehensively embraced all the women, on both sides of the door, but now coalesced around the Filipina. 'You have to get in there, and talk to her,' he said urgently. 'It's all up to you now.'

The young woman flinched and took several steps

towards Clara, who was still some distance away. Thea dimly figured out that Blake believed Mariella was the best person to persuade Yvonne to accept that Victor was dead. The shouting, she supposed, had been his own way of reacting to the news of the second death. There was no sign now that he thought Mariella had committed a murder herself.

Inside the house, the phone began to ring. It was not answered, as far as they could tell, but stopped after six peals for the automatic messenger to take over. 'Why doesn't she answer the phone?' asked Thea, still aware that many important answers were somewhere inside her head if she could only give herself time to explore them. Every time she thought she was close to understanding something, a new external distraction drove it away again. There was no time or space for methodical thought, with all these incomprehensible people crowding in on her. She fancied she knew just how Yvonne must be feeling.

The road past the house was as quiet as always, but the three cars parked against the garden wall made it seem as if some unusual event was taking place in Hyacinth House. A party, probably, people would think. Another one or two would make a crowd, forcing anything trying to pass to squeeze through slowly, with time for a good look at whatever might be going on. The bumpy atmosphere of dawning crisis was intensifying. Blake was rubbing his chin with a large hand, apparently thinking about his next move. Clara was eyeing Mariella with narrow suspicion, as if trying several hypotheses out, to explain her presence and her effect on Blake. Thea was feeling in her pocket for her mobile, with a growing certainty that the only way out of the impasse was to call Gladwin. And yet nobody seemed actually on the brink of genuine violence or criminality. If there had not been two murders already, it would seem that little more than a heated discussion had taken place. As it was, Thea's thundering heart was insisting that there would be no calm or easy outcome to this bewildering evening.

Chapter Twenty-Two

Before she could make the call, a fourth car arrived, as she had somehow known it inevitably would. Clara saw it first and emitted a little yelp that sounded more pleased than alarmed.

'It's Mark!' she announced, going to meet him and hopping impatiently as he got out of his car. She grabbed his arm the moment he emerged, and shook it like an importunate child. 'Hey, Mark, come and see to your mother. She's locked herself in the house. Blake's having one of his rages and there's a strange woman. Come *on*. Oh, by the way, I saw your car here on Sunday afternoon. I thought you'd come to see us, but you never showed. I want an explanation for that. I got Baskerville all saddled and ready for you, for nothing. I was sure you'd come for a ride.'

Much of this was incomprehensible to Thea, but her attention snagged on the reference to the car. That surely had to be important.

The foppish young man appeared unfazed by this sudden stream of information, smiling uncertainly from face to face until he reached that of Mariella. 'Hello, Elly,' he said with a kind of regretful politeness. 'What are you doing here?'

She made no reply, seeming less than delighted to see him.

'You know her, of course,' said Thea. 'And you know about your father.' She searched his face for signs of grief, and discovered grooves around his mouth and shadows under his eyes. It made absolute sense that he would rush to his mother's side on hearing the news – whether to comfort her or himself was probably unclear even to him. 'Did you know Yvonne would be here, as well? Isn't she meant to be in France?'

He ignored her, leaving Clara to address herself to Thea, apparently reassured by the arrival of Mark. 'Has something happened to Victor?' she asked.

'It seems so. That's what all this is about – I think. I'm sure Yvonne will settle down now Mark's here and everything'll be fine.'

'Right,' Clara nodded uncertainly. 'I hope you're right. Now I do have to get back. I was already late. My husband's got the horses in the trailer and he'll expect me to be there when he unloads them. Sorry if I intruded,' she added stiffly. 'I just wanted to see Vonny, that's all.' She was already walking back to her car.

'Everybody wants to see Vonny,' said Blake, watching her departure with no hint of his earlier fury. Even he, it seemed, was mollified by the arrival of Mark. Only Mariella appeared to have grown more uncomfortable rather than less. Apparently Mark liked her rather more than his sister did, sons being generally a lot more forgiving of their fathers' peccadilloes than daughters were.

'But why is she home so early?' Thea mumbled. 'What's everybody *doing* here?' There were some basic truths coming into focus, which she was trying to use as the foundation for a full explanation. Somebody had stabbed Victor, and his girlfriend had abandoned his dead body. Something suspicious involving Mark's car had taken place on Sunday – the day Stevie Horsfall had been murdered. Blake thought she, Thea, was stupid for not seeing something obvious. Belinda . . . Here she ground to a halt. The role of Yvonne's daughter remained obscure, beyond being the one to discover Victor's body, prompted by Thea herself. Yvonne had aborted her trip to France and returned in a weirdly blithe mood, which quickly turned to an insane level of avoidance.

Somehow, the thread led to Mariella. Her behaviour was the most bizarre, and she currently appeared to be the most agitated person. Had *she* killed Victor after all, screaming as she did so, and disappearing for the next two days while she waited for someone to find him?

'Do you think she's hiding from . . . um . . . Mariella?' Thea asked Mark. 'I thought it was Blake, but if he wanted to confront her with her husband's killer, that would be scary, wouldn't it?'

Mark shook his head at her. 'I have no idea what you're talking about,' he said. Then he squared his shoulders. 'Look – I know where there's a broken window catch, round the side. I can get in and see if Mum's okay. You all wait here.' He spoke in a low voice, which could only mean he did not want Yvonne to hear him from inside the house.

It seemed as good a plan as any to Thea and she nodded.

Blake was glaring at her, his scowl back again. She realised he might not take kindly to her remarks. 'Do you think Mariella killed Victor?' she asked him boldly.

For reply he merely sighed dramatically and spread his hands. At least he didn't call her stupid again, she thought ruefully.

'I did not,' said the Filipina.

'But the police might well think you did,' Blake told her severely. 'You were an idiot to run away like that.'

Mariella looked warily at Thea, seeming to hope for some female solidarity. 'This man is very angry with me,' she confided. 'For my failings and cowardice. He shouted at me for it. Shouted and shouted.' She put her hands to her ears at the memory. 'I told you, both of you. I do not have the right papers to stay here. I cannot speak to the police.'

'Irresponsible cow,' said Blake calmly. 'All this could have been settled days ago if you'd had any guts.'

'How?' demanded Thea. 'How could it?'

The conversation had made a good smokescreen for Mark at least. He had disappeared around the side of the house, and might well already be inside. Blake gave no reply to her question, which was hardly surprising. They waited, in the last rays of the sun that came across the garden, turning the red and orange flowers vividly exotic. Thea wished she had simply driven home an hour ago, when she had the chance.

'I still think I ought to call the police,' she said stubbornly.

'Whatever for? What good would that do?'

'We have here a witness to the murder of Victor Parker. That in itself is reason enough. Now we've got Yvonne going off her head as well. I think we need backup.'

He laughed contemptuously. 'Backup! Just who do you think you are, anyway?'

It did seem a fair question, now she paused to think about it. 'Believe me, I never asked to get involved in all this. You can't accuse me of that. My loyalties are to Yvonne, when it comes down to it. I think you should just leave her alone.'

'You're a fool,' he said flatly. 'And an uncharitable one, at that. Why did you turn this poor girl away?'

'She's not a poor girl, she's an illegal immigrant. I'd be harbouring a criminal.'

He gazed at her probingly, his dark eyes searching hers. 'Really? Is that really what you think? Look at her, damn it!'

Thea shifted uneasily from one foot to the other and glanced at Mariella. Was she truly such a cold-hearted bigot as Blake was suggesting? 'Yes, I know,' she muttered. 'She's probably a victim of the system. But . . . I've got a daughter in the police. The DS here is my friend. I had to make a choice.'

'Rubbish!' he scoffed. 'You're in an ideal position to argue her case for her, to make them see she's no more a criminal than you are.'

'Okay,' she capitulated. 'You're probably right. But can we discuss it some other time? Mark's in there trying to convince his mother that his father's been killed. That's the important thing now.'

Something softened in Blake's fierce expression, and she was reminded of his kindness when the hornet stung her, and his affable manner on their early encounters. 'Poor old Vonny,' he murmured.

As if released from a strong grip, Thea stepped back, and gazed at an upstairs window, which she believed to be that of Yvonne's bedroom. 'She's sure to let him talk to her, isn't she?' she said.

'Who knows?' he shrugged.

'I thought you did,' she shot back, needing to correct the balance between them, after his verbal mauling of her. 'I thought you knew just what had to be done. I thought you had the key to the whole wretched business.'

'You thought wrong,' he said. 'You heard Clara.'

She had forgotten Clara. Her accusations about Blake's bossy interventions had gone unheeded. 'Oh. Yes,' she said. 'I suppose I did.'

The front door opened without warning and Mark's face appeared. 'Thea – will you come in please. Blake – you'll have to go away. She's not going to talk to you or Mariella, however much you try to force her.'

'That was quick!' Thea said, as she looked around for her dog, and made for the door. 'You've only been gone a minute.'

'Yes . . . well . . .' he said unhelpfully, and almost dragged her inside, closing the door in Blake's face.

'I can climb through windows as well as you,' Blake shouted from outside. 'Just see if I can't.'

'Don't be a fool,' Mark called back. 'I haven't locked you out. I'm relying on you to be sensible. Just go. I'll come and see you in the morning. Nobody's going anywhere before then.'

It seemed a very rash promise, to Thea. How could he be so sure? The whole surreal situation began to feel like a parody of a thriller film, where instead of people charging around with guns, shouting threats at each other and climbing onto roofs in a highly unintelligent bid to escape, they just stood around being very British and reasonable until somebody broke down and explained how and when and why they'd committed the crime.

There was no sign of Yvonne, but Mark pointed towards the kitchen, where Thea went to find her. She was sitting placidly at the table, as if nothing unusual were happening. A cat was on her lap and a sheet of yellow paper lay on the table in front of her. 'Have you been in here all along?' Thea demanded.

'Most of the time,' she said. 'I locked you all out because you were being so noisy.'

Was the woman actually mad, Thea wondered? Should this thought not have occurred to her earlier? With responses so inappropriate to the situation, madness had to be the reason, almost by definition.

But what *was* the situation? Blake had been shouting. The Filipina was carrying vitally important information about a murder. Clara had been curious to learn why Yvonne had returned early. Victor was dead. There definitely was a situation to be addressed, but when she tried to grasp the essential bones of it, it evaporated into smoke.

Mark was tinkering with cutlery on the draining board, tapping two teaspoons together meditatively. Nobody would ever guess that he had just climbed in through a side window, Thea thought. 'Mu-u-u-um,' he said, very slowly, 'Clara just told me she saw my car here in the village on Sunday. I thought it was in Evesham all day, while I was at the conference. Isn't that weird?'

'You came here in it on Monday,' said Thea helpfully. 'You told me you'd driven from where you live, on the Welsh border.'

'No, I didn't say that. I just told you where I lived. I was in Evesham on Saturday and most of Sunday, staying at the Royal William Hotel, which was holding the conference. I'd been looking forward to it for ages. It's the high spot of my year. I came here early on Monday, straight from there.'

'Why exactly *did* you come here?' It wasn't the question she wanted to ask. The important thing lay somewhere else, but she could not quite identify the spot.

'Belinda thought something was up. I told you – I had to come and see if you were . . . I mean, exactly how you got involved with Gudrun and Stevie.'

'But Clara said the car was here on Sunday, not Monday.'

'It wasn't. It was in Evesham.'

'So Clara got it wrong? It can't have been here, can it?'

'Mum?' Mark tried again. 'Say something.'

Yvonne met his eyes with an untroubled gaze. 'I borrowed it,' she said simply. 'You know I've got a spare key.' She looked at Thea with a little smile. 'It was mine originally, you see. I gave it to Markie when I got the new one.'

'But you were in *London*,' said Thea urgently, desperate to deny the implications of the three calm words – *I borrowed it.*

'Yes. But I came back. After I'd seen Victor.'

'And you went to France.' Thea was almost pleading for confirmation that at least some of her most solid assumptions were based on firm ground.

'I found the letter.' Yvonne spoke dreamily, tapping the paper in front of her. 'Victor had it in his Filofax. It's from the DNA people.' She looked at Mark as if expecting him to understand. 'About Stevie.'

Something was happening to Mark. He had become sharper, his eyes tightening in sudden acute focus. 'Letter?' he repeated, in a low voice.

'He dropped it, when he was looking for Belinda's wedding list. I recognised it. It came here, five years ago, and I thought it was telling him he had cancer or leukaemia or something.' She laughed. 'I was worried about him. When he said he was leaving me, for no reason, I thought he was trying to protect me. I pleaded with him to explain, to give me something to tell the neighbours – and you and Belinda, of course. He just said the marriage was over and he was going to start a new life in London. I searched for this letter afterwards, but never found it. I thought he was *dying*.'

'Don't laugh, Mother. It isn't funny.'

'Hang on,' begged Thea. 'Are we talking about Stevie's paternity?'

Mother and son both turned towards her. 'It has nothing to do with you,' said Yvonne politely. 'I confronted him, of course, on Sunday,' she went on. 'He told me they'd muddled it up, and you were the real father.' She looked at Mark. 'He said you'd been to bed with Gudrun when you were nineteen.'

Thea's mind was moving sluggishly, clogged with implications and wild guesses that led nowhere. But Yvonne's transparent lie was unmissable. 'Rather a big muddle,' she remarked. 'Seeing that Mark's DNA would be totally different from Victor's.'

'Honestly,' insisted Yvonne, with a dreadful little giggle. 'That's what he told me. I wasn't sure whether or not to believe him for a few minutes.' She looked timidly at Mark, as if hoping for his support.

'He's a bloody liar!' roared her son, after a long silence in which it seemed his brain was as stunned as Thea's.

'Yes,' nodded Yvonne, smiling. 'That's what I thought.'

'But you're something even worse,' Mark choked out. Then he flung out of the room. Seconds later, sounds of terrible breakage came from the living room.

'Stop him!' cried Yvonne leaping up from her chair. 'He's smashing all my things.'

Drew had never been to Snowshill, but knew it was west of Broad Campden, which he could find with little effort. Every time he tried to focus on the right section of the map book on the seat beside him, he got no further than the crossroads at Moreton-in-Marsh before something made him drop it and watch the road ahead. It was only by luck that he spotted a sign indicating Snowshill to the left, off the A44, directly opposite the road he would normally take to his new burial ground. Reproaching himself for his deplorable lack of observation at never registering this sign previously, he turned left and followed the straight hilltop stretch, with a flamboyant red sky directly in front of him.

The abrupt alteration of landscape was disorienting. Within yards, hedges had vanished and there were long sweeping views on both sides, and virtually no hint of human habitation. The road narrowed and undulated and he wondered whether he might have missed another sign along the way. A small crossroads pointed out a lavender farm, and a National Trust sign to Snowshill Manor, and he continued slowly, wondering how he would ever locate the actual property that Thea was occupying. Somehow he had failed to plan for this final challenge, thinking he could simply circle the lanes until he saw her car outside a house. Eventually he would have to phone her, he supposed, but he very much preferred to take her by surprise.

Then, with scarcely any warning, he was in the village of Snowshill. He emerged from a T-junction, to see ahead and below a cluster of the familiar beautiful stone houses sitting in a charming jumble alongside a squat-towered church. He took the little street that plunged down amongst the buildings, crawling along slowly enough to inspect each house as he passed it. They were of a fairy-tale beauty, with gabled roofs and stone-framed windows, all built of the same extraordinary material that conjured words like *honey* and *caramel*, as if you could eat it.

Ahead was a long wall decorated with circular stones that gave it an odd character. They had been incorporated into the wall itself, at intervals, for no obvious reason. They could even be old cannonballs, he supposed, utilised as a way of making some sort of historical point. The house beyond could only be glimpsed, but it appeared to be substantial.

At random he turned left, still going downhill towards a patch of trees. The road snaked around again to the left and he expected to find himself back where he had begun in another few minutes. Instead, he was suddenly out of the tiny settlement and climbing upwards towards the far more open and treeless landscape he had traversed five minutes earlier.

A pair of houses could be seen on the right, with several cars parked outside. One of them was a green Peugeot – the *same* green Peugeot he had so cleverly found in Crouch End, only the previous day. And next to it was Thea's red Fiesta.

Chapter Twenty-Three

He had found her! The relief was laced with delight and excitement. They were going to have another adventure; that was obvious. The reactions he felt at the prospect were becoming reliably predictable. Thea exuded something vibrant and magnetic, even when sitting placidly in a pub garden with her dog. She was not so much a distraction from his unhappy home life as a whole different realm of experience. It was like stepping into a dream or a story, relinquishing all control in the process.

There was, he noticed, another house set back behind the first one. Yet another car sat on a tarmacked area in front of a small garage attached to the further house. Daylight was almost gone, subduing the colours of the massed flowers in the garden, adding to his sense of unreality.

There was no reason to expect trouble, or even adventure, in this quiet little Cotswold settlement. He could see no signs of movement. And yet he knew with complete certainty that there was trouble close by. There *had* been a murder here, only a few days ago. Perhaps that accounted for his heightened adrenaline levels. The green car had somehow found its way home, trailing clouds of suspicion and violence. It was more than enough to render him cautious, eyes and ears strained for information.

There was barely space for another vehicle, but he pulled in onto the verge and hoped no large lorries would want to pass. He had to scoot over to the passenger side to get out, having left so little space between the car and the garden wall. Treading carefully, he went through the gate labelled 'Hyacinth House' and up the path to the front door. There he paused, hearing unusual sounds coming from the house. The owner of the green car was also the owner of this house – that much he remembered clearly. She was not supposed to come back for another week or more. And somebody inside was smashing china and glass, while somebody else howled in protest.

Before he could approach the front door, two people emerged from the other house. A dark-haired man and a small foreign-looking woman crossed the unfenced gardens and stood listening. Drew went up to them. 'What's going on?' he asked. 'Is Thea in there?'

'Who are you?' asked the man.

'My name's Slocombe. Drew Slocombe. I came to find Thea.'

The crashing sounds were continuing unabated. 'Can we get in?' Drew demanded. 'We'll have to do something.'

'I've called the police. They'll be here any minute now,' said the man, with a glance at the woman. 'From the sound of it, the truth about his father has just got through to young Mark Parker.'

337

'Truth?' Drew repeated. 'Look – I need to make sure that Thea's all right. It sounds nasty in there.'

The man stepped aside and swung his right hand in an inviting arc, plainly giving Drew permission to go ahead. 'Feel free,' he said. 'I'm not stopping you. I've done all I intend to.'

Drew strode to the door of Hyacinth House and tried the handle. To his surprise it turned and the door opened. With a strong sense of trepidation, he walked in.

Thea was standing in the hall, her dog in her arms. To the left, through a doorway, Drew could see a young man swinging a chair with complete abandon, scything ornaments, plates, glasses from shelves and surfaces with an appalling look of dedication on his face. A woman stood in the midst of the destruction, blood and tears on her face, making no attempt to interfere.

'W-what . . . ?' Drew stammered. 'Can't we stop him?'

'We did try, but he's beyond reason.' Thea's voice was strained and tight. 'I should call Gladwin.'

'There's a man outside who says he's already done it. They should be here soon.'

'We should go outside. We've no place here.' Stumblingly, she went out of the open door and into the garden, still clutching Hepzie.

'Here they are!' called Blake. 'At last.'

Two uniformed police officers got out of a car and walked steadily, shoulder to shoulder, across the garden. Instinctively they looked to Drew for an explanation, which even in the midst of chaos surprised him. 'There's a man in there, completely out of control. He's smashing the whole place to bits.'

'Is he alone?'

'No,' said Thea. 'His mother's there. You'd better hurry. She's getting quite badly cut from the flying glass.'

The officers exchanged looks. 'Does he have a firearm?' asked one.

'Of course not. He's not armed at all, except with a chair. He might stop when he sees you.'

'But watch out for her,' warned Blake. 'She might have a knife.'

The cautious policeman activated his phone. 'Backup needed at Snowshill,' he barked importantly. 'Violent domestic incident, one male, one female. Possibly armed with a knife.'

Thea gave a cry of frustration. 'You wimps,' she accused them. 'Just get yourselves in there and use some common sense for a change.'

The officers stood straighter and squared their shoulders. 'Madam,' said the one with the phone, 'we have orders not to approach dangerous individuals until we can assess the level of risk.'

'Mariella!' called Blake suddenly. The Filipina had crept away from the group and was disappearing into Hyacinth House. The four others automatically followed her, as if her action had somehow changed the whole situation.

Mariella crunched fearlessly through the shattered porcelain and smashed glass, and put a hand on Mark's arm. 'Stop,' she ordered him. 'This can do no good.' She turned to Yvonne. 'You are Mrs Parker, then,' she stated. 'You are the murderer.' She seemed to feel more curiosity

339

than anything else. 'You have sent this boy crazy by what you've done.'

In the doorway, Thea and Drew exchanged blinks of amazement. 'Murderer?' repeated a policeman softly.

'Where's the knife?' said the other one.

In reply, Yvonne bent to gather a shard of glass from the fireplace and flew at Mariella with it, swiping wildly, ignoring the blood springing from her hand, where she grasped the lethal edge.

'No!' shouted Drew, plunging forward. He was not quite close enough to get his own face slashed before the two policemen grabbed him and pushed him out of Yvonne's reach. Then they finally tackled her, one on each side, valiantly risking personal damage. She dropped the glass without resistance, holding her streaming hand up close to her face, eyeing the flowing blood with interest.

Mark had dropped his chair at some point, his frenzy over as suddenly as it had begun. 'Mariella's hurt,' he said quietly.

Everybody looked, to see a deep gash in the young woman's bare upper arm, where she had raised it to defend herself. Blood was pumping out steadily and her face was white. Drew began to think that two hesitant police officers were nowhere near adequate to the crisis. They still held Yvonne tightly between them, as if their work were done. 'Call for paramedics,' said one to the other. 'That's an artery, that is.'

'For heaven's sake,' said Thea, thrusting the spaniel into Drew's arms. 'Come out here,' she ordered Mariella, 'and sit down.' She led the shaking woman into the kitchen and started to wrap tea towels tightly around the bleeding arm. Blake joined her, holding the bindings in the right place without being told. Both murmured calming reassurances to their patient, knowing instinctively the value of slowing her heart rate and conserving all available energy. 'Pressure,' muttered Thea. 'That's right, isn't it?'

'Exactly. It's not as bad as it looks.' The slippery blood was gathering on the floor beneath the chair, giving off a hot metallic smell that made Drew want to panic, as he watched the first-aiders go into action. He had all the training necessary for stemming rapid blood loss. He had done it before. But he had been given permission to sit this one out. He had a spaniel to hold. The awkward dog in his arms wriggled, and almost escaped. He badly wanted to put it down, but could not see a good place to do so.

Mark Parker was the only person left to his own devices. He drifted into the kitchen and stood with his back to one of the worktops, watching intently. Slowly he began to speak, addressing nobody in particular. 'Dad was Stevie's father, then,' he said. 'Belinda was right all along. I never believed her. I didn't see how Dad could ever have disowned him, after the way he was so protective of us. His own kid. We were just adopted, after all. This was his real biological boy. Mum never had the slightest idea, of course. It would never occur to her. She's so naive.'

For want of anyone else to pay attention, Drew cocked an encouraging ear. 'You think she strangled the kid?' he prompted.

'I know she did. She took my car on Sunday, came here, then parked it back where she'd found it, in Evesham.'

'We saw hers in Crouch End,' said Drew in confusion.

'Must have left it there for days, and got the train to Evesham and back. She'll be on some CCTV somewhere, I imagine.'

'But why? I mean, why now?' In truth, he wasn't sure what he meant, but he definitely needed a lot more elucidation.

'Dad was fool enough to keep the evidence – he must have had a paternity test some time ago, and it confirmed his suspicions. But he kept the secret from Mum. Didn't he, Mother?' he called to Yvonne, who was hanging limply between the policemen, her lacerations causing them some concern. 'You never had any idea. Why do you think he left you? Wasn't it because he couldn't bear to see Stevie every day, with you so maddeningly trusting and innocent? So he invented some horrible Internet sex thing to give you some sort of explanation for him going.'

Yvonne smiled crookedly. 'No – I invented that,' she said. 'I wanted people to think badly of him.'

Thea thought of Janice, mother of another of Victor Parker's offspring. Would Yvonne have murdered Ruby as well, if she'd known?

'Why didn't he just tell her the truth?' wondered Drew, quietly.

'It's not easy to tell Yvonne things,' said Thea, still focused on Mariella's arm. 'I can vouch for that.'

'Here they are at last!' said one of the policemen in relief, as further footsteps crunched up the front path. 'Took their time, didn't they?'

* * *

Despite – or perhaps because of – rigorous procedures for debriefing, it took Gladwin until well after dark to ascertain the whole story. Injuries had to be dealt with first, and the dangerous condition of the living room assessed and made safe. Everyone appeared to be generously smeared with blood from head to toe, apart from Drew and Hepzibah. Blake Grossman flashed some kind of secret identity card at the police officers, earning himself exoneration from all questions and a nod of respect from Gladwin. Only Thea seemed to notice this exchange. Was he Mossad, she wondered wildly. Or merely MI5?

Mark Parker adopted a sweetly reasonable manner, even when confronted with the destruction he had wreaked in the living room. 'I was very angry with her,' he said simply. 'She killed that poor little boy, who I could have known as my little brother, who could have been a part of our family – which was bad enough. But I couldn't let her get away with killing my father. She had to take what was coming to her for that.' Gladwin eyed him doubtfully, and made a mental note to check his medical records for any history of psychological disturbance.

Yvonne said nothing when she was finally formally arrested and charged. She said nothing for the following week, during which scarcely any evidence was gathered to demonstrate that she had indeed killed both Stevie Horsfall and Victor Parker. And yet nobody doubted that she was guilty, or refrained from speculating as to her motives. 'Jealous revenge, I guess you can call it,' said Gladwin to Thea.

'But it was all so perfectly *planned*,' protested Thea.

'With alibis at every stage.' She had had plenty of time to think it all through since the climax on Wednesday evening. Gladwin had asked her to meet her in Cirencester, to check whether she had any further testimony to give.

'No, I don't think it was. She just acted instinctively.'

'But the car thing.'

'Yes, that was rather brilliant, I admit. Simple, but effective. Even now, if we can't see her on the Evesham CCTV there'll be hardly anything concrete to use against her. Nobody saw her, as far as we know, she left no physical evidence and she hasn't said a word to incriminate herself. We know she did it, but we're having a hard time proving it.'

It was Drew who suggested the solution, five days later. 'They just need to tell her they're arresting Belinda for the murders, on the basis of new information, and Yvonne will soon admit it,' he said, when Thea phoned and reported Gladwin's frustration to him, before giving him much of a chance to speak. 'After all, she did it all for her children.'

'Did she?'

'Of course.' He cleared his throat. 'Actually, it was Maggs who explained it. She's adopted, you see.'

'Er . . .'

'I told her the whole story. She insisted I should, and I couldn't see any reason not to. Anyway, she says Yvonne would have been incandescent when she realised there was a natural child as well as the other two. Not just because it threatened their inheritance of his money, but because of the *biology* of it. There was a little piece of Victor in the world, but not of her. It might not have mattered to her so much while they were still married, but once divorced, she couldn't cope with it at all. So she had to kill Stevie – it must have seemed inescapable.'

'But she was nasty and cunning enough to get poor Gudrun blamed for it.'

'Possibly not deliberately. That shoe might just have fallen off unnoticed, when she grabbed the boy. But it worked very well as a double revenge on Victor and Gudrun.'

'And why dump him behind my car?'

'Maggs thinks that's as far as she could carry him, and it made a good hiding place. Or else, Mark's car was sitting close by, and it just worked out that way.'

'I'm wildly impressed by all this,' she told him. 'You and Maggs must have talked about it for ages. Have you worked out why she killed Victor as well?'

'Probably because of Mariella.'

'Ok-a-a-y,' said Thea slowly. 'That makes sense, I suppose.'

He elaborated patiently. 'Not just the sordidness of it, and the natural fury of the older discarded wife when faced with a prettier, younger model. But the idea that he might yet father *another* child, if she didn't stop him. It looks as if she had no idea Mariella existed until she must have seen her coming out of his flat on that Monday and followed her around the streets. Well, that's all a big guess, assuming she never went to France, of course.'

'She can't have done – and I was so convinced,' moaned Thea. 'It never occurred to me she could just pretend all that.' Another puzzle presented itself. 'And how did she know about Mariella in the first place?'

'Most likely she saw evidence of a woman in the flat, when she was there on Sunday morning. Or maybe Victor simply told her – showed her a photo, even. Anyway, we think she must have hung around Crouch End on Sunday evening, or somewhere close by that does B&B. When she saw Mariella go back in with the shopping, and heard Victor greet her, her suspicions would have been confirmed. Then when she went in and saw he wasn't wearing any clothes, she lost it completely and let fly. Funny, really, after what that nanny said to us. Remember?'

'Not really.'

'She said Mariella would scratch the eyes out of any woman moving in on Victor. She got that wrong, didn't she?'

Thea was deeply impressed at his ability to keep up and remember every detail she'd passed to him over recent days, during their phone calls and taxi rides in London. She accepted his reasoning, with one or two reservations. 'You think she killed Victor on an impulse? But she had a knife.'

Drew paused for thought, the phone line making a hollow silence while Thea waited. 'Maybe she used one that was in the flat. Maybe she took it when she went after Stevie, and it was still in her pocket.'

'They obviously haven't found anything as nice and easy as a murder weapon covered in fingerprints.'

'What about the B&B or wherever it was she spent those three nights? Saturday, Sunday *and* Monday, presumably.'

'Last I heard, they haven't traced it. She didn't use a card to pay, so it must have been a very small low-tech place.'

'Which is why Maggs says they have to outwit her, and threaten to prosecute Belinda instead.'

'I'll tell them, but I very much doubt they'll take the advice. It'll all come down to boring donkey work in the end. She's sure to have left some sort of trail, if they can only find it.'

He said nothing. Only then did Thea ask, 'And how's Karen?'

He made a small sound that sent a chill right through her. 'She died,' he said thickly. 'Yesterday afternoon.'

'Oh,' said Thea. 'Oh, Drew.'

REBECCA TOPE is the author of three bestselling crime series, set in the stunning Cotswolds, Lake District and West Country. She lives on a smallholding in rural Herefordshire, where she enjoys the silence and plants a lot of trees, but also manages to travel the world and enjoy civilisation from time to time. Most of her varied experiences and activities find their way into her books, sooner or later.

rebeccatope.com

To discover more great books and to
place an order visit our website at
allisonandbusby.com

Don't forget to sign up to our free newsletter at
allisonandbusby.com/newsletter
for latest releases, events and exclusive offers

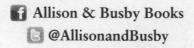 **Allison & Busby Books**
@AllisonandBusby

You can also call us on
020 3950 7834
for orders, queries
and reading recommendations